HAYLEY
AND THE
HOT FLASHES

JAYNE JAUDON FERRER

SMALL TOWN GIRL PUBLISHING

Library of Congress Control Number: 2022936224

Cover Design by: Purple Penguin Designs

For information please contact:

Small Town Girl Publishing

www.smalltowngirlpublishing.com

ISBN: 978-1-7378411-5-9

ISBN: 978-1-7378411-8-0 Ebook

Acknowledgments

This book began as a fun collaboration; Monica Weber and I spent many months with Hayley and her Hot Flashes—independently at our homes in Greenville, SC, and Hendersonville, TN, and together during intensive weekend sessions every few months in Franklin, NC, and Pigeon Forge, TN. Then, as it so often does, life took an unexpected turn; Monica became a single parent and seminary student and, suddenly, giving this story a happy ending fell to me. I am grateful for Monica's contributions and for the laughter we shared during the initial draft. On behalf of Monica, I extend thanks to Klair Kimmey and Carol Webster for their support during her involvement.

My own thank you list is long and heartfelt. For encouraging words and helpful edits, my thanks to Angie Baker. For insider information about the world of country music, I am grateful to Eleanor Dicks, Roger Jaudon, and Stella Parton. For reading, laughing, and being the world's best "assisterant", a big hug to Vera Stanfield. Thank you to Dr. Jennifer Smart for treatment information regarding Alzheimer's and menopause, and to Deputy Chief of Staff Jon Adams of the Davidson County Sheriff's Office for clarification of law enforcement protocol. Thank you to Melissa Carrigee and her team for giving this story wings, and to Gwen Gades at Purple Penguin Book Design for a fabulous cover. To my beloved husband and sons, you have my unending gratitude for your love, support, encouragement, and tolerance: I know life with a "wordwoman" can be a challenge!

I hope you enjoy the saga of Hayley and her friends and, remember: it's not age that matters, it's attitude!

—Jayne

Introducing

HAYLEY
AND THE
HOT FLASHES

and their supporting cast

CHAPTER ONE
Home Again, Home Again, Jiggety-Gig

Hayley Gayle Swift, once-upon-a-time-country music diva, wiped away a tear as she sat sprawled on the soft, white leather sofa in her Nashville den. She scanned the letter in her hand once again.

> Nothing much exciting going on around here (as usual!). C.J.'s mom's Alzheimer's is about the same, Amanda stays busy with the twins (who are so darn cute!), Meg's working at a pawn shop, and I'll go back to teaching kindergarten when school starts. A bunch of us have been working on plans for our 35th high school reunion. Think you could come? We still don't have any place fancy around here, so it'll be in the school gym, or maybe the VFW building; at least the gym is air-conditioned now!
>
> I hope everything's good with you. I still call Jerry at the radio station and request one of your songs at least once a week! We miss you, "Sister!" Take care of yourself.
>
> Love, Sue

"Thirty-five years? Unbelievable," Hayley sighed aloud to Bubba Troutt, the well-worn, fifty-something handyman/gardener/ Father Confessor who was tightening the last bolt on a chronically leaky drainpipe under her kitchen sink. "It just doesn't seem like it's been that long." She rested her head against the back of the sofa and stared for a few seconds at the cell phone that lay within arm's reach. "Why haven't I done a better job of staying in touch, Bubba?" She picked up the phone and gripped it as if feeling for a pulse. "I *loved* those girls. Maybe I could ... nah, you can't go home again. Isn't that what they say?"

There was a grunt from under the sink.

"I've been in Nashville thirty-five years. *This* is home now, not South Carolina—even if nobody here remembers who I *am* anymore." Hayley kicked a foot in frustration and sent a grey pillow sailing off the sofa. "Gaa! If I could just shake this writer's block ... come up with a new song ... get back on top where I belong ..." She snapped her fingers and sat up. "Hey, Bubba, that reminds me: Carrie Underwood never called me back. We were supposed to get together and work on a song this week."

"Ungh," came another grunt.

Hayley rose and ambled over to the large French doors that flanked the west side of the room. The sun streamed in, reflecting off her swimming pool—her *green* swimming pool—next to which a buxom platinum blonde, wearing a bikini at least two sizes too small, flipped through a *National Enquirer*.

"Bubba, why is my pool green? And who is that *Playboy* reject sitting in my chaise lounge?" Hayley stood with her arms folded across her favorite t-shirt—the turquoise one that always made her

Jayne Jaudon Ferrer

think of the ocean she grew up next to, the one she always reached for when she was having a day like today.

"I told ya, the pump ain't workin'. I also told ya if we had any really hot days, the water was gonna turn. Ow!" Bubba yelped as he emerged into a sitting position on the tile floor. "And that's my new girlfriend, Suzette. I met her at church."

Hayley snorted. "Musta changed the dress code; she doesn't look like anybody *I've* ever seen in Sunday School."

Bubba rolled his eyes as he stood up, then winced, bracing his back. "And your last trip to Sunday School was when—1990?"

"Hush up. I pay you to look after my house, not my soul." The sulky brunette, graceful and shapely despite her baggy comfort clothes, turned and sank into an overstuffed chair. "So why isn't the pump working?"

Bubba paused as he passed in front of the woman who was more buddy than boss, his bald head cocked in a patronizing tilt. "Because it's gonna cost nine hundred dollars to replace it and you said, and I quote, 'Screw *that!*'" He grinned as Hayley flinched.

"Fine. I'll figure something out. Maybe I'll fire *you*," she threatened. "But the green has to go. Get it fixed. Throw some bleach in there, or something."

There was a sudden tapping on one of the French doors. "*Bubbaaa*," the chubby blonde whined through the glass. "You *said* you'd only be a few minutes!"

"I'm done, I'm done," Bubba said as he opened the door and waved the girl inside. "Suzette, I want you to meet country music superstar—and my boss—the one and only Miss Hayley Swift."

"*Swift*? Oh, my gosh! Are you, like, Taylor's *mother*?" Suzette's transformation from bored to blissful was instantaneous and Hayley wasn't sure if she wanted to laugh or cry. Bubba cleared his throat and wrapped a reassuring arm around his boss.

"Honey, Miss Hayley has been one of the biggest names in country music for decades! You ever hear that great song, "*Sister Serenade*?""

Suzette shook her platinum spiked head as boredom once again engulfed her pouty face.

"Well, take my word for it; Miss Hayley here is a bigger star than ol' Taylor has ever *thought* about bein'!"

Hayley smiled in spite of herself. She kissed the hairy hand clutching her shoulder, then gave her handyman a bump with her hip. "Thanks for not using past tense on me, Tonto. Now you and"— the phrase "Bible School Barbie" flashed through her brain— "Suzette toddle along. Pool. Blue. ASAP," she reminded the receding bald head.

Good grief—Taylor Swift's mother?? she thought as she closed the door behind them, then fell into a favorite recliner. Curling into a ball, she imagined some smart-aleck Nashville deejay chortling, "What happens to has-been country queens? We shove 'em back into the closet!" *Ba-dump-BUM.*

As tears trickled down the clear, unlined face that looked a good ten years younger than its fifty-three years, Hayley let her eyes drift around the room. The walls were filled with trophies and mementos of her many achievements. *Newcomer Award, 1988 . . . Best Country Song, 1992 . . . Nashville Woman of the Year . . . 1996 . . . Songwriter of the Year, 1999 . . . Best Entertainer, 2002 . . .*

The fireplace mantle was cluttered with framed moments in time: Hayley at the Grand Ole Opry with Minnie Pearl; with Bush

Number One and Two at the White House; curtsying to the Queen in London; singing to troops in Iraq. So many songs, so many stages. When did it start to end? When did she start to find herself at home more than on the road, in front of a TV more often than in front of a camera, getting more attention from *Where Are They Now?* than *People*? Her gaze fell on a small, pink pillow half-hidden in a pile of bigger, brighter ones stacked on the sofa. Crying softly, she stumbled from the chair and snatched the little pillow to her breast—a handmade gift from her best friends back in Skerry on that euphoric May day when she'd boarded a bus bound for fame and fortune. She'd hauled that little pillow to all fifty states and most of Europe; more than once, it had cushioned her head as she faced fear, doubt, and fatigue on her way to the top.

But even as she had clung to that bedraggled memento like a cherished talisman—its cross-stitched reminder to *"Remember: there's no place like home!"* bringing comfort time and again—she had let slide the friendships that spawned it. As her tears spilled on threads that were faded but still stitched tight, Hayley indulged in a bleak walk down Memory Lane. Images of her "gang"—brilliant Amanda, sassy Meg, lively C. J., and loyal Sue—tugged at her heart. She knew only the barest facts about their lives now, sent a perfunctory card now and then, *thought* about calling, but rarely did. Bless Sue, who had faithfully stayed in touch and kept her up to date on significant events. Her friend's loyalty stabbed like a knife.

And what of Keith Parker? Handsome, faithful, focused, devoted Keith. Thirty-five years after the fact, Hayley still flinched when recalling the look on her boyfriend's face at the bus station the day she departed. Commitment was the last thing on her mind at that point; fate had dealt her a golden opportunity in the form of a bus ticket to Nashville, and she grabbed it like the brass ring it was. She'd loved Keith, but the timing was all wrong. She'd never meant to abandon him—he was the standard by which she compared every man who came after—but somehow, the time slipped away, she never made her way back home, and then it seemed too late to try. Now, with a career dying of malnutrition, her parents and her Aunt Beatrice long gone, no siblings, no husband, no children—not even a dog!—Hayley felt, for the first time, mocked instead of comforted by the pillow's clichéd admonition. Drained, she pulled an afghan around her legs as she tucked the pillow under her head and drew into a fetal position. "Oh, y'all," she whispered raggedly, "I'm so sorry."

♪

The shrill trill of her cell phone jerked Hayley back to consciousness before she could make sense of anything. *Is that the security alarm? What time is it? Where's Bubba?* Slowly, her brain began to process the facts: it was late afternoon, and the phone was ringing, and ringing, and *ringing*. "Oh! Phone!" she exclaimed as the last synapse finally fell into place. She lunged out of the chair and toward the granite-topped bar that separated the den from the kitchen. "I'm here! I'm here!" she promised, hoping fervently it wasn't a vinyl siding salesman or cable TV deal-of-the-week that had wrenched her back into this pathetic day.

"Hayley Gayley! How's my girl?" Through the receiver came the irrepressible—and unmistakable—voice of Clarence "Tipsy" Mack, talent agent extraordinaire. Just this side of hustler for a two-bit record company when he happened upon Hayley at Skerry's 1987 Basket-Flower Festival, Tipsy was now one of Nashville's most respected names, and had enjoyed a golden reputation for years. Promoters adored him because Tipsy always delivered a hundred and fifty percent. Label execs loved him because he'd sent them one chart-topper after another for the past three and a half decades. Radio stations in every market carried his weekly one-minute commentary, *"Bullet Train,"* and the execs of the hit TV show, *"New Country Superstar,"* had offered him an insane amount of money to join their panel of judges for the upcoming fall season.

Holding the phone in place with her shoulder, Hayley returned to her nest in the chair. "I've been better," she admitted frankly.

"Well, cheer up. I've got good news. How'd ya like to take a little road trip?"

She sat up. "You got me a *gig*? Oh, Tips! Where? When?"

Tipsy chuckled. "The good ol' Bible Belt. All those little towns we used to love—Dickson, Oneonta, Fletcher, Westminster, Macclenny, even the Orange Blossom Opry!"

"Yee-haw, hold me back. When?"

"You kick off Labor Day weekend for an eight-week run."

Hayley took a moment to do the math. "Promo deadlines for those dates would have been months ago. What gives?"

There was a split-second pause, then a kinder, gentler Tipsy spoke. "Well, Candy Cutler had to cancel; she's havin' some health issues."

Hayley felt a knot constrict in her stomach. "*Candy Cutler* is headlining a tour?" The copper-tressed adolescent coquette was being touted as Generation Z's LeAnn Rimes, but had only released one single and was just beginning to make her way onto radio playlists.

There was another pause. "She's not exactly headlining. She's . . . opening for Cal Taylor's "Retro Rodeo" tour."

For a full fifteen seconds, there was dead silence. Then Hayley managed to rasp out a pitiful wail. "I'm not the *headliner*?"

Tipsy was grateful he couldn't see the look on his client's face. He and Hayley had been together through good times and bad. It hurt him that her time in the spotlight had long ago ended and he hadn't been able to pull her back into the game. The cold-hearted suits in today's country music industry kept telling Tipsy he should dump the only losing member of his current roster, but Hayley was his first triumph and the reason for most of his success, and he remained loyal to a fault. He wouldn't bail until she did. "Aw, honey, this is a great fit," he soothed. "Cal's fan demographics are the same as yours, and y'all enjoyed working together in the past. I thought it'd be fun for you." He hesitated. "Singing old songs is better than singing *no* songs, sugar. Will you at least think about it?"

"Sure, Tipsy. Thanks, hon. I . . . uh, I gotta go." Hayley clicked off the phone and let it slide down into the folds of the crumpled afghan. For a moment, she sat perfectly still as new tears began to flow. Then she poked around the afghan, found the phone and, with an anguished sob, hurled it across the room.

She was waiting when Tipsy walked into his Music Row office the next morning. "Am I in for good news or bad?" he asked as he grinned, dropped his briefcase in a chair, and engulfed his favorite singer in a hug.

Hayley sniffed. "Depends on whether you're the windshield or the bug, I suppose." She extracted herself from his arms and adjusted her hair and clothing. "How much does this gig pay?"

"Thirty thousand, fifteen shows. Expenses covered separately, and you'll bunk on the tour bus, but get your own compartment."

"Less than I used to make in a single night," she observed wryly.

"Yeah, and once upon a time, women used to think I was a hunka-hunka burnin' love," Tipsy commiserated with a shrug. "Look, it was gonna be *twenty* thousand, but I reminded them they're dealing with the one and only Hayley Swift. I don't think we can expect better. Life ain't always grand, honey, but it goes on with or without us." He sat tapping a pencil, gnawing on his lower lip.

"Wait a minute," she demanded, her eyes narrowing. "You don't chew your lip unless you're holding back. What haven't you told me?"

Tipsy pushed back his swivel chair, stood, and swayed to the left, then to the right. His hair, backlit by a window that overlooked Music Row, surrounded his head like a grey halo. His dark suit, well-cut as it was, failed to hide the paunch most people would associate with beer—especially given his name. But Tipsy was an absolute teetotaler. The swaying that earned him his moniker was the result of an inner ear condition he'd stopped trying to cure when he realized it had become his trademark. He swayed and gnawed his lip for several more seconds, then abruptly sat back down. "There's no budget for rehearsals. You'll have to pull it together on the road. And I can't go with you; I got too much goin' on here." He paused and looked her straight in the eye. "And the tour starts with the Basket-Flower Festival."

Hayley groaned and put her head in her hands. "Right back where I started from. This is pitiful."

"There's more," he said quietly, and she lifted her head, the expression on her face somewhere between incredulity and disgust. "The Friday before the festival is your thirty-fifth high school reunion. The mayor — some guy says he dated you in high school—called me yesterday to see if you'd be their guest of honor and sing at the dance."

Hayley felt her legs go numb. "Dear merciful Lord in heaven."

"Are you swearin' or prayin'?"

"I'm not sure," she admitted. "Keith Parker is mayor of Skerry?"

Tipsy frowned. "Naw, Parker ain't the right name. Wiley? Wilding? Wilder? That's it. Wilder!"

Hayley gave a hoot. "Darryl Ray Wilder is mayor of Skerry? That's rich. But why on earth would they want *me* to be a guest of honor? I haven't been back since the day I *left*."

"Honey, you're that little town's biggest claim to fame—their *only* claim to fame, for that matter! They're proud of you."

"Maybe. They *oughta* think I'm the biggest snob on the planet. And, for the record," she added, "I did not date Darryl Ray Wilder. I went on a hayride with him in the seventh grade."

"Didja kiss him?" Tipsy asked with a lurid wiggle of his bushy eyebrows.

"No!"

"I'd bet he remembers it different. Boys do that, ya know. Anyway," he continued, reaching to pat the hand Hayley had flung on his desk, "home towns are mighty forgiving. They'll think you've been so busy with your glamorous, celebrity life you simply couldn't get away, but you always wanted to. That's what they wanna believe, that's what they wanna hear, and that's what we're gonna tell 'em. Illusion is everything, darlin'." He smiled reassuringly.

"But my career is *over*, Tipsy. I don't want to go crawling back home as a *loser*!" Despite her resolve not to cry, Hayley felt puddles welling under her contacts.

Tipsy's smile vanished and he raised a finger to point in her face. "Listen here," he said sternly. "Your career is not over till I *say* it is, and if you never sing another dang *note*, you're not a loser! You had a heck of a ride before you were even dry behind the ears, little girl, and you still have more loyal fans out there than most in this business can ever *dream* of. You are *not* washed up, you've just . . ." he paused, struggling for the right image, ". . . been waitin' for the right soap!"

The fierceness of his face, the ridiculous analogy, and the absurdity of it all hit Hayley hard and she suddenly burst out laughing, tears of mirth replacing those of self-pity. Regaining control, she grasped Tipsy's hand and covered it with her own. "Oh, Tips, even if you're lying through your teeth, I love you for your loyalty."

Embarrassed now by his impassioned outburst, Tipsy grunted. "Hey, I'm runnin' a business here, missy. I don't do charity."

"Well, dig out some contracts and let me sign away what little dignity I have left. I have things to do if I'm going on the road," Hayley challenged, then she smiled. The tour, humiliating as it was, would keep her sinking ship afloat a little longer.

"A tour? Hot diggety!" Bubba whooped when Hayley delivered the news. "I'm orderin' that pool pump today! You'll get to see all your old friends! Ain't that great?"

"I don't know," Hayley sighed. "Once I left, I never went back, and I never *looked* back. I may have burned some bridges I didn't mean to."

Bubba gave a dismissive wave. "Come on, now, it's a *gig*, ain't it? I say we throw a party to celebrate!"

She gave him a long look. "And invite who—Suzette?"

Ignoring the sarcasm, Bubba rubbed his hands together in anticipation. "No! The press! And fans! We should have your fan club do a contest and let the winners come to the party! We'll make it a send-off event, the night before the tour begins."

Hayley looked at the employee who had long ago become family, her eyes narrowing. She mused for a moment then said, "You know, that's not as hideous an idea as it sounds."

"Thanks for *that*."

"Let me run it past Tipsy. If he likes the idea, you're on!"

As Bubba left the room, Hayley turned and sauntered toward the master bedroom that adjoined her office, pausing in front of the full-length mirror that flanked her closet. "Fitness center," she muttered aloud, casting a critical eye at the image facing her. "Fitness center, wax, body wrap, facial, pedicure, manicure, highlights." She put her hands on her hips and pivoted left, then right. "You're slippin' a little, honey—sweats and tees are not your best look—but not bad, old girl, not bad. I think we can repackage the goods and give 'em their money's worth." She leaned toward the mirror and affected a sexy pose. "So, tell me, Dr. Parker, how've you been?" she purred. Then, slowly, she backed away and blinked. "I'm sorry; do I know you?" she said dully, as she turned and walked away.

CHAPTER TWO
...But I Still Feel Eighteen!

"Ooh, didn't we think we were gorgeous?" Sue Campbell sat with the 1987 edition of the *Cusabo Spirit* open in her lap, where a picture of five faces surrounded by abundant bangs and curls smiled up at her from the yearbook's yellowed pages.

Amanda Brooks leaned down for a closer look. "We *were* gorgeous," she confirmed. "Still are," she added, giving Sue's chair a firm bump with her denim-clad hip.

The sunny South Carolina kitchen was redolent with the tantalizing aroma of fresh-baked cinnamon rolls. Celia Jo Fleming, the kitchen's attractive blonde owner, nodded agreement with Amanda's assessment as she licked icing from her fingers. "That's what my mama always said: 'Skerry girls, best in the world!'" she quipped, as she whisked the plate of hot pastries off the counter and onto the oak table around which sat her three best friends.

"Why aren't you a *cow*?" Meg Dorris groaned as she claimed

one of the huge, sugary treats. "I never come over here that you don't have something fabulous baking in the oven! *How* do you stay so skinny?"

"Marital bliss," C. J. deadpanned. "Pete complains constantly, but I tell him it's the only way I can keep my girlish figure, so he just has to deal with it. Don't you feel his pain?"

"Do *not* talk about 'marital bliss' when I haven't had so much as a lukewarm kiss in five years!" scolded Sue. Widowed at thirty when her husband was killed in a boating accident, the plain but popular kindergarten teacher had dated only sporadically in the ensuing years, though her friends constantly sent eligible men her way.

Amanda hooted. "I keep telling you, Suzie—Bag Boy Barney over at the Piggly Wiggly is ripe for the picking. All you gotta do is let him know you're interested!"

"But I'm *not*!" Sue protested, as Meg made a face and squealed, "Ewww!" Everyone laughed.

"If I hadn't been kissed in five years, I'd go hunt up Matthew McConaughey," mused Meg. "Might as well start with the best!"

"Oh, no," countered C.J. "The *best* would be Ben Stiller."

"Ew! And too short," pronounced Amanda, as she reached for a cinnamon roll then folded her long, lithe body into the chair next to Sue. "Tom Selleck," she sighed. "Now *there's* a man you could kiss."

"An *old* man," Meg snorted, but Sue gave an enthusiastic thumbs-up.

"Definitely more interesting than Bag Boy Barney, bless his heart. I always thought Keith Parker looked a little like Tom Selleck—all that thick, dark hair, and those a-maa-zing shoulders." She drew out the last two words in a slow moan, and an audible sigh went up from all four women.

Meg harrumphed. "Wonder if poor *Keith* has had a kiss in the last five years? In the last *ten*, for that matter?" She narrowed her eyes as she took a sip of coffee. "I keep wondering if he's gay. It's weird someone that good-looking isn't married."

"He's not gay. He just never got over Hayley," Sue offered quietly.

"Well, she sure got over *him*," Meg grumbled. "I still can't believe she got on a bus to Nashville and never came back. The poor guy was devastated!"

C. J. shot Meg an odd look. "How do *you* know what he was? For that matter, how do you know he and Hayley never reconnected?"

Meg shrugged, her square jaw tensing defiantly. "We were all *friends* back then, C. J.; we talked. Keith came to see me a few times after Alice was born. And I still see him around town every now and then."

Amanda moaned. "Me, too—and it's always pure pleasure. He is *so* handsome."

"And nice," said Sue. "Keith Parker is a genuinely *nice* man. Skerry is very fortunate he chose to come back here and set up practice after medical school."

"We are, indeed," agreed C. J. "I figured he'd stay in Nashville to be close to Hayley and they'd get married and have lots of beautiful babies and live happily ever after."

"Would that have been before or after she stole our song?" Meg sniffed.

Amanda sighed heavily and plunked down the mug of chai

tea she was holding. "Here we go again." She fixed a level gaze on the voluptuous but aging blonde across from her. "*Hayley* wrote "Sister Serenade," Meg. It was never 'our' song."

"It was enough ours that we sang it at graduation, *and* we won the Basket-Flower Festival talent show with it!"

"Yes, and that was *our* moment in the spotlight. You can't blame Hayley for catching a break, Meg. She had no way of knowing there was a talent scout in the audience that night."

"She knew we were a quintet—a fact she conveniently forgot to mention!"

"No, she didn't!" Sue protested. "I heard her tell that man we were a group. But he didn't think the rest of us had that . . . whatever it is you have to have to be a star." She smiled ruefully. "Not many people do."

"We *might* have," Meg retorted, "but nobody gave us a chance! And when Hayley Swift left town, she never even bothered to look back.."

"Oh, Meg," soothed C. J. "The rest of us couldn't have picked up and left like that. Amanda was headed for early admission at Mars Hill, Sue had a job, I was engaged, and you, well . . ."

Tears welled in Meg's blue eyes and spilled down her cheeks. "It always comes back to that, doesn't it? Thirty-five years and it still gets thrown in my face."

Amanda lifted one brow. "People do tend to remember when someone shows up at senior prom in a maternity dress."

"Bitch!"

"Trollop!"

"Girls!" C. J. scolded, as Meg and Amanda sat glowering.

"We've stuck together way too long to have this fight again. And as you, yourself, just pointed out, Meg, this really *is* ancient history! The point is, not only was Hayley far more talented than the rest of us, she needed a *break* more than the rest of us. We had college, and families, and futures to look forward to; Hayley had nothing but a sick aunt and a prehistoric Cadillac."

"She had *us*, but she threw us away," Meg returned. "You were her best friend, Sue. Are you still writing letters to her? Does she ever answer you back?"

Sue blushed at the memory of the letter she'd just mailed to Nashville. "She does, sometimes. Her life is different from ours, Meg. I doubt she gets to enjoy a daily routine like running to the post office or the drugstore, or grabbing a pizza after work with girl-friends. I'm not sure our life isn't preferable to hers."

Meg snorted. "Loyal to the end, every one of you a suck-up, just because Miss High-and- Mighty Country Diva made good. Well, *I* say she dumped us and doesn't deserve to be fawned over and I can't believe she's coming back to rub it in after all these years."

Sue stared at Meg. "What are you talking about? Hayley's coming home?"

"She's coming *home*?" Amanda echoed.

"Don't you people read your mail? We got a flyer about the reunion, plus it was in today's newspaper."

C. J. jumped up from the table and dug down into a bas-ket on the kitchen counter. "Oh, my gosh!" she exclaimed, scanning the front page of the latest *Skerry Herald*. "*Hayley Swift to Serenade Class of '87.*"

Amanda grinned. "Good play on words, there, Keats," she

said, referring to the paper's editor, Eddie Keats, a fellow member of their graduating class. "Guess we're not the only ones who remember '*Sister Serenade.*'"

"Oh, I'd love to have her stay with me while she's here," murmured Sue. "Wonder if Eddie has a phone number for her?"

"It says she's going to play at the Basket-Flower Festival, too," said C. J. as she continued to scan the page. "What fun!" She looked up, her face beaming. "I'm thinking this calls for a party!"

"Um, isn't that what a reunion *is*?" Amanda inquired with a wry expression.

C. J. stuck out her tongue. "We need a bash for just us. It's '*The Girls Next Door*' together again! Time to dig out the hair crimpers and Whitney Houston CDs!"

Amid the others' laughter, Meg abruptly pushed back her chair and rose to leave. "I can't believe you're welcoming her back with open arms like nothing ever happened."

"Hayley was a good friend, Meg. I've missed her. We *all* have—I thought," said C. J. "I don't bear her any grudges, and if you *do*, you're being unfair. Hayley got lucky, but we did, too—just in different ways."

Meg put her hands on her hips. "Don't talk to me about being lucky, Miss 'My-Husband's-Rich-as-Midas-and-I-Have-the-Perfect-Life.' Try raising a kid when you're eighteen, and the hot shot who knocked you up marries you just long enough to run up a pile of bills. Try keeping a decent job when you're raising a kid by yourself with nobody around to help. And try feeling good about yourself when that kid leaves home the day she turns eighteen. There is *nothing* lucky about my life, C. J.; my life *sucks*!"

The kitchen was silent but for Meg's ragged sniffs as she

plundered her purse in search of a tissue.

When C. J. finally spoke, her voice was controlled but passionate. "I'm sorry life didn't turn out the way you wanted it to, Meg, but Ty Dorris didn't get you pregnant all by himself. And in case you've been feeling too sorry for yourself to notice, the rest of us have our own problems. Amanda went through pure torture to have children, Sue lost Bill when they were barely back from their honeymoon, and my mother has Alzheimer's. She doesn't even remember there *was* a 1987, for Pete's sake!" C. J.'s voice cracked and she fought to regain composure. "*Everybody's* life sucks, at one time or another, but you can look for the blessings and go on, or you can wallow and drown. If looking for the blessings makes me Pollyanna, then so be it."

"Once a cheerleader, always a cheerleader," Sue interjected in a solemn stage whisper and the stony silence was broken as all four women began to giggle.

"Oh, C. J., I'm sorry." Meg threw her arms around her friend. "I don't mean to be hateful, and I guess I love Hayley as much as you do." She straightened and wiped her eyes. "I'm just going through a really hard time right now. Every time I think maybe Alice and I can patch things up, something goes wrong. And, inevitably, that will be the day I run into Ty and his bimbo-of-the-month."

"Let's roll his house," suggested Amanda.

"Amanda Brooks!" reprimanded Sue. "And you a Sunday School teacher!"

Amanda's look of contrition was not convincing.

C. J. reached to smooth a wayward strand of Meg's long, over-processed blonde hair. "Maybe Hayley coming home will be a fresh start for everyone. She's bound to feel bad for not doing a better job of staying in touch; let's just plan to focus on the positive."

"Cue the violins," trilled Amanda, and C. J. picked up a crumpled napkin and threw it at her.

"So, what are we wearing to the reunion?" Sue asked as she rose and started collecting dishes. "Anybody still have the halter dress C. J.'s mom made us for the talent show?"

"Got it," confirmed C. J., "but don't know that I can get *in* it!"

"Oh, please. I bet even your cheerleading outfit still fits!" Meg challenged.

"I kept my dress, too," said Amanda, as Sue and Meg nodded agreement. "I can probably do a little altering for those of us who— for *whatever* reason," she interjected, tossing a devious look at C. J., "—haven't kept our girlish figures."

"Mama had such fun making those dresses," C. J. smiled. "I wish she could do the alterations for us."

Sue brightened. "Do you think if we carried the dresses down to the nursing home, she'd remember making them?"

"What a great idea!" said Amanda. "What do you think, C. J.? Would that trigger any memories?"

C. J. turned off the water at the sink where she was rinsing cups and saucers. "It might," she shrugged. "You never know what will get through to her, or how she'll react."

Sue crossed the kitchen to give her friend a sympathetic hug. "Poor Louise," she sighed. "She didn't deserve to end up like this."

"Who does?" C. J. responded. "But the Alzheimer's is harder on us than it is on Mama. She's blissfully unaware. I guess that's a blessing."

"Pollyanna lives!" sang Amanda as she leapt triumphantly across the room. This time, C. J. heaved the wet dishcloth she was holding and hit her target square in the face.

CHAPTER THREE
It's My Party and I'll Go Berserk If I Want To!

"Miz Swift, we got company!" Bubba hollered through the bathroom door. "Caterer's here, and that bossy woman that heads up your fan club just called. She says she's on the way with some reporters *now*, so they can get an 'exclusive.'"

Hayley yanked open the door, toothbrush in hand, hair in hot rollers, eyes bulging.

"Oh, and I forgot to ask: it's okay if Suzette comes tonight, right? She's become a real fan since that day I introduced y'all."

"Mm-hmm," Hayley responded, then turned to spit a mouthful of toothpaste foam into the sink.

"Well, she *has*!" Bubba insisted. "She's been listenin' to all your old albums . . . and there's plenty of food and I figure the more people that's here, the better it'll lo—"

"I'm sure Suzette would become a fan of the Mormon Tabernacle Choir if it meant more time with you, 'Studly.'" Hayley grabbed a towel, wiped her mouth, and sighed. "Invite the whole neighborhood, I don't care. I'm leaving in the morning for the 'Retro How-Low-Can-You-Go' tour, so I have no dignity left, anyway!" As Bubba turned to leave, she grabbed him back. "Did you ever look at those e-mails I told you about? I got another one this morning. It's starting to scare me."

"Been too busy workin' on the pool, which," he retorted as he made a point of removing her hands from his shirt sleeve, "is now perfectly turquoise, thank you very much. I'll look at 'em tonight. Meanwhile, get ready! I cain't be entertaining reporters while I'm fixin' food platters!" he sassed as he disappeared around the corner.

♪

Hayley stood in the midst of the throng that filled her living room. Some of the people she recognized; most, she didn't. Some were sneaking surreptitious looks at her—while smiling, waving, or whispering to companions behind their hands. Others were aiming cell phones in her direction, documenting proof of their brush with a sort-of celebrity. Most were juggling cups and plates as they made their way around a buffet table that stretched from one end of the room to the other. A large woman wearing a red hat and an odd-looking fellow in an antiquated frock coat sat on either end of the sofa beside her. Hayley took a deep breath, sat between them, and tried to look convivial. The woman wore bright red-and-purple tennis shoes and a nametag that read 'HEATHER, 2nd PLACE, LAVERGNE.' The man, whose dingy, ruffled shirt was in desperate need of bleach, had jet-black hair slicked back from his forehead and a long, greasy mustache; whether the oil was meant as an enhancement, or was residue from the fried mozzarella sticks on which he was gorging, Hayley couldn't tell. His nametag boasted 'RHETT,

1st PLACE, NASHVILLE.'

HEATHER, 2nd PLACE plopped a shrimp into her mouth, then prodded Hayley on the thigh. "I'm a Red Hat," she said proudly, nodding with such vigor that the gigantic purple feather adorning her hat swished down into Hayley's eye. "Let's see; you're fifty-three now, right? So you could be a Red Hat, too! I'll sponsor you!" HEATHER, 2nd PLACE paused to stuff another shrimp in her mouth. "You know, just because you turn fifty, that's no reason to slow down, don't you agree? The women in our group have exciting jobs, they travel...we meet on the first Monday night of every month and have a big buffet and a guest speak—*oh!*" HEATHER, 2nd PLACE's mascara-caked eyes went wide. "After you join, *you* could be our guest speaker! Oh, my goodness, wait till I tell our Chapter President I've got Hayley Swift lined up as a speaker! Which month do you want? August, for your birthday, or October, for Country Music Month?"

Hayley feigned a coughing fit. "S'cuse me," she said, rising and turning just as 'RHETT, 1st PLACE, NASHVILLE' did the same. "Oh, my!" she exclaimed as she collided with his plate of hors d'oeuvres. "I'm so sorry!"

"No worries," smiled the man as he shifted his plate back into position with one hand and reached for one of Hayley's with the other. "I've been looking forward to meeting you—and what better way than up close and personal?" Before Hayley could react, he brought her hand to his lips as he bowed slightly. "May I get you a beverage?" he asked as he straightened. His eyes were intense, his grip on her hand firm.

"Actually, I need to go find my agent," Hayley said, reclaiming her hand and taking a step back. There was something about the man that made her uncomfortable. Of course, this whole night was making her uncomfortable; why had she let Bubba and Tipsy talk her into throwing this shindig when—she inhaled deeply and glanced at her watch—she had to climb on a bus and hit the road in twelve hours? "Please, enjoy yourself. It was nice meeting you," she said and started to leave, but RHETT, 1st PLACE held out a hand to stop her.

"Oh, please. Now that I've finally met you, there's so much I want to say." He bent to put his plate on the sofa then, with a napkin, slowly and carefully wiped his mouth as he straightened. "I am a connoisseur, Miss Swift. I drink only pure, unpasteurized milk, I sleep only on 2000 thread-count, pure Egyptian cotton sheets, I build my computers component by component, and my ears listen to only one voice: yours." He closed his eyes and smiled. "I listen to your songs upon waking, as I work, in my leisure, and as I sleep. You have become a part of me, of my very essence, and being here with you now—," he opened his eyes and stared at her intently, "—in your home, in your presence, is something I've dreamt of for years."

Speechless, Hayley glanced around, hoping to spot Tipsy or Bubba. *Where* are *you guys? Don't I have any* normal *fans? Somebody* rescue *me!* "My goodness, how you do flatter me!" she finally said. "I'm honored, sir, especially since I haven't had a hit in a long, long time. I appreciate your loyalty."

RHETT, 1st PLACE frowned and moved a step closer. "*Shhh,* none of that," he scolded. "You are timeless, madam—your talent, your beauty . . . I have cherished you from the depths of my soul for as long as I can remember and, now, finally, here we are together!" He reached up to cup Hayley's chin in a sweaty palm. She flinched as his damp fingers made contact with her skin. "I have a secret," he continued. "I've just taken an eight-week leave of absence from my job to pursue my dream—indeed, my prayer. Miss Swift, may I be your escort on your impending Grand Tour of the South?"

Hayley forced a cordial expression even as her stomach did a back flip at the thought of being near this eccentric stranger a moment longer than necessary. A disturbing itch began in her brain; why did this man's archaic language seem vaguely familiar? *And where is Tipsy?* she thought again for the hundredth time.

"I can tell I've surprised you."

His voice quavered with, what? Passion? Fear? Insanity? Hayley wasn't sure which.

"I beg you, let me be your devoted servant and I will bring you tea with honey every morning, anoint you with oil every night, commit myself to your every desire . . ."

Suddenly Hayley stiffened and she jerked away with such force that her would-be devoted servant lost his balance and fell back onto the sofa, causing HEATHER, 2nd PLACE's plate of food to go flying into the air. "'Devoted servant!'" Hayley yelped. "You! *You're* the one who's been sending me those disgusting e-mails! Everett Wilson!" Her shock turned to rage and she bent and shoved him, sending the man sprawling and the sofa sliding. "Who *are* you? How did you get in my house?! *BUBBA! TIPSY! GET IN HERE NOW!!*"

HEATHER, 2nd PLACE had made a quick trip back to the buffet table during the early part of Hayley's conversation with her other seatmate. Since returning, though, she'd been listening with rapt attention until the moment Everett Wilson came crashing down beside her. Now she struggled to keep from joining him on the floor as her hostess lunged at the man again. The sudden lurch caused the cracker which HEATHER, 2nd PLACE had been nibbling to aspirate into her windpipe and the woman began frantically choking.

Hayley whirled at the horrific sound. "Somebody *help*!" she cried as she stopped pounding the chest of the man on the floor to begin pounding the back of the woman beside her.

Tipsy and Bubba, coming from opposite directions, finally appeared. Agog at what looked like utter pandemonium, they began elbowing their way through the clamoring, confused guests that were rapidly congregating around the calamity in the center of the room. Tipsy broke through first, patting his face with a handkerchief as he reached Hayley and grabbed her by the elbow. An old hand at mob scenes after years in the music business, he put on a game face and summoned forth his best hail-fellow-well-met tone.

"Well, now, what's going on here?" he greeted, giving a jovial wave to the room at large even as he shot Hayley a look of censure. "Everybody havin' a good time? We sure appreciate all y'all comin' out tonight and your devotion to Hayley over the years."

A trembling, traumatized Hayley, double checking one last time to make sure HEATHER, 2nd PLACE was breathing again, collapsed on the sofa beside her. "This is the scumbag who's been sending me those awful e-mails," she barked at Tipsy, turning to jab her finger in Everett Wilson's face. "He's planning to kidnap me and...oh, I can't even tell you. How did he get *in* here? Who let him *in*?"

"Why, you–," Bubba Troutt's growl was positively primal as he charged through the crowd gathered behind Hayley to slam a knee in Wilson's chest.

HEATHER, 2nd PLACE gasped and Hayley shrieked,

ready to begin pounding again until the woman waved her away, yanked off her hat, and began fanning herself vigorously. As Bubba did his best to pummel the living daylights out of the foppish-looking fellow on the floor, Hayley did *her* best to wrench them apart. Meanwhile, Tipsy was trying, unsuccessfully, to redirect everyone's attention as a reporter from *MusicRow* alternated between scribbling furiously in a notebook and shooting video on his cell phone of what would undoubtedly be the lead story on Channel 5 that night.

"Scuze me just one minute," Tipsy finally said as he bent and, with considerable effort, pulled Hayley off Bubba and Bubba off Everett Wilson, giving all three a look that could have vaporized steel. He then threw his arm around Hayley and dragged her to a standing position beside him. "Let's everybody take a deep breath and calm down. I'm sure we've just got ourselves a little misunderstanding here." When Hayley spun her head to protest, Tipsy tightened his grip on her arm and hissed, under his breath, "Ssh!" Then he patted the same arm he'd just almost severed, beamed a benevolent smile, and continued. "Now, this poor fella, he won our 'Favorite Fan' contest fair and square, just like the rest of you did, and maybe he's had a little too much to drink, but I'm sure he's not done anything improper. Meetin' Miss Hayley here, face to face, for the first time, he prob'ly just got a little carried away. She has that effect!"

As the crowd whistled and hooted and laughed, Tipsy lowered his head to speak directly into Hayley's ear. "This is not the time to be hollerin' about kidnapping and such. Do you hear me? That don't fit well a'tall with your image, little missy—and you've got reporters hyperventilatin' over there, they're so hungry for a piece o' this." Straightening back up, he said, "Y'all listen up! Where's that purty girlfriend of Bubba's? . . . Suzy-Q? Suzanna? . . . Suzette! . . . that's it! Come on over here, honey. Now Suzette here is gonna be givin' away free CDs—that's right! absolutely free!—out by the pool to the first fifty folks who get out there in a nice, straight line. This is one of Hayley's best—*Christmas in the Country*, with duets by Hayley and Randy Travis, Hayley and Mel Tillis, Hayley and Willie Nelson . . . somebody told me this was former President Reagan's *and* President Carter's favorite CD." An "Oooo!" rose up from the crowd. "So y'all head on out there! Take your food, your drinks—get you a refill on your way past the buffet—and get on out there so you can take home that free CD. No shovin', now—we're all friends, here . . . well, not you, Irv," he said as he winked and pointed a finger at a reporter from the *National Enquirer*. "But even *you* can have a free CD—and you're gonna love that gospel version of "*White Christmas*!" Go on, everybody! We're gonna let Miss Hayley catch her breath here a minute, then we'll be right out there with ya. She's so pumped up about this Retro Rodeo tour, she's hot as a firecracker and twice as excitin'!"

As Hayley struggled to free herself from Tipsy's iron grip, party guests surged toward the patio. Tipsy relinquished his hold on Hayley to corner Irv the reporter and extended a hand. "How ya doin', Irv? Good to see ya. Look, what you saw here tonight was a big mix-up, but if you've got a minute, I can scoop you some news on the ghost of Hank Williams that'll put you in line for a Pulitzer. A real *exclusive*. How 'bout it?"

The reporter raised his eyebrows, gave a thumbs-up, closed his notebook, and headed for the pool. Tipsy turned back to the sofa and glanced down at Bubba, who'd sat perched all this time beside his prey—smug lion with hapless gazelle.

"Ease up there, Bubba. Give him some room." Tipsy gave a hard look at the man as he slowly got to his feet and began straightening his clothes. "Wait a minute. I *know* you."

"Yes, you do," he said, in an indignant voice, "I'm Everett P. Wilson, and I am Hayley Swift's most devoted fan. I did *indeed* win the contest to be here tonight, but I'm also the person you hired to build Miss Swift's exceptional website, which I was glad to do for next to nothing because I have loved Hayley since the first time I saw her on TV in 1987. I was five. I have devoted my life to her, and winning this contest was my reward." He turned to look at Hayley. "You are, frankly, my only reason for living, Miss Swift. Several counselors have tried to convince me that you're an addiction, like alcohol or drugs. But I'm not drunk, or high; I'm in love—so in love I would do anything to be with you. I've spent my entire life working toward this moment." With an expression that fell somewhere between benevolence and disdain, he continued to look at Hayley while nodding his head to either side to indicate Tipsy and Bubba. "If you'll just get rid of these unnecessary people, we can resume our conversation and continue making plans."

As Hayley stood speechless, Bubba disconnected from 9-1-1 on his cell phone. "Didn't I tell you there was something fishy about this guy, Mr. Mack? That day he showed up at your office while I was there, an' offered to take all them old photos and press kits off your hands? And then you hired him to do that Internet stuff and sent him over here to install somethin' or other . . . I shoulda never let him come through the door. Shoulda never . . ."

Hayley wrenched from Tipsy's grasp. "You mean this creep has been in my house *before*? Tipsy, what is going on here?"

As the sound of a wailing siren became audible and drew closer, Tipsy Mack swayed to the left and the right, then steadied himself by closing his eyes for a moment. "*Darlin'*. I'm sure this is blown all out of proportion. Bubba, would you kindly escort Mr. Wilson to the front door? Tell the police to turn off them dadblame sirens, then tell 'em what happened here, and make sure they follow up with Mr. Wilson's probation officer. Ask the Captain to holler back at me on my cell phone when he gets a minute."

Bubba grabbed Everett P. Wilson by the nearest arm. The man gave him a cold stare, then adjusted his collar and smoothed his coat before reaching to place the hand from his other arm on Hayley's shoulder. Gasping, she shrank away.

"Not to worry, my love. They can imprison my body but not my soul, and they can never extinguish my love for you. 'Til next time," he declared with a slight bow.

Tipsy turned beet red as he pointed Bubba and his charge toward the door. "That's about enough out of you," he growled and then turned to grab the sofa as his knees buckled under him. "Law-zy, my head's spinnin' like a top."

"*Your* head's spinning? What do you think *mine's* doing? *Probation* officer??? Am I to understand you hired a convicted *criminal* to build my website, work in my house, come to this party, and now you're going to blithely send him on his way after he's sworn to stalk me for the rest of my life? Tipsy, did you *read* those emails I sent you? The man is *crazy*! Kuh-*RAZY*! I'm getting ready to romp around Picket Fence America in a dilapidated tour bus with *zero* security, and you're leaving that guy on the street? *I don't think so!!!*

Tipsy raked a shaky hand across his forehead. "Would you calm down? There are probably a hundred people by now out there by your pool, and if you don't lower your voice, you're gonna be tomorrow's headline and out of a gig you need more than you realize." He sighed as she flinched. "I'm gonna shoot straight with you, Hayley-Gayley. I love you like a daughter and if I hadn't discovered you singin' your heart out all them years ago, I'd likely be workin' on the General Jackson or serving up well drinks at Tootsie's—and you know that—but you need to face some facts."

Hayley crossed her arms and scowled as Tipsy sat up straight to look her in the face. His eyes reflected the burden of having to share the truth, pain, and disappointment of sixty-plus years of dealing with life.

"You've had a bad run goin' on ten, fifteen years now, darlin', and I'm about played out on how to jump-start your career. You still got the voice, you still look great, and if you'd get down off your Songwriter High Horse and sing somebody else's material, you *might* have another hit! Did you ever think—just once—you might show me the courtesy of trustin' my judgment? You say you trust me, but you never take my advice about pickin' songs. It's always been your call. Well, sugar, you keep callin' the wrong number. And, yeah, you pay me to be your manager, but you don't listen to a thing I say."

Hayley swallowed hard as Tipsy's blunt words stung her ears. She'd been prepared for his *other* lecture—the one where he told her what she wanted to hear: how she'd pen another hit any day now, how if she'd written all those hit songs she could surely write another, how that song simmering just beneath her subconscious would surface any time. Feel-good phrases he'd kept repeating when she refused to hear the truth.

Tears welled in Hayley's eyes as she gazed at the man who was much more father than manager. "Oh, Tips, I'm so sorry!" She flung her arms around him, then retreated and took his hands in hers. "But just because I'm sorry for being difficult doesn't mean you're off the hook for what happened here tonight. That pervert could have killed me! He might yet! You and Bubba—and the *police*!—need to read those e-mails! If somebody doesn't lock him up, I'm hiring a bodyguard!"

Tipsy sighed. "I promise you, Hayley, the guy's harmless. He's just got the hots for you."

"Hots I can handle. It's homicide that worries me, or hand-cuffs—on *me*!"

"Aw, he did a little time in juvy for hacking, that's all. He's a computer wiz. He contacted me about updating your website a while back, and said he'd give us a discount because he was a fan. Since you don't have a record label to cover costs like that anymore, it seemed like a good deal. He told me he'd been in some trouble, and I checked, but it didn't look like anything beyond teenage pranks. He built the site, did a good job, then kept hanging around. I figured he needed money, so Bubba suggested I hire him to be the site administrator. I did, and we gave him a bunch of your old show merch and photos to see if he could sell 'em online. But he's off the payroll as of tonight. This minute! He did a dang good job, though. I kinda hate to lose him."

"*Tipsy*!" Hayley's eyes widened in disbelief and she smacked him. "Are you not listening to me? Here you are accusing me of not trusting you about a song and I'm trusting you with my *life!* What if there's somebody else like him out there? What if Rhett Wilson's not the only one? Answer me this: Was there any kind of screening process for this 'favorite fans' contest? Do you know anything *about* these people you invited over here tonight?"

"Quite a bit, actually." Tipsy sat, chewing his lower lip.

"Wait a minute. There *wasn't* a contest, was there? Then who *are* all these people? Cousins? Vagrants? Most-wanted? How low did you have to go to find me some 'fans'?"

Tipsy looked distinctively uncomfortable. "Now, it ain't like that. Most of 'em are *big* fans, but I might have called in a favor or two to fluff up the crowd." As Hayley walloped him again, the beleaguered manager flinched and raised his arms in self-defense. "Now hold on a minute!" he protested. "Remember what I said a few days ago about illusion bein' everything? The more common interpretation of that is 'fake it 'til ya make it,' but the bottom line is that, sometimes, reality can benefit from a little enhancement—and this is one of those times. This gig is givin' you a chance to reclaim your place in the spotlight, and if it means stackin' the deck with an administrative assistant or two—"

"A FedEx driver? Mailman? Your favorite barista?" Hayley interrupted with a snort.

"Well, who knows? Maybe they'll start playin' your records at the coffee shop!" Tipsy retorted.

Outside, in the swelter of the early September evening, at a sprawling home set beneath Tennessee starlight, eighty-three country music fans and a half-dozen journalists, in sundry stages of inebriation, frolicked in a once-pristine swimming pool now littered with soggy sandwiches, assorted fruit, shrimp tails, a big red hat with a broken purple feather, and a torn eight-by-ten glossy of former country music superstar Hayley Swift. Not one of them noticed that the diva herself was missing all the fun.

CHAPTER FOUR
Home is Where the Hard Is!

As the black stretch limousine slowly rolled up to the rambling Skerry Inn, the driver killed the engine. Alone in the cavernous back seat, surrounded by the twilight darkness, Hayley Swift mentally assessed her clandestine return to the town where she'd spent the first eighteen years of her life.

Well, well. Same three stoplights, same Dairy Dip. But would you look at old man Denton's place? Turned into a cozy bed and breakfast. No sign whatsoever of that sleazy old reprobate who made my mama and daddy's life—and mine—so miserable. Wonder what Mama would say if she knew I was spending the night here, after all her warnings to stay away from this house?

Hayley shook her head to dispel the unpleasant memories, then took advantage of the limousine's spacious back seat to stretch lazily. In a last-ditch effort to make amends, Tipsy had sent his long-time personal chauffeur to Hayley's front door that morning. Wearing a crisp black uniform and a smile that rivaled the sun, Bernie Gambrell had presented her with Tipsy's American Express card and a note that said, *"Even second fiddles deserve to go first class. Enjoy the ride—all 10 hours of it! Bernie's the best, and so are you. P.S. The band bus will meet you in Skerry. P.P.S., Almond Joys in the fridge. Love, T."*

Grateful to have only her own company as she came to terms with returning home after all these years, Hayley smiled now as she recalled the final moments of her send-off party the night before. Her favorite image was Tipsy Mack, Agent Extraordinaire, patiently and politely urging the inebriated guests to get out of her pool and into the shuttle bus he'd spirited up from somewhere. Taking a deep breath, she leaned forward and pressed a button to lower the window separating her compartment from the driver's. As the tinted glass slipped down to reveal the grey-haired, kind-eyed man behind the wheel, Hayley cleared her throat. "Bernie, would you do me a favor?"

"Sure thing, Miz Hayley. You name it." He turned toward her and smiled.

"Well, I don't know if Tipsy told you, but I haven't been back home in thirty-five years, and I'm a little gun-shy. I wondered if . . . well . . . would you mind going in and making sure they've got my room ready, so I can just slip in quietly?"

"No problem. I'm ready for a good leg-stretch anyhow. Be right back."

Bernie exited the sleek car and lumbered up to the handsome old house, its wedding cake columns and curlicued tiers resplendent in their restored glory. Hayley watched as he entered the house, then slumped back against the smooth leather seat. She pulled out her compact and checked her lipstick a third time.

"You can do this," she whispered fiercely as she stared at her reflection. "You're a pro! You've won every award there is, earned more money than most people will ever see, but now you're broke and, if you don't knock 'em dead *this* time around, game's over, girl. This may be just a little two-bit gig, but you're gonna play it to the hilt, and prove you've still got what it takes! Right? *Right!*"

She exhaled and snapped the compact shut as Bernie opened her door and held out his hand. "They're ready for you. Got the best suite all set; lady name of Miz Ellen's gonna make you some tea if you like. All you gotta do is walk up them steps and I'll take care of everythin' else." He squeezed her hand. "You doin' okay?"

Hayley pursed her lips, then smiled faintly. "I'm fine. Just tired. Thanks for driving me all the way down here. I really appreciate it."

As the driver's face crinkled in a broad smile, an evening breeze lifted a sheaf of papers off the seat beside Hayley and sent them scattering onto the manicured lawn. Bernie stooped to catch them as Hayley sighed and shook her head. "Thanks," she said as he handed her the slightly damp pages. "Guess Tipsy figured if he put me in a limo with pen and paper instead of on a bus with the band, I might get inspired to do some writing. Lord knows I could *use* a new hit song!"

Bernie gave her arm an affectionate pat. "It'll come, Miz Hayley. It'll come," he assured her, then moved to unlock the trunk. As he removed three enormous suitcases in succession, Hayley stood silently, staring into the dark abyss of the limousine's gaping trunk.

"Bernie, can I ask you a question?"

The chauffeur paused as he heaved the last— and heaviest—

bag out of the trunk. "Is this the kind of question I should go ahead and set this down?"

Hayley chuckled softly. "Probably," she said, and leaned back against the limo. "Look, you've known me a long time. You know how hard I worked to make it to the top. But I haven't . . . well, I didn't exactly stay in touch with my friends here in Skerry. I'm . . . um . . . kind of embarrassed to be coming back after not paying anyone much attention all these years. What if they don't like me anymore? What if they've asked me here just to gloat, now I'm down on my luck? I truly *care* about these people—I never meant to ignore them; it's just that there are a lot of bad memories here along with the good. I meant to come back, I *meant* to stay in touch but . . . I was so glad to get *away* and then . . . time just disappeared. *Years* disappeared." She looked up with tears in her eyes. "I don't know how to handle this, Bernie!"

The man scratched his chin and straightened his cap before speaking. "Miz Hayley," he finally said, "You been all over the world, singin' to folks old and young, workin' yo' tail off since you was just a kid. You sung for sick people, for soldiers, for queens and presidents. You can go up these steps; this ain't nothin' to be afraid of. This is home."

Hayley looked up at the night sky and tried to ward off the tears that wanted so badly to flow. "That's just it. These people know who I *really* am; all the sequins and make-up in the world don't hide the fact that I was cheap white trash with a song and a prayer."

"You mighta been poor, little girl, but you weren't trash. You were a good girl, raised to live right and love the Lord and no matter what happened or didn't way back then is a long time ago and needs to be laid to rest." Bernie put a hand on Hayley's shoulder and looked straight into her brooding, troubled eyes. "Now you listen to ol' Bernie. You go in there and get yourself a good night's sleep, then tomorrow, you put on your best Sunday-go-to-meetin' clothes, you paint that pretty face like Jesus was comin', and you waltz in to that fancy party with your head held high, because *somebody* wanted you here bad enough to *pay* you to come home. Then you sing your heart out, and any people who been thinkin' bad about you, once you commence to singing, is gonna remember how proud they are you came from their hometown, and how they maybe had a hand in makin' you famous, and how they wanna see you twinkling back up there with the stars where you belong. Ol' Bernie's predictin' this time tomorrow night, mosta Skerry's gonna be standin' in the gym, cheerin' they fool heads off. We can make a small wager on that, if you care to." He turned away, hoisted all four bags and turned back toward the house. "Everbody has to face their past sooner or later, but not everybody gets a chance to make things right. You say what you need to say to the folks that need to hear it, and let the good Lord take it from there." He nodded toward the inn. "Now, let's get you in outta this night air; I don't want Mr. Tipsy on my case for getting' you sick."

Hayley inhaled deeply, then leaned forward and kissed Bernie on the cheek. She followed him up the walk and held open the door as he entered the lamp-lit lobby of the Skerry Inn. Delicious aromas permeated the air—a mixture of cinnamon, roses, and baking bread. The walls were painted a bold blue, with creamy white wainscoting accenting doors that led to the parlor, a massive dining room, and a handsome library Hayley remembered as old man Denton's study.

She swallowed hard, her brain struggling to both recall and repress the awful memory of how Otis Denton had summoned her into this very room the day after her parents died in a car accident.

They'd been delivering a custom sedan to a car dealer in Myrtle Beach when the brakes went out and sent them careening over a bridge. Mr. Denton blamed the brake failure on Ernest Swift himself, since he was Denton Auto's chief mechanic. But when the ensuing investigation brought to light two sets of accounting books for the dealership, Denton suggested his bookkeeper, Ernest's wife Sara, had been pocketing money from the business and could, perhaps, live with the guilt no longer.

A "confession" note found in the Swift's tiny apartment over Denton's garage was proof, he claimed, of her parents' guilt, but Hayley knew the note wasn't in her mother's handwriting, and she suspected her parents were being used as scapegoats to cover up Denton's own misdeeds. In retrospect, Hayley supposed she could have sued her parents' employer on any number of grounds, but at the time, she was an awkward, self-conscious girl of sixteen whose sole living relative was a phlegmatic aunt, and whose sole material possessions suddenly consisted of a few clothes, a small box of photos, and a transistor radio.

The day after the accident, Otis Denton, wrapped in a red silk robe and smoking his ever-present stogie, stood on the staircase she now faced and, jabbing the *Wall Street Journal* at her with every point he made, barked at Hayley that she had three days to be out of the apartment and there was a past-due rent balance of four hundred dollars. At the look of horror on her face, Denton smirked and. abandoning his bark for a smoother, softer tone, proposed to Hayley that, due to his magnanimous nature, he might be willing to overlook her father's incompetence and her mother's dishonesty and consider a cash-free resolution of the debt—a 'labor exchange,' he called it. An 'even trade.'

You know, Pretty Girl, I put up with a lot from your parents, for your *sake, because I wanted them to take good care of you. I hired them when you were just a little bitty thing—a little bitty thing with the voice of an angel. You remember how you used to sit on my lap and sing to me when you were no bigger than a minute? I'd let you ride around with me in my big ol' convertible while your mama made lunch for my men, and you'd come over with your daddy to the house when he came to pay the rent, and you'd always give me a big ol' hug. Every Easter, I'd buy you a fancy dress and a big ol' basket of candy; you remember that? I've looked out for you, Pretty Girl, and I can keep on doing that. You got yourself a mighty fine talent, and if you'd dress yourself up, you could be a real looker, too. I got connections, sugar. I can set you up; you just say the word. Now, come on in here, darlin'. Let's you and me seal the deal with a hug, and maybe a little kiss. You always have had the purtiest little mouth. Mouth like yours can open doors. Whatcha think about that, Pretty Girl? Wanna open some doors?*

That was the day that transformed Hayley's life forever. As she stumbled backwards out of Otis Denton's house and raced to remove her few belongings from the garage apartment, she pledged to leave Skerry as soon as possible. In the meantime, her daddy's Aunt Beatrice reluctantly took her in. The only escape from Aunt Beatrice's tiny, stifling house was to work as many hours as she could at the Dairy Dip, or babysit. She paid Denton the four hundred dollars in less than six months, but the shame of the old man's suggestion of a 'labor exchange' had haunted her ever since.

Now, standing in the spot where that odious offer was made all those years ago, Hayley fought to maintain her composure as a silver-haired woman glided to the antique table that served as a registration desk.

"Good evening, Hayley! I don't know if you remember me; I'm Ellen Gibbs. I bought this house from the Denton family and restored it several years ago. We're so honored you'll be staying with us! Your driver tells me you're exhausted, so, if you'll follow me, right up those stairs . . . well, I suppose *you* know your way around this house better than I do, don't you? The old master suite is the biggest room, and—"

Hayley raised a hand to interrupt. "I appreciate your hospitality, Ms. Gibbs, and I don't want to be a bother, but there is no way I'm sleeping in Otis Denton's bedroom. He was a vile, loathsome man who made my life miserable, and as beautiful as this house is now, and even though he's rotting in his grave, I *cannot* sleep in a room where I know he laid his head." Remembering Denton's proud boasts about the KKK robe that hung on the back of his bedroom door, Hayley suddenly grinned and gave a nod toward Bernie. "How 'bout you put Mr. Bernie in the big bedroom and give me something else?"

Ellen Gibbs blinked a few times but managed to muster a wan smile. "Why, certainly, if that's what you'd prefer. I have a sweet room at the back of the house that gets a lovely evening breeze. It's small, but it has a private bath. Just give me a moment to turn down the bed. Y'all go on in the dining room and help yourself to some tea and cookies."

Bernie followed Hayley to the brocade-papered dining room. Raising a hand, he gave her a hearty high-five. "That's the gal I been knowin' all these years!" he chuckled. "I reckon you gonna handle this homecomin' just fine, Miz Hayley." He lowered his head, shook it, and chuckled again.

Hayley put her hand over her mouth and tried to restrain a nervous giggle. "I can't believe I said that!" she whispered, and gave Bernie a conspiratorial squeeze. "Thanks for the pep talk. You're a good friend. Now, let's chow down on these cookies. I'm starved!"

CHAPTER FIVE
You'll Never Go Alone

"Did I just hear a *flush*? Hayley, darlin', where *are* you? Is everything all right?" Tipsy Mack's voice crackled through the cell phone, the signal strength wavering as Hayley fled one tiny stall and slipped into another.

"Tipsy, this was a horrible idea! I can't believe I let you talk me into this." Teetering between tears and hysteria, Hayley rubbed her taut stomach in an effort to calm the flock of hyperactive butterflies dive-bombing her entrails. "The band's not here, the people at the registration table had no idea who I was, and my old gang is sitting like a bunch of vultures right in front of the stage. I feel like a lamb going to slaughter!" she wailed.

"Hay . . . ca . . . down . . . ov . . . .acting . . . it . . . fine . . . " came her manager's fractured voice.

"You're breaking up, Tipsy; what?"

"There . . . crash . . . bus . . . not . . . " she heard and then the phone beeped and went silent. Almost immediately, it warbled to life again, a synthesized version of *"The Hallelujah Chorus"* echoing across the black and gold ladies' restroom inside the Skerry high school gymnasium.

"Tips? Is that you?" Hayley gasped into the tiny receiver.

"Naw, honey, it's Jack."

"Where *are* you?" she demanded of the man who'd served as road manager for almost every gig she'd ever played and would be backing her tonight.

"Calm down," drawled the deep, mellow voice. "We're almost there. Pinky lost a contact and we had to hunt for it."

Hayley gave an exasperated sigh. "I have one word for that man: LASIK!!!"

Jack Bisbee cackled. "Ain't it the truth? We could've already retired if we had a nickel for every time we've had to crawl around on the floor, looking for them things. Listen, we got a slight problem."

Hayley felt the hair on the back of her neck prickle and the butterflies do a triple-somersault. "Jack?"

"Calm down, everything's gonna be fine. But your back-up singers had an unpleasant encounter with a chicken truck on I-95 outside of Florence."

"Didn't they come with you?"

""Naw, somebody had somethin' goin' on so they rented a car and didn't leave Nashville 'til this morning."

Panic constricting her vocal cords, Hayley's voice came out as a squeak. "Can't they get off the interstate and come down Highway 52 instead?

"They could, if they weren't on their way to the hospital to get chicken feathers plucked outta their butts. It's already almost eight, sugar; the Class of '87'll be sawin' logs before we can get another bunch of singers out here. Listen, we're just pullin' into the parking lot. Come on out to the bus and let's go over the line-up. I can do the harmony on "Love Me, Love Me Not" and "Mr. Cool," and Willard and Bo can handle "Rodeo Be-Bop.""

Hayley coughed, trying to open her rapidly constricting throat. "I can't *do* this," she rasped. "Even if you guys help out on the other songs, you can't do "Sister Serenade," and you *know* that's the first thing they'll wanna hear."

Suddenly four women burst through the door into the ladies' room. "*Hot flash! Hot flash!* WATER! AIR VENT! *MOVE!*" the tallest woman shouted as she fanned herself with flapping arms. The others—an overweight bleached blonde, a Katie Couric lookalike, and a mousy redhead—were laughing and fanning their purses at the agitated flashee.

As Hayley sobbed silently in the bathroom stall, with Jack's tinny voice chirping out of the cell phone now smashed against her neck, recognition slowly came to her. *No. God wouldn't be this cruel.* She rested her head against the metal wall, pondered her choice of actions then, deciding there *was* no choice, opened the stall door and walked out.

Amanda Brooks' long arms ceased flailing and she stared into the mirror like she'd just seen a dancing giraffe. "Hayley? Oh, my *gosh*! *Hayley*!" She shrieked and spun around, nearly falling off her three-inch heels. "Oh, Hayley! Oh, *Hayley*!"

There was an onslaught of arms and bodies and squeals, then a small, muffled sniff rose up that C. J. interpreted as the beginning of tears. "Don't you dare, Hayley Swift!" she warned. "If you start crying, we *all* will!" She pulled back and held her old friend at arm's length. "Wait a minute! You're *already* crying. What's wrong? Oh, honey, what's *wrong*?"

That was all it took. The dam broke, the years disappeared, and five women whose lives had taken very different paths were all eighteen again—hearts full, spirits high, ready to take on anything that threatened their alliance. Hayley was relaying her road manager's bad news about the backup singers when she suddenly blinked and took a step back. "Why are you all dressed alike? Ohmigosh! Those are our Basket-Flower Festival dresses! Oh, my *gosh*! How *sweet*!" She teared up again, then giggled. "And how *incredible*! How many women our age can still wear the clothes they wore in high school? Y'all are amazing!"

"Devious, too," chuckled Meg. "C. J. went digging in her mama's scrap bag and found some remnants to provide a little—um—*expansion*—for those of us who've grown!"

Suddenly, Amanda pulled away from the group and began fanning furiously again, then stopped and shrugged. "Over," she pronounced. "Oh, well." She stood looking in the mirror at the five of them, then smiled. "*Sing with me, sister, 'cause we . . .*" she abruptly began to croon.

"*. . . all share a history . . .*" chimed in C. J. and Sue.

"*We're all in this together,*" Meg intoned—reluctantly, but on perfect pitch.

"*Life is short, but the ride is wild . . .*" Hayley's face beamed as her pure soprano voice finished off the first verse of the chorus and the five voices came together for the payoff.

"*I'll watch your back, you watch mi—*"

They yelped as a knock on the door made them all jump.

"Hayley?" said a deep male voice.

Amanda took a step forward and pulled open the mirrored door to reveal tall, dark, and stunning Jack Bisbee, final apologetic concession by Tipsy Mack to his diva gone home. After the send-off party debacle, Tipsy's guilt—along with his concern for Hayley's safety—led him to call Jack, Hayley's former lead guitarist, to see if he and his band, Road Kill, could back her for at least part of the Retro Rodeo tour, bolstering Hayley's spirits and acting as body-guards. Tipsy figured if Jack did nothing but show up and soothe Hayley's nerves for the Basket-Flower Festival, it would be money well spent. Now, the lean, muscled musician nodded slightly and grinned at the ladies who stood gaping at his oversized presence in the tiny bathroom.

"Hel-*lo*, and look what the cat dragged in!" cooed Meg.

"Ladies," acknowledged Jack, as he removed his black Stetson and, obviously enjoying the attention, bowed with a flourish.

Very much aware of how good Jack looked in his black t-shirt and tight, black, boot-cut jeans, Hayley pursed her lips in an amused smirk as the women treated themselves to a moment's pleasure. "Girls," she said finally, "meet Jack Bisbee."

"No *wonder* you never came home," Sue whispered in Hayley's ear as Meg and C. J. extended hands and Amanda gave a quick adjustment to her French twist.

Hayley snorted and gave Sue a squeeze. "Any good news about the girls?" she asked Jack hopefully.

"'Fraid not. Everybody's gonna live—well, maybe not the chickens--but it sounds like they're all pretty banged up." He gave the women a quick once-over. "How the heck did you find back-up singers—much less, costumes! — that fast?"

Hayley looked confused. "What?"

Jack flashed another crooked, dimpled smile. "If you girls sound as good as you look, nobody'll ever know we brought in ringers."

"Hold on, cowboy!" Meg said, with a provocative thrust of her hip. "We *used* to sing with Hayley, but unfortunately, we got left behind when she went to Nashville. Your offer's a little late—by about thirty-five years."

"Oh, Meg!" groaned Amanda, throwing back her head in frustration.

Now it was Jack's turn to look confused.

Meg reached to rest a hand on Jack's shoulder and gave him a dazzling smile. "You see, Jack, Hayley started her career in a quintet—*our* quintet. But when the talent scout came around, she could only find room on the contract for one name: hers. Just think—you could have had *all* of us all these years, not just 'Miss Queen of the Rodeo.'"

"I knew this was a mistake," Hayley mumbled as she turned to slump against a wall.

"It most assuredly was not! Listen here, Meg Dorris," Sue snapped as she whirled away from Hayley and put a finger in Meg's face. "I've had just about enough of your whining. Nobody stopped you from going to Nashville except *you*. If you think you're so goldarned talented, here's your chance. Hayley needs help and, apparently, all she has is us, so I expect to see your fat butt up on that stage in a few minutes with the rest of us!"

Stricken, Meg stood in open-mouthed silence, as did Hayley. But Jack grinned, Amanda attempted to muffle a snicker, and C. J. stared at Sue in rapt admiration. "You *go*, girl!" she said in an admiring voice.

Suddenly Meg wheeled around to face Hayley. "Why *should*

we come to your rescue? You walked out on us! And would it have killed you to pick up a phone every ten years or so, just to see if your four best friends were still alive?"

Unblinking, Hayley stared back into Meg's angry face. "I thought leaving Skerry would let me forget all the pain of that last year. I didn't walk out on *you,* Meg; I walked out on *me.* I tried to block it all out—my parent's accident, the rumors, the insinuations, the shame. I missed you guys so much I cried myself to sleep for months!" She paused a moment and swallowed hard. "That pillow you guys gave me saved my sanity more than once. But every time I picked up the phone to call, it all came back. I tried, Meg; I really did. But I couldn't reconnect. It was too hard."

"So why now?" Meg challenged, her blue eyes still blazing. "Why'd you finally come back home?"

Hayley gave a sad smile. "I—I guess because somebody finally *asked* me to."

Jack pointed at his watch. "I hate to ruin a Hallmark moment, but you gals have to make a decision. It's about ten minutes till showtime. Are we cuttin' '*Sister Serenade*' or are you ladies gonna step up to the plate?"

The five women stood looking at each other, their expressions ranging from tentative to bemused. Finally, Amanda gave a whoop. "Oh, *heck,* yeah! Why not? Do we all still know the words?"

C. J. hooted. "Will we ever *forget* them?

Jack nodded. "Looks like we're set, then. I'll see y'all on stage." He turned and pushed open the door but Meg grabbed his arm. "Hold on! This is what I wanted thirty-five years ago, but I've smoked way too many cigarettes to pull it off now. Sorry, Hayley, count me out."

Jack jerked his arm away and whipped back around. Using

one finger to tip back his Stetson, he leveled a challenging look at the belligerent blonde. "Didn't I just hear you complainin' about gettin' left behind? Darlin,' you've got a rare second chance. You gonna grab the brass ring or not?"

Meg smirked. "Maybe. Are you the prize?"

The guitarist guffawed. "Careful what you wish for, Blondie!" He grabbed Hayley, gave her a quick peck on the cheek and smacked her shapely rear end. "Go get 'em kid, I'm outta here! There's enough estrogen in this ugly bathroom to neuter King Kong!"

As the door eased shut behind Jack, Meg sighed deeply. "I gotta use the john." She slammed a stall door shut as C. J. and Amanda exchanged amused grins. Sue leaned close to Hayley and whispered, "Is there something we should know about you and Jack?"

Hayley gave a rueful smile. "We tried once, years ago, but it freaked us both out. I love him to death—he's always been there for me—but he's just a friend. Jack's a loner; his only love is his guitar." She took a deep breath, felt the butterflies in her stomach go into hyper-drive again, then studied Sue's and her reflection in the mirror and grinned like a four-year-old entering Disney World. "I can't believe this is happening!"

"It's happening, all right!" Amanda whooped as she headed into another of the stalls. "Yee-haw!"

"Ladies and gentlemen—The Girls Next Door!" Jack swept the Stetson off his head with a wink as the five women strode out to take center stage. Amanda, Sue, C. J., and Meg stood paralyzed behind their microphones and, for a moment, there was absolute silence. Then Hayley reached to take her mic from its stand, and the Skerry high school gym erupted in an explosion of cheers and applause. Relief washed over Hayley. She glanced backstage and saw Bernie standing in the wings. She smiled as he pointed a finger and mouthed, '*I told you so!*' Then she looked at her four best friends, now holding hands like nervous beauty pageant contestants, threw back her head, and laughed.

"Hello, Skerry! I'm Hayley Swift, and I'm *home!*" The Class of '87 roared. "It's been a long time, but say hello to The Girls Next Door!" As the crowd roared again, the drummer hit the downbeat of the song that put Skerry's prodigal daughter on the map.

At the back of the gym, Dr. Keith Parker stood listening in the shadows and smiled. "Welcome home, Hayley," he murmured softly.

An hour later, as she rested her head on Keith Parker's shoulder and swayed to the strains of Reba McEntire singing "What Am I Gonna Do About You," Hayley took a deep, cleansing breath and closed her eyes. *I can't believe I'm home! It's like we picked up right where we left off. Our harmony was dead-on! Meg even hit that high 'C' she said she'd never be able to hit again.* She giggled as Sally Field's famous paraphrased line came to mind: '*You like me! Right now, you like me!*'"

Keith pulled away. "What? You think it's funny I still can't dance?"

"I think it's funny we're back here in this gym just like we were thirty-five years ago."

Keith cocked an eyebrow. "As I recall, I suggested—thirty-five years ago—that we step out to get a little fresh air."

"And as *I* recall, it wasn't just the air that got fresh!" Hayley retorted.

Keith looked chagrined. "Hey, can't blame a guy for trying."

Hayley made a coquettish face. "Can't blame a girl for hoping he'll try again." She met his dark gaze and he opened his mouth to speak and then, as his pants pocket buzzed, didn't. Instead, he reached down for his cell phone.

He pressed a button, scanned the screen, then leaned to kiss her cheek. "Sorry. I'm on call tonight. I have to run." He touched a finger to her nose. "Don't get on a bus until I see you again. We've got some unfinished business." With a quick wave and a nod, he was gone.

Hayley watched as, this time, Keith walked away from *her*. "I guess turnabout's fair play," she sighed, and crossed the dance floor to look for Sue.

CHAPTER SIX
Dang, Darlin', You Want Fries with that Shake?

"Okay, I need a large cherry Coke, two Cheerwines, a strawberry freeze, a sweet tea, a large black coffee—Mr. Gene, is that *you*? It's me! Hayley! Yeah!—okay, and then an order of chili cheese fries . . . five loaded Dipsy burgers— wait, make it six! We need one for Bernie—and, um . . . five orders of tater tots. Oh, and hold on! Don't total it up yet—we gotta have dipped cones. But don't make 'em yet; we'll drive back around when we're ready. And come out here so I can hug your neck!"

Hayley plopped back against the leather seat of the limousine as it cruised past the drive-through speaker and rounded the corner of her teenage place of employment. "I can't believe this," she squealed, looking around the interior of the car at her four best childhood pals. "Here we are at the Dairy Dip, after a dance. It's like high school all over again!"

Amanda fluttered a *Class of '87 Reunion* program at her bosom. "It is most certainly *not* like high school! I'm having hot flashes, you're not wearing roller skates or a red satin miniskirt, and the Dip now takes plastic!"

As Bernie maneuvered the big vehicle into a vertical space on the edge of the parking lot, Hayley glanced around at what had been Skerry's most popular late-night hangout for decades. "This place doesn't look a bit different! Why on earth hasn't Mr. Gene remodeled?"

C. J. rolled her eyes and set her mouth in an imitation of the Dairy Dip's crusty elderly owner. "*Aw, now, I did the whole place over in 1980. I cain't be wastin' money on such as that!*"

The friends chuckled, but C. J. shook her head. "Don't laugh! He's probably a millionaire. That man is tight with a penny and smart with a dollar; I swear he owns half the county. I heard him say one time, if he could just find a good woman to share it with, he'd be the happiest man in Skerry."

"There you go, Hayley: a million bucks and free Dipsy burgers for the rest of your life!" laughed Sue. "What a deal!"

"You first!" Hayley grimaced as Amanda began fanning.

"I am *melting*!" she yelled, and pressed a button that opened the sun roof. "Hot dog! Cool air!" she exclaimed as the Dairy Dip's blue neon lights mixed with the South Carolina starlight to cast a soft glow on the limo's interior. As a light breeze cut through the sticky night, Amanda bolted up, thrusting her head and shoulders through the roof.

"Lawzy, I may have to start sleeping in the deep freeze!"

"You know, I don't think I've *had* a hot flash yet," said Hayley. "I mean, I've always been hot-natured, but I don't remember having a meltdown just all of a sudden. Could I have had one and not known it?"

The chorus of cackles caused heads to turn all over the parking lot.

"Oh, sure—about like you could get hit by a Mack truck and not know it," Meg hooted, as she, Sue, C. J., and Hayley clambered up to squeeze through the sunroof next to Amanda. They looked around at the cars scattered across the parking lot. A few contained groups of teenagers, or families with small children, but most were filled with young couples.

Sue narrowed her eyes as a truck on the highway cruised through a yellow light. "Well, well, well," she said. "See that old Chevy pickup coming around the corner, Hayley? That would be Doctor Keith Parker. Guess his emergency is over."

Hayley's eyes followed the blue truck as Meg moaned. "Oh, man, did he ever smell good tonight! We slow-danced three times— then he found *you*. What'd you say to run him off?"

"Nothing!" Hayley objected. "He got called in."

They watched as the ancient truck drove past and disappeared.

"Hmm. Guess he's not hungry," Amanda sniffed. "He'll be back. The call of Gene's chili cheese fries is a powerful thing."

"I— didn't notice a ring when we were dancing," Hayley said quietly. "Didn't Keith ever marry?"

Sue shook her head. "Nope. You can pick up right where you left off. How long are you in town?"

Hayley gave a weary chuckle. "Oh, please," she admonished

with a roll of her eyes. "There's enough water under *that* bridge to sink the Queen Mary."

Sue shrugged. "You're both strong swimmers. I think you owe it to yourselves to try again. Would it be so awful to admit you made a mistake and tell him how you feel?"

Hayley sighed deeply. "And how *do* I feel? I've been trying to figure that out all night!"

"Hey, there's Keith's truck again!" Amanda interjected. Hayley Swift, I *dare* you to flag him down." Her eyes narrowed. "I *double* dare you—and there's another round of chili cheese fries riding on it."

With a defiant lift of her chin, Hayley brought her fingers to her mouth and let rip an ear-splitting whistle. Fifty feet from the Dairy Dip entrance, Keith Parker grinned broadly as he saluted in response to Hayley's whistle and 'come here' wave, then turned in and aimed his ancient truck toward the limo.

"I can't believe I did that!" Hayley shrieked as she shot down onto the seat below.

"Time for a swim under that bridge, girlfriend," Sue teased as she lowered herself down beside Hayley.

"Oh, *man*! I'm all sweaty, my hair's a mess . . . do I need lipstick?"

C. J. smoothed a stray strand of hair away from her friend's panicked face. "You look beautiful. Pheromones do that to a girl."

"Pheromones and *sequins*," Amanda quipped, poking a finger into Hayley's sparkly silver dress.

Hayley stuck out her tongue at Amanda, gave Sue and C. J. a quick hug, then climbed out of the limo and headed toward Keith's beat-up truck, parked just a few feet away.

"Well, hello, again! What brings you to this heartburn party?" She knocked on the hood of the vehicle she'd last seen three and a half decades earlier.

"Hey, careful there! This baby's now an antique!" Keith said as he climbed out of the cab.

"By several orders of magnitude! You should see if there's a registry for National Historic Vehicles," she teased, pausing to inspect a dent in the door she thought she remembered contributing.

"My patient lives, I'm happy to report, but *I'm* dying of starvation. Have you eaten yet?"

"I have," Hayley said, then turning so Amanda would be sure to hear her, added loudly, "BUT I BELIEVE I MAY HAVE AN ORDER OF CHILI CHEESE FRIES COMING!"

Keith gestured toward a rustic picnic bench, half-hidden behind a cedar tree next to the parking lot. "It's cooled off a little; we could sit over there, if it won't mess up your dress. Will the Posse turn you loose for a while?"

Hayley chuckled at Keith's old nickname for her girlfriends. "Go place your order while I tell Bernie to take them for a spin around town." When she arrived back at the limo, however, she found no one except Bernie, who was munching contentedly on his Dipsy burger, a book perched on the steering wheel. "Where'd everybody go?" she asked.

"I believe they headed toward the ladies' room."

"Okay, well, if they come back any time soon, take 'em for a spin around town, would you, please? I'm gonna sit with Dr. Parker while he eats."

Bernie gave a nod. "Will do."

"Okay, then, back in a few," Hayley said as she spotted Keith coming her way with a bulging food sack.

They met midway in the parking lot then walked together to the picnic bench and sat, mostly hidden from view by the scrubby cedar. Hayley sipped her drink and watched as Keith took an enormous bite of his burger, closed his eyes, and chewed politely, but in obvious pleasure. His hair, thinning slightly, was still dark and wavy; his eyes—when open—were the same deep blue pools she remembered, though framed now with a few congenial, middle-aged crinkles.

"Do you still come here a lot?" Hayley asked, and Keith laughed.

"More than a man with a medical degree should. I cling to the hope that science may still find healing power in a cheeseburger."

"Isn't it funny? When I worked here, all I could think about was leaving. Then when I left, for a long time, all I could think about was coming back. I guess we never value our treasures till we lose them, do we?"

Keith raised an eyebrow. "You've been pining away over the Dairy Dip all these years?"

Hayley gave him a look of reproach.

"Sorry," he grinned, then sobered. "So is that why you finally came home? To find a lost treasure?"

She met his gaze briefly, then looked away. "Maybe. No. Not really." She stared at the man she'd thought, at seventeen, she would marry. "I have to be straight with you, Keith. I'm here because playing this reunion was the first gig I've been offered in months. You don't have to be a country music insider to know I'm pretty much a has-been at this point—haven't had a hit in years. This was the kick-off for an eight-week run my manager scraped up for me—the 'Heat & Humidity' tour, I'm calling it." She tried to laugh, but it came out as a cough. "I'm not the headliner, but I need the money, so here I am, right back where I started." Their eyes met again, Hayley's glistening with unshed tears. "Any treasure to be reclaimed, well, that'll be a bonus—one I've thought about for thirty-five years." She looked away, again. "I never dared to hope for that."

They sat in silence for several seconds, then Keith cleared his throat. "Thirty-five years is a long time to leave something unresolved. I guess we're both at fault; you never called me, I never called you. I did go to one of your concerts, once—first time you played the Grand Ole Opry. I was at Vandy, in med school."

The tears finally spilled as Hayley lifted her head. "You *lived* in Nashville? Why didn't you call me? I had no idea!"

Keith took one of Hayley's hands into his, then shrugged. "When you got on that bus, you made a choice. I knew you loved me, but I also knew you had to leave—and I understood why. I loved you so much, I couldn't interfere—even if it meant letting you go. You followed your dream, Hayley, and I'm proud of you. But I followed mine, too. I wanted to be a doctor as much as you wanted to get out of Dodge. I certainly didn't plan to come back *here* to start a practice, but dreams don't always turn out like you think they will when you're eighteen."

Hayley gave him a sad smile. "Yeah, mine's sort of turned into a nightmare. I'm out of work, I'm broke, I'm lonely . . . there's not a day goes by I don't think about you, Keith—about what it would have been like to be with you."

"Yeah, I've wondered that a few million times myself. I guess you know by now I never got married; I *tried* to fall in love," he confessed, with a lopsided grin, "but it just didn't feel right trying to be with someone else. I guess I hoped you'd feel the same, eventually." He smiled. "A lot of folks say I've wasted my life, waiting on you; what do you think?"

"I never asked you to wait for me, Keith."

"I know, and I didn't *consciously* wait, I just nev— "

The opening drum/bass riff of the "Ghostbusters" theme song suddenly pierced the stillness, startling them both. "Oh, for—" Keith pulled his phone from his pocket, read the message, and gave an annoyed snort. "I have to go again." He let go of Hayley's hand and stood. "Look, we still have a lot to talk about. I'm off tomorrow; can we spend the day together?"

Hayley laughed as she blotted her face with a wadded-up napkin. "Only if it includes air conditioning. I'm staying at the bed and breakfast. Pick me up at ten?"

"Eight-thirty—but I promise to make it worth your while." He leaned to kiss the top of her head. "Sleep tight, and welcome home." As he sprinted off to his truck and sputtered away with a loud grinding of gears, Hayley collected herself and sipped the last of her Cheerwine.

"You okay?" asked Sue, suddenly appearing from behind the cedar tree.

"Gettin' there."

"Keith go home?"

"No, he got another call from the hospital. He's off tomorrow; we're going to talk some more."

"I think you should skip the talking and start making up for lost time," Sue started toward the limo then turned back and wiggled her eyebrows. "Or would that be making *out* for lost time?" she taunted, then took off running. Hayley raced after her and, together, they collapsed against the vehicle door, out of breath and snickering.

"You promised we could cruise Main Street in this thing; let's do it!" Sue demanded as she shoved Hayley aside, opened the door, and clambered in.

Amanda, who'd been stretched out on the wide back seat, barefoot, eyes closed, and balancing the remains of a Dipsy burger on her belly, rose up in a panic. "Whoa, *napping* here, do you mind?" She lifted the burger box off her stomach and swung her feet into the floorboard to make room for the others. "Bernie said you were with Keith. I want details—*all* of them. Sweet nothings, smooches, true confessions, the works."

"My lips are sealed," Hayley stated. "Where *is* everybody?"

"Well, C.J.'s gone to the potty—*again*, Bernie went to get our dip cones, and who knows where Meg is?" Amanda readjusted her dress and looked down to brush away some crumbs. "Last time I wore this, I swear my cleavage was a foot higher. Gravity is a terrible thing. Well, I'm with Sue. I think it's time to make good on your promise to cruise Main in this monster—but we can't go past the church." Sue and Hayley looked at her, perplexed. "The twins are at a lock-in—if they happened to be outside, they'd die if their friends saw me sprouting from a limo in a halter dress from high school!"

"Isn't 'lock-in' the operative word there?" Hayley inquired. "As in the kids would all be LOCKED INside? Besides, they might think it's *cool* for Mom to be shakin' her groove thing."

Amanda rolled her eyes. "Oh, you soooo know nothing about motherhood." She leaned back and laced her hands behind her head. "I must say, I had a blast singing with you up there on-stage tonight, Hayley. Brought back a lot of memories, didn't it, Su-zie-Q?"

"I'm sorry? What?" Sue looked confused.

"Singing with Hayley tonight. It brought back a lot of memories, didn't it?"

"Oh. Yes. It did. Sorry. Hey, didn't . . . that guy in the cowboy hat say something happened to your back-up singers and they're going to be out of commission for a while? Does that mean you'll have to get someone to fill in for them? You should hire us! Wouldn't that be a kick? I thought we weren't half-bad tonight!"

"Are you kidding? We were faaaabulous!" Amanda howled, and she and Sue began warbling a falsetto refrain of "Sister Serenade."

Hayley suddenly sat straight up, slapped the seat with one hand and, with the other, grabbed Sue's arm, bringing the impromptu duet to an abrupt halt. "That is a *phenomenal* idea, Sue! I love it! It's perfect! We could share Road Kill's bus . . . it would be like a two-week slumber party until my back-ups get out of the hospital!

Where's my cell phone? What time is it? I'm calling Tipsy!"

Right then, the limo door flew open and C. J. dove in, stiletto heels and halter dress upended as she collapsed into the seat with Meg right behind her. Both women were laughing so hard they were crying.

"What in the *world*?" Hayley demanded.

"Oh, my gosh, y'all missed it. It was *hysterical*!" C. J. rolled down into the floor and lolled in uncontrollable mirth, colliding with Meg, whose face was as red as an August tomato.

"We were coming out of the bathroom . . . " C. J. managed, before convulsing again in a gale of laughter.

"And this old man . . . " interjected Meg, but then she doubled over, unable to say more.

As Sue sat wide-eyed and Amanda's eyebrows met in a perplexed scowl, C. J. drew a deep breath. "Okay, okay," she said. "I'm calm now. Almost." She chortled again. "So. We were coming out of the bathroom, heading this way, when this gross old redneck *geezer*, parked next to the walk-up window, pokes his head out his car window, and yells, '*Dang, darlin' you want fries with that shake?*'"

Meg and C. J. fell over each other again as they snorted and pounded their fists on the floorboard. "We didn't know whether to hit him or hug him!" Meg guffawed. Amused by their friends' reaction, if not by the corny remark, Hayley, Sue, and Amanda began to giggle as well, and several minutes of hilarity ensued until Hayley sent forth another piercing finger whistle.

"Wow! Twice in one night!" she exclaimed as her girlfriends startled to attention. "Still got my touch! Listen up, I have an announcement."

Cross-legged in the corner of the floorboard, Meg rolled her eyes. "Let me guess: Keith Parker confessed his undying love for you, you're going to give up show biz, get married, and live happily ever after."

Hayley made a face. "I think you've read one romance novel too many. Look, I've missed you guys so much, and I know I screwed up, but maybe this is a chance to make things up to you. How 'bout if y'all come on this tour with me—as my official backup singers—until my regulars have recovered? Our first gig is the Basket-Flower Festival."

"That's three days from now!" Amanda protested.

"I know it's last-minute, and I know you have lives and commitments to get out of, but it would be *so* much fun to finally travel and sing together on the road, just like we planned."

"Some of us *work* for a living, Hayley," said Meg as she reached in her purse for a cigarette. "I can't just call my boss and tell him I'm taking off; I have *bills* to pay."

"I'll figure out a way to pay you as much as you'd earn from your regular jobs for however long you take off, and I know Tipsy will cover all your expenses." Hayley looked around the car from one face to another. "I know it may be too little too late, but I feel like this is an opportunity and I'd love to take advantage of it. Please, y'all? *Please?* We can spend all day Sunday practicing, and if the only song you're comfortable with by then is 'Sister Serenade,' that's fine. Jack and the guys can do the others until the next show, which is Wednesday."

Sue took a deep breath and looked out the sun roof; as a long-tenured teacher, she had plenty of time off accrued and, widowed and childless, her time was hers to spend as she saw fit. But she knew the others had obligations: husbands, children, parents, schedules.

"I *am* off Sunday," Meg admitted. She inhaled deeply from the cigarette she'd just lit, then lifted her head to exhale out the sunroof. She looked at C.J., who looked at Amanda, who looked at Sue. Then they all looked at Hayley.

"This is crazy to even think about," sighed Amanda, "but I gotta say, this is the most enticing offer I've had in years! I say we go for it. There's one condition, though." She leaned close to look Hayley in the eye. "There is *no* way we can be called the 'Girls Next Door' at our age. This time around, we're 'Hayley and the Hot Flashes,' or the deal's off."

"Deal," said Hayley.

"Woo-hoo! Road trip!" shouted C. J. and everyone except Meg burst into cheers and applause.

"How about it, Meg?" Hayley held out a hand. "You know you want to. You did then, you do now. Forgive me and let's move on! Who knows? Maybe the man of your dreams will be sitting in some audience in Alabama."

Meg exhaled another long stream of smoke, then pitched her cigarette out the window and took Hayley's hand. "You're right; who knows? Maybe he will."

"Yee-haw! Let's roll, Bernie!" commanded Amanda, as

the driver appeared beside the limo balancing five cones of choco-late-encrusted ice cream perched upright in a pasteboard container. As the women claimed their treats, one by one they ascended back up through the open sun roof, bathing in the fragrance of the sultry southern night as, slowly, the black stretch limousine made its way up Main Street.

CHAPTER SEVEN
If You're Gonna Swim with the Big Dogs...

Meg Dorris emerged from the stockroom at Paulie's Pawn Shop with her arms full of Steven Seagal DVDs. She'd thought Hayley was joking on Friday night, but danged if she hadn't shown up on Meg's doorstep Sunday morning with a tour itinerary and the $500 advance Meg said she would need to have before she'd approach her boss about time off. "Here's the schedule, in case you want to give it to your daughter," Hayley had said. *Right. Like Alice would care where I am.*

Meg reached the cash register and gingerly lowered her arms to set the stack of DVDs on the counter. She walked around to enter the check-out area and absentmindedly ran her hand through the drop-off bin to see if any returns had accumulated since her last sweep. *Hayley and the Hot Flashes. Cute name. It'll make people laugh.* Although Meg wasn't sure she wanted to be laughed at. She had no illusions about becoming a star at this point in her life; there were only so many Helen Mirrens who earned their fame after forty. But she was certainly as good as—no, better than!—those wannabes who hogged the stage at Cowboy's on Karaoke Night. People told her so. Even the ones who weren't hoping to trade flattery for a little action. *Man, if I was a little younger* . . . But thirty-five years ago, any shot she might have had at making a name for herself burned up in a blaze of hormones in the back seat of Ty Dorris' vintage T-bird.

Her own parents were no more supportive than Ty; as Meg recalled, her mother's exact words were, "You stupid little slut! That boy was gonna start at fullback for Ole Miss!" Two days after the wedding, a hastily arranged private affair held in her daddy's study at Calvary Temple, the good reverend and his wife felt an urgent call to start a mission church in Hood River, Oregon. They never returned to Skerry, and their only communication in the ensuing years was an annual Christmas card addressed to "Meg Dorris and Family" containing a $50 bill and that year's December issue of their church newsletter. The connection was severed permanently when a letter arrived from a Hood River attorney ten years ago, informing her of her parents' death in a car accident.

So much for family. It was her girlfriends who'd been there—for holidays, birthdays, good days, bad days . . . when Alice left, when her dog died. She smiled thinking about the rehearsal yesterday, which had gone better than any of them had expected.

"Anybody ever tell you kinda look like Pamela Anderson?"

"Excuse me?" Meg was startled to look up and find a burly man standing in front of the register, a worn DVD case for *Ol' Yeller* clutched in his beefy hand.

"Pamela Anderson," he repeated. "You look a little like her."

Meg wasn't sure if she considered that a compliment or not,

so she merely smiled and held out her hand. "Cash or credit?" she asked, as an image of Pamela, dressed in a powder blue halter dress and belting out the chorus of "Sister Serenade" flashed through her mind.

♪

The day after Labor Day, The Girls Next Door—now officially billed as Hayley and the Hot Flashes—crowded into a faded red leatherette booth at the Dairy Dip. Hunkered down over Gene's legendary banana splits, they traded tales of the frantic two days past and assessed their first "professional" gig at the Basket-Flower Festival the night before.

"Who knew Backup Singer 101 would be so grueling?" Amanda groaned. "My feet *still* hurt from all those encores last night."

C.J. rolled her eyes. "You know you'd have stayed on that stage all night, as long as the crowd kept cheering. Could you believe it was standing room only?"

"That was so sweet when Tom and the twins brought you roses onstage," Sue said with a wistful smile.

"Not nearly as sweet as when Pete rushed the stage to plant a big one on C. J. in front of God and everybody!" Hayley laughed.

"Nothin' shy about *my* guy!" C.J. giggled. "So this backup thing is gonna be a *boatload* of fun for us, but I hate that your regular singers got so banged up in that wreck they'll have to miss the whole tour. I left a card and a package of my cinnamon rolls with Pete, to mail to the hospital in the morning. I hope it gets there; he kept sniffing the box!"

Hayley leaned to hug her friend. "That's really thoughtful of you."

"I still can't believe your manager—what's his name? Flopsy?—wants us to fill in for the entire tour," said Sue. "What did he say when he called you last night?"

"You mean Tipsy. He said—," Hayley paused and furrowed her brow. "I thought I already told you this."

Sue shook her head.

"Okay, well, he said the doctor said there's no way the girls could be in shape for a road trip in two weeks, and a 2-month tour was totally out of the question so, based on what Jack told him about how things went Friday night at the reunion and last night at the festival, he's going to send y'all a contract. But he said to be sure and tell you that you don't know what you're getting into!" She looked each of her friends in the eye, one by one. "He's right; I've been doing this so long I forget how hard life is on a tour bus—being in a different town every night, washing your hair in a shower the size of a phone booth ... "

"Not turning on a stove or a dishwasher for two months . . . or hearing the word 'MOM!' two hundred times a day . . . oh, the horror!" vamped Amanda, flinging her hand against her forehead in a melodramatic pose. "I don't know if we can stand it!"

Hayley chuckled. "Okay, but don't say I didn't warn you. And if you have any doubts about this, tell me now. Y'all are saving my neck here—Tipsy's, too . . ."

"You mean Flopsy," C.J. deadpanned, and they all laughed as Sue blushed.

"What's so funny?" Keith Parker rounded the corner beside the cash register, a towering container of chili cheese fries in his hands.

"Parker, how do you keep that boyish figure?" Amanda challenged. "That's the third batch of those artery cloggers I've seen you eat in the last hundred hours!"

"Fourth, but who's counting? What are you girls up to?"

"Planning our new career as harmony divas!" said Amanda. "The doctor for Hayley's backup singers said no way can they do her tour, so, look out, world, here we come!"

"I mean it! Are you sure?" Hayley interjected. Two months is a long time to be away from your homes and families. I will understand completely, and there will be no hard feelings if . . ."

"Yeah, yeah, whatever," Amanda interrupted. "Have you asked Dr. Parker if he wants to ride shotgun with us on the tour bus? What would Jack Bisbee say to having a *male* Hot Flash?"

Keith grimaced. "I don't even know how to *process* that concept! Thanks for the offer but, unfortunately, doctors don't get 8-week vacations—not this one, anyhow. I'll try to catch some of your weekend shows, though; make sure I get a copy of the schedule." He winked and hefted a chili-heaped fry to his mouth. "Later, ladies," he said as he headed out the door.

Spoons scraping up ice cream was the only sound for a moment or two, then Meg broke the silence. "So if you and Keith are a thing again, does that mean Jack's fair game?"

Hayley rolled her eyes. "I *told* you, Jack is strictly my road manager. We've been through a lot together, and I definitely love the man, but it's purely platonic."

"Are things purely platonic with Keith?" Sue asked. "You've been with him a lot this weekend. Are you dog-dipping through those troubled waters yet?"

C.J. hooted. "*What*?"

"Sorry, I meant *dog paddling*," Sue said, looking embarrassed. "The other night Hayley and I were talking about water under the bridge and I said she should jump back in and try again, and, well, you know . . . when a dog swims, he *paddles* . . . and he doesn't get very far very fast, but he keeps at it . . ."

The four women looked at Sue, then looked at each other, then erupted into laughter. Hayley took a breath and rubbed her hands over her face. "Let's just say we're taking it step by step. And now, let's change the subject! Meg, how did the conversation go with your boss when you asked about taking more time off?"

The blonde shrugged. "He said if I wanted to go, I could go—but I shouldn't plan to come back."

"Whaaat?" the women chorused.

Meg shrugged again. "That job's days were numbered anyway. I stopped in and talked to Florene Honeycutt on my way home from practicing Sunday and she said I could come work for her at the Feed & Seed when I get back. She wants to add a garden center manager."

"That would be perfect for you!" C. J. exclaimed. "You love plants!"

"And have an incredible green thumb," Amanda added. "You grow the best tomatoes and the prettiest roses of anybody I've ever known. Florene is smart to hire you."

Meg blushed at the praise. "Well, a lot could happen in two months, but I think the timing for all this is gonna work out." She took a deep breath and looked at Hayley. "One more thing: I think I'll take you up on your offer to send Alice a ticket to the fair in Newnan."

"I thought you and Alice weren't speaking!" C. J. said in surprise.

"We aren't; I thought this might be a way to break the ice."

C. J. shook her head as she finished off her last bite of banana split. "I can't imagine not talking to my daughter on a regular basis. That must be so difficult. Good for you, Meg, for making the first move."

Meg sighed. "She may ignore me. But I figure if I'm in Newnan anyway, with Jack Bisbee on my arm—" she slid a sidelong glance at Hayley, "—it'll be a chance to show Alice her mama's not the loser she thinks I am."

Amanda rolled her eyes, then cleared her throat. "Well, I'm set. My mother-in-law will be here this afternoon to collect the gift she's always wanted: the chance to take over my house and my children!"

Hayley grinned. "Aren't you afraid she'll have the locks changed while you're gone?"

Amanda made a face. "Are you kidding? There's a high probability she'll move my entire family over to her mansion in Birmingham!" She sighed. "I know I should be grateful she's willing to come help Tom with the twins, but I *hate* knowing she's going to go through every drawer I own."

"Why don't you leave her some little surprises?" C. J. suggested. "Like a note in your lingerie drawer that says 'Aha! Caught you!'"

"Or a picture of Tom in his underwear that says, 'Isn't he the sexiest thing you've ever seen?'" Meg chuckled.

"Well, hopefully, your lives won't be *forever* turned upside down by this adventure," Hayley said. "Meanwhile, I will be forever grateful!" She licked the last of the strawberry syrup from her spoon, then set it down with a contented sigh.

"I hate to break up the fun, but I have to go see Mom and

finish packing," C. J. said as she stood and reached for her purse.

"And I have to go tuck those notes in my lingerie drawer," Amanda deadpanned, and the others snickered.

Hayley gave hugs all around. "The bus will come to your house first in the morning, Sue, then Amanda's, then C.J.'s, then Meg's. You'll pick me up on the way out of town and, if all goes according to plan, we should be on the road by noon."

"You sure Flopsy is gonna have our outfits ready?" Amanda questioned. "I'd hate to make my big debut in mom jeans!"

Hayley chuckled. "Trust me. Tipsy Mack does detail like Donald Trump does deals. You'll look like an old pro by the time you take the stage in Easley. That's our first stop—the Upper South Carolina State Fair."

"Woo-hoo!" Amanda shouted, lifting her hands in the air for high fives all aound. "Bring on the stilettos and the sequins!"

"Gee, and I had you pegged all this time as more of a bandanna and blue jeans kind of gal," Hayley teased as she rose from the booth, the others following.

Amanda grinned. "Are you kidding? I've been waiting *years* for an excuse to wear silver Spandex in public!" And with a swivel of her hips and an unladylike "Booyah!", the middle-aged mother of twins slam-dunked her napkin into the trash and sashayed out the door.

CHAPTER EIGHT
The Wheels on the Bus Go 'Round and 'Round

"Oh, dear Lord in heaven!" Sue Campbell gasped when she opened the door of her tidy, two-bedroom home the next morning. Parked in front of her hand-painted mailbox sat a 40-foot, black and silver bus with the words "Hayley and the Hot Flashes" painted in hot pink, foot-high letters across the side.

There was a loud whoosh of air as the door to the bus opened, and a heavy-jowled, silver-haired man appeared. "You must be Sue," he called out as he stepped down and strode up the sidewalk, his Tony Lama python-skin boots gleaming in the glare of the mid-day South Carolina sun.

"And you must be Hayley's manager," Sue responded as she extended a hand, which Tipsy Mack grasped in his own.

"I can't tell you how nice it is to meet you, after hearing so much about you," he said. "And I want to thank you for welcoming my girl back home so warmly. I know it was hard for Hayley to come back here, but it was time. Past time. I appreciate you making it easier."

Sue assessed the big man for a moment, taking in his tired brown eyes, unguarded smile, and well-cut but rumpled suit. Billowing televangelist hairdo notwithstanding, she decided she liked him.

"I've heard a lot about you, too. According to Hayley, your talents place you somewhere between Superman and The Almighty."

Tipsy chuckled as he pulled a handkerchief from the pocket of his jacket and wiped a light film of perspiration from his face. "Well, she's kind, if given to exaggeration." He stood for a moment, looking out across Sue's meticulously manicured lawn. A calico kitten made its way through the hedge of purple basket-flowers that separated Sue's yard from her neighbor's. Tipsy's eyes met Sue's in an honest gaze. "So is this road trip a good idea or a bad one?"

"Truth? Probably bad." Sue leaned back to rest against the door jamb. "But it's also probably the best way to leave the past behind, once and for all, and move on."

"I understand Miz Meg Dorris's enthusiasm for this undertaking has been a tad less than wholehearted."

Sue laughed. "Well, the specter of 'what might have been' looms large at middle age. But maybe this adventure will let her move on, too." She lifted a brow. "How about you? Are you coming along for the ride?"

Tipsy raised his hands and widened his eyes. "No, ma'am! I'll be as close as a cell phone—but no closer. You gals'll have to slug it out on your own." He glanced down at the Rolex on his wrist. "Speaking of which, if you're ready, we need to rock and roll."

"My box is right here," Sue said, stepping inside the foyer and gesturing to a small tweed suitcase.

"That's it?" Tipsy asked in amazement.

"What can I say? I'm a no-nonsense kind of girl."

Tipsy grinned broadly as he picked up the suitcase and preceded the slim, close-cropped woman out the door. "You are a rare and wondrous species, Miz Campbell. I may very well be falling in love with you as we speak."

Amanda Brooks' twins, Tommy and Diana, were sprawled in the grass, eating popsicles, when the tour bus groaned to a stop on Chariot Way, then made a wide right turn and lumbered toward their cul-de-sac.

"Mom! Mom! It's here! It's here!" they shrieked, leaping up in a flurry of flailing arms and legs. With their mother's lean, leggy build and their father's fair coloring, the eleven-year-old Brooks twins brought to mind an image of Golden Retrievers frolicking on the lawn.

Millicent Brooks opened the front door of her son's handsome Tudor-style stone house and peered out cautiously. In a platinum French twist and stylish charcoal pantsuit, she looked nowhere near her seventy-three years—though a smile would have gone a long way to soften her stern features. "Tom Junior! Diana! Settle down! People will think you're nothing but common riff-raff!" She gestured impatiently for the children to come inside but, completely ignoring her, the twins bounded up to the bus, waving and smiling as it rolled to a halt with a shuddering hiss.

"Hello, there, chilluns!" boomed Tipsy Mack as the door fanned open and he emerged like a preening peacock.

"Wow! Your boots are *cool*!" breathed Tommy.

"Is our mama really gonna *sleep* on this bus?" Diana asked, eyes wide.

Tipsy dismounted with a labored grunt. "Thank ya, sir, and yes, ma'am, she is," he said as he tousled both on the head. "Climb on in there and take a look, little missy. That there is Fred," he said, waving a hand toward the curly-haired, rotund man behind the steering wheel. "He don't bite and he *might* let you pull some levers!" He chuckled as the twins pushed past him to clamber up the stairs and into the bus.

Amanda stuck her head out the door and yelled, "Mornin', y'all! Be right there!" as Tipsy made his way toward the scowling woman standing cross-armed at the top of the steps.

"Good morning, madam. My name is Clarence Mack, of Nashville, Tennessee. Whom do I have the pleasure of meeting?"

"Millicent Brooks of Birmingham, seventh-generation," came the crisp, austere reply.

Tipsy laid his hand across his heart in a gesture of reverence. "Birmingham! One of our finest southern cities," he intoned.

Taken aback, Millie nodded slightly. "Why, yes, yes, it *is* . . . do I— *know* you, Mr. Mack?" she asked hesitantly.

With a wistful smile, Tipsy shook his head. "I'm afraid not, and more's the pity. If I didn't have to get these gals on the road, I would dearly love the chance to *get* to know you, Miz Brooks, over a fine china cup of Earl Grey tea . . . "

"Big red bags, comin' through!" Tipsy's flirtation came to an abrupt end as Millie's son plowed through the doorway and down the sidewalk with Amanda's luggage. "Tom Brooks, how ya doin'?" he offered with a nod, huffing past.

"Tom! Really!" scolded Millie, as she reached to smooth

her hair and smile apologetically at Tipsy. "You'll have to forgive my son's manners. Amanda *abandoning* her family has everyone in a bit of an uproar."

Amanda appeared behind her mother-in-law just in time to hear her comment; she stuck out her tongue and made a face, but Tipsy winked and gave just the slightest shake of his lustrous head. "Abandon? Oh, my dear, *no*! Your beautiful daughter-in-law is committing an *incredible* act of kindness! Why, Hayley would have had to cancel her tour if these ladies hadn't stepped in to save the day! The fact they've turned their lives upside down, canceled their plans, and come to the aid of an old friend in distress—at the last minute . . . why, it touches my grizzled old heart. You don't see sacrifice like that anymore."

Amanda stepped forward then, her enormous duffle bag and only slightly smaller tote bag jostling Millie. "Oh, it's nothing," she cooed, batting crossed eyes at Tipsy as she passed. "But I couldn't have done it without our precious Mama Millie! *She* should get all the credit."

♪

By noon, they were all on the bus and barreling north on 501. Tipsy stood in the middle of the aisle and swayed a little. "I'm told you girls did a fabulous job at the Basket-Flower Festival. Mayor Wilder said it was a record crowd. Now then, we're headed to Columbia to pick up Jack Bisbee, who I believe you've already had the pleasure of meeting, and his band. It's been a little tricky tryin' to honor Road Kill's previous commitments while they pinch-hit for Hayley on this tour. The boys had to play a gig there last night, so we're kind of goin' 'round our elbow to get to our thumb today, but bear with us; it'll all work out." The bus bounced over a rough spot in the road and Tipsy grabbed a seat to steady himself. "Easy there, Fred. One more mishap and this tour is history before it ever gets started!" Fred honked the horn in response, and Tipsy turned his attention back to the girls. "I know y'all have been goin' over the charts and workin' out your harmonies, so you're prob'ly all set but, just remember, the boys can step in and help out if you feel the least bit uncomfortable. They're pros, so they can cover a multitude of sins."

"*That's* a relief!" breathed C. J. "I'm scared to death!"

"Aw, sugar, I'm bettin' by showtime, you'll be slick as a pig on butter," Tipsy assured her. "Besides, you just flash them big ol' dimples, and people won't care if you howl like a hyena."

"We might actually be *good*, you know." Meg sat cross-legged behind a table in one corner of the bus's lounge, a defiant tilt to her chin that made Tipsy suspect this woman had had to fight to be heard for most of her life.

"You might, indeed," he agreed. "Frankly, I hope you knock ever'body's socks off. But in case you don't, my job is to make sure Hayley doesn't go down with the ship. In other words—" He struck a pose and, in a horrible mimic somewhere between Weird Al Yankovic and P Diddy, began punching his hands into the air. "'Yo-part-is-ta-do-yo-best; my-part-is-ta-do-thuh-rest. Uh-HUH!'"

As the women groaned, Tipsy removed his jacket, laid it across the back of a seat and began rolling up his sleeves. "All right, ladies," he said, waving them closer. "Gather 'round and let's see if these costumes meet with your approval. Hayley? Start handin' me them boxes back there."

Hayley held up a hand. "Hang on, Tips. Before we get sidetracked, I wanted to tell everybody about Rhett Wilson."

"Who's Rhett Wilson?" Sue asked.

"Him!" Hayley said, as she turned and taped a photo on the bus console. "This is that stalker I told you about. Take a good look. If you see him, *anywhere*, find Jack immediately. The guy's a lunatic."

Tipsy patted her shoulder reassuringly. "Now, the last I heard, the police issued that restraining order, so I don't think you need to be worried about Mr. Wilson. Still, it's good to be cautious. "Now, let's try these costumes."

For the next hour, they played dress-up as they rolled along I-20 West. True to Hayley's promise, the girls were amazed at how well the fit and color of each outfit matched its intended wearer.

"I have boobs!" Sue crowed.

"I have 'em where they're *supposed* to be!" marveled Meg.

"And I'm *perky* again!" beamed C. J., pirouetting with her chest thrust forward.

Pink to the tip of his ears, Tipsy shook his head and put his face in his hands. "Well, I'm glad you like them, but, Lawdy! It's time for me to get off this bus!"

Hayley laughed and gave the big man a hug. "You're the best manager in the whole world, Tipsy."

"Certainly the most *versatile*! What would the suits at the Talent Managers Association say if they knew I'd added pantyhose selection to my repertoire of services?"

"You go, Tips!" Amanda whooped, as she pumped her fist in the air and paraded up the aisle wearing a hot pink, tiered gauze skirt and said pantyhose, adorned with silver glitter.

In a heartbeat, the other women leaped into the aisle, whooping and gyrating as Amanda chanted, "Tipsy! Tipsy! He's our man! If he can't sell us, NOBODY can!"

Fred pushed a button and triggered an earsplitting air horn

rendition of the seven notes of "Shave and a Haircut (Two Bits)" to cap off the cheer, causing all six of his passengers to jump in startled surprise and the car in the right lane to nearly run off the road.

"Look out, world—here we come!" yelled Amanda.

♪

A short while later, the bus lumbered into the parking lot of a Cracker Barrel in Columbia, South Carolina. As she made her way toward the door, Hayley noticed that, somewhere along the way, the photo of Rhett Wilson had acquired a jaunty red Sharpie beret, and an "autograph" that read, *Flopsy, I'll never forget you!* In spite of herself, Hayley giggled. Jack was with her now; she would be safe.

A weary Tipsy Mack, who despite his tee-totaling philosophy, thought he might be in serious need of an alcoholic beverage for the first time in his life, eased down the steps of the bus.

"They're all yours," he warned, as Jack Bisbee reached out to extend a hand. "Hope you ate your Wheaties, son: you're gonna need 'em!"

Jack cackled. "What's the matter, Tips? Too much estrogen for a man your age?"

Tipsy mopped his forehead. "For a man of *any* age!"

Graham Frazier, Road Kill's lean and lanky fiddle player, ambled up from the wooden porch where he'd been stretched out in a rocker. "Bring 'em on, big daddy! I've died and gone to heaven! If you'd told me two weeks ago I'd be spendin' the next two months with a bunch of hot middle-aged, newbie girl singers, I'd have said you were crackin' smoke!"

"How 'bout you just deactivate your radar, Frazier," cautioned Pinky Brown, the band's short, chubby, piano player, who'd been having to take two steps for every one of his fellow musician's.

"Most of these ladies are mamas!"

Tipsy pointed a cautionary finger. "Or *wives*. Listen here, Frazier, there'll be no monkey business on this tour. You got it?"

Graham just grinned.

Jack turned and leveled a stare. "Let me tell you somethin', Casanova: you get outta line and you and your fiddle'll be back in Nashville faster'n you can spell 'furlough.' Now go get the gear. We got a schedule to keep."

"Yes, *sir*, Mr. Boss Man," Graham muttered, and sauntered off.

Jack turned back around in time to see the Hot Flashes clambering down from the bus, one by one. "You may be right, Tips," he chuckled, as Road Kill's bass player, Willard Taylor, and drummer, Bo Whitfield, joined the party just in time to escort the ladies into the restaurant. "It for sure won't be a *dull* tour. Hey," he continued, turning all business as he pulled a card from his shirt pocket. "We played a packed house here last night, and I feel obliged to tell you a guy from Tugalo Records told me to give him a call when we get back to Nashville." He handed Tipsy the card. "Have you had that conversation with Capitol Records yet?"

Tipsy twitched uncomfortably. "It's hard enough to get a *new* band a record deal these days, much less one that's been around as long as y'all have. And then there's your *name*."

A grin returned to Jack's handsome face. "Nobody forgets a name like Road Kill!" Then he sobered. "I'm serious. You need to know if Tugalo Records makes us an offer, we're gonna consider it. Fair enough?"

The older man nodded. "Fair enough. And listen—I really appreciate you boys comin' to Hayley's rescue on this tour."

"No problem; she's a class act. Cal Taylor oughta be countin' his blessings to have her on board. I've always got Hayley's back; you know that. She believed in me when nobody else did."

"She's loyal to a fault," Tipsy agreed, as he laid a hand on Jack's shoulder. "The right song and she'd be back on top in a heartbeat, but she won't look at anyone else's material and she's had a long dry spell. Maybe you can talk to her—or help her write a song."

"Yeah. Maybe." Jack put his fingers in his mouth and gave a shrill whistle. "Move it, Frazier. We ain't got all day." He turned to lift the luggage compartment door just as Bernie Gambrell slid his shiny limousine into a space next to the bus. "Bernie, my man!"

The long-limbed chauffeur got out and raised a hand in greeting. "Missin' anything?" he asked, as he walked over and held up a cell phone. Jack's eyes grew wide and he patted his chest and hip simultaneously. "You left it in the back seat when I dropped you boys off last night. Limo's gassed up and ready to go, Tipsy," Bernie said as he reached to drop Jack's phone in the man's shirt pocket. "I'm gonna run in here and get us some Moon Pies and root beer for the road."

"Tell those 'Hot Flashes' time's a wastin' and we're leavin' in ten minutes, with or without 'em!" Jack called as he began helping Pinky and Graham load equipment into the belly of the bus.

♪

"I thought you were looking *forward* to being away from home for a few weeks!" Hayley's expression was one of complete bafflement. She was standing in the toy corner of the Cracker Barrel Old Country Store, watching Amanda Brooks sob into a huge, stuffed Kermit the Frog.

"I . . . I was. I . . . I . . . am! But I m-miss my baaaaabies!" Amanda wailed as she wiped away her tears on Kermit's left arm.

A clerk frowned in her direction. "Ma'am, I hope you realize you've just *bought* that frog!"

Hayley shushed the woman with a nod and a wave, then put an arm around her friend. "Oh, they'll be fine. And think about it: no dishes, no cooking—"

"No hugs, no kisses!" Amanda interjected pitifully.

"You get used to it," Meg muttered as she and C.J. walked up to join them. "At least you'll have a *husband* waiting when you get back."

C.J. poked Meg in the back.

"I have an idea," said Sue, as she approached the trio from the t-shirt section. "Why don't you collect a souvenir for the twins from each town we play in? Let's see . . ." she mused, looking around for a possibility. "That looks like a nice man. Maybe he can help us find something the twins would like."

Hayley looked past Sue's finger to Bernie, who stood at the register with an armload of Moon Pies. She turned back to Sue. "Do you mean Bernie?"

Sue smiled vaguely. "Oh, right. *Bernie*. Yoo-hoo, Bernie! We need your help!"

As Sue headed toward the driver, Hayley gave Amanda a big hug. "I don't have children, so—in all honesty— I *don't* know how you feel, but it's only been a few hours since we left your front yard. Are you sure you're gonna be okay with this?"

"I don't know!" Amanda confessed, her eyes still brimming with tears.

Meg rolled her eyes. "This is nothing but a hormone attack. Girl, you *so* need intervention." She waved her arms at the still scowling clerk. "Y'all got any herbal estrogen pills?" The clerk, who had distanced herself from the trio but was still scowling in their general direction, didn't hear.

Meg took a couple of steps in the clerk's direction. "HEY! DO YOU HAVE ANY HERBAL ESTROGEN PILLS?" The clerk, who, this time, heard her loud and clear, flushed bright red as every single person in the room turned to stare.

"You really think that would help? You think this is just another hormone thing?" Amanda asked as she started to wipe her face with Kermit again, then—noting the clerk's glare—used her shirt sleeve instead. "As if the hot flashes aren't enough, now I've got mood swings to deal with!"

The surly clerk suddenly thawed. "Oh, the mood swings aren't *half* as bad as the night sweats! Have you had any of *those* yet?"

A petite woman in a pink track suit looked up from the sweater she'd been admiring. "I had to sleep 'au naturel' for six months, mine were so bad." She shook her head. "But *my* biggest problem now is confusion. Some days, I swear I can barely find my way home! I have to leave Post-It notes for myself all over the house!"

"*I'm* having to do that!" Sue exclaimed from Housewares.

A rotund redhead in a lime green muumuu called out from behind a candle display, "Confusion ain't *nothin'* compared to overactive bladder! Don't it just kill ya to have to visit the ladies' room every fifteen minutes?"

"And ringing in your ears!" A sophisticated-looking brunette laid down the afghan she'd been fondling and drifted toward Amanda. "Sometimes it's so loud, I think my head's going to explode!"

Bernie sidled up to Hayley, his expression unreadable but his eyes downcast. "I hate to break this up," he whispered, "but Jack says he's leavin' with or without you, and y'all best get on out to the bus. Now if you'll excuse me," he said, beating a quick retreat toward the door, not even slowing down when Meg bumped into him on her way back from the register.

"Shoot!" she complained. "No teas, no pills, no nothin'. Well, 'til we can get our hands on some ginseng or red clover, the next best cure is chocolate!"

A whoop of approval erupted from women all over the store. Meg yelled, "Costumes be damned! Where's the Whoppers?"

The petite woman in the track suit piped up. "Oh, no, dear. What she needs is a 6-pack of king-sized Hershey bars—with almonds!"

"Uh-unh," interrupted the woman in the muumuu. "My mama taught me there ain't *nothin'* like chocolate-covered raisins to get through 'hormone hell'!"

The surly clerk—who, by this time, was an old friend and had wrapped Kermit in a bag and was handing him back to Amanda with her credit card, said, "What you *really* need is some Chocolate Fudge Ripple ice cream, which we don't have, I'm sorry to say. But if you wanna hoof it down the road to the Piggly Wiggly, I'll give you some plastic spoons to take with you!"

This last met with an enthusiastic round of cheers and applause, which continued until a tiny, grey-haired woman raised her cane from the cookbook section and waved it in the air. "Excuse me," she said softly as she returned the cane to its rightful position, "but I'm afraid *all* of you ladies are misinformed." She smiled sweetly as a hush descended and, then, in a quavering voice, continued. "I wasted a lot of years waiting for St. John's Wort and chocolate to work, before I discovered the *real* key to getting through 'the change' is a good gardener—one who'll make your bed inviting, shovel in some treats, scatter a little sunshine, and keep the pests away." She winked. "And if you're lucky, he'll keep the bloom on your roses for years to come!"

CHAPTER NINE
Much Ado About Nothing

Amanda was stretched out in the tour bus on the tiny bunk she'd claimed as hers. Shifting to get more comfortable, she put her backside against the wall and curled around a pillow as she listened contentedly to her bus mates laughing and talking up front. It had started to rain, and the swish of the tires on the highway sang a high-pitched harmony to the low rumble of the diesel engine. She checked her watch; they'd be in Easley shortly, with just enough time to squeeze in a sound check and quick bite before show time. Amanda let her eyelids close and her memory drift back to Tipsy's parting exchange in the Cracker Barrel parking lot:

"Now, you boys listen up: don't be gettin' frisky with these gals. Y'all are too old to be tryin' to live up to the reputations you think *you have, and these ladies actually* have *good reputations, so don't screw 'em up!"*

"Speak for yourself, you old goat!" Bo had called, his long,

grey ponytail bouncing as he brandished his drumsticks in a series of showy riffs across a seat back. *"Women still swoon when I walk in the room!"*

Fred had looked up in the rear view mirror and grinned. *"Yeah, they say, 'Lord a'mercy! Who is that ugly thang?'*

"Tipsy, will you leave already?" Willard, the bass player, had then complained. *"We got a bus full of beautiful women here. Time's a-wastin!"*

Then Sue had stood up. *"Flopsy, don't you pay any attention to them. You are a real gentleman and we appreciate you looking out for us!"*

"Oh, Flopsy, thank you SO much for protecting our virtue!" Graham mimicked.

"We love you, Flopsy," Bo had fawned in return.

And then Pinky had bowed in Tipsy's direction, fluttered his pale eyelashes, and intoned in his best soprano voice, *"Mister Flopsy, you is a fine, fine specimen of manhood!"*

Amanda giggled at the recollection, then started as a deep male drawl intruded on her reverie.

"Knock, knock."

The privacy curtain on her bunk fluttered and Amanda slid it back to find Graham Frazier sitting on the bunk across from her.

"You okay?" Graham's shaggy dark hair and handlebar mustache made him look like a gunslinger straight out of the Wild West—an image Amanda suspected the fifty-ish musician worked hard to cultivate.

"I'm fine," she nodded. "Just thought I'd lie down and relax for a few minutes."

As the fiddle player pulled off his boots and stretched out

on the bunk across from her, Amanda panicked. "Th...that's your bunk?"

Beneath his mustache, Graham's lips spread in a lazy smile. "No such luck, darlin.' I just thought I'd keep you company for a while." He twisted sideways and propped up on an elbow. "Jack tells me this is all new to you gals."

"About as far removed from our everyday life as you can get," she said, chuckling. "Hopefully, what seems like a dream won't turn into a nightmare!"

"Aw, from what I've seen so far, y'all are gonna do just fine." Graham rolled over on his back, the faded blue t-shirt he wore stretching taut across his chest.

Amanda's heart raced, and she was fairly certain her blood pressure was spiking to stroke level. *Holy chocolate macaroons! I'm going to spontaneously combust!* she thought as she flopped backwards on her own bunk and tried to breath. She hoped the heat her body was generating wouldn't incinerate the tantalizing source of this problem that lay less than four feet away. *Married woman! Married woman! Mother of twins! Stretch marks!* she scolded silently as she closed her eyes and attempted to will away the sweat she felt streaming from one end of her body to the other.

Again, the velvety bass voice interrupted her mental self-flagellation. "Hey, when's the last time you rode a Ferris wheel?"

There was a pause. "Um, it's been a while. Why?"

Graham flipped over on his side and offered up another heart-melting, slow-as-molasses smile. "I was thinkin' maybe you and me could take a spin around the midway after the show tonight."

"You *do* know I'm married."

Joe Cowboy lifted his eyebrows in amusement. "I wasn't

plannin' to run off with ya, darlin'.' I just thought you might like to ride the Loop-de-Loop!"

Amanda's face burned in embarrassment. "Oh. Right. Just thought I should mention it." She took a deep breath, then rolled into a sitting position. "Well, gee. I think I've rested enough. Guess I'll go see what the other girls are up to."

Graham rose as she did, causing their bodies to graze in the narrow passageway.

"You let me know if you change your mind and decide you're up for a ride." He leaned closer as she tried to slide past. "You look a little flushed. That Loop-de-Loop would cool you right off."

Amanda heard him chuckle as she fled the way-too-close-for-comfort scenario.

"Okay, ladies, let me hear you again where Hayley finishes up the verse and y'all come in on the 'oohs.'" The bus was parked near a drag race track, a sea of carnie trailers and RVs flanking it, an enormous Ferris wheel and colorfully lit midway just beyond. In contrast to the laid-back demeanor he'd displayed thus far, Jack Bisbee was all business now. As road manager, it was his job to see that everyone knew what to do—and did it. "Pinky, you're gonna have to punch up the harmony till they get a little more confident there." He caught a slight sigh from Meg and looked up. "You're doin' fine. Don't worry about it."

She gave him a "yeah, right" look. "This is a lot tougher than I thought it would be. It's hard to hear myself over all these instruments."

Willard elbowed Pinky. "Well, dang, sugar. You been a professional backup singer for . . . let's see . . . all of five or six hours now.

You prob'ly don't even need 'all these instruments.' We'll just stop playin.'"

Hayley gave him a look as Meg tried to determine whether Willard was teasing or being rude. "Ignore him, Meg; Jack can give your amp a little nudge once we get on stage." She turned from one woman to the other with an encouraging smile. "Remember, Tipsy said, by tomorrow, you'll be singing these harmonies in your sleep."

"Oh, Lord, I hope not!" C. J. wailed. "They're already echoing in my brain like broken records!" Without missing a beat, Sue and Amanda leaned in on either side of their friend and began wailing the chorus from C.J.'s least favorite song, "Love Me, Love Me Not," and everyone—even C.J.—laughed.

"Okay, let's get back to work," said Jack, directing attention back to rehearsal. "Pinky? One, two, one, two, three, four..."

Pinky Brown's chubby fingers danced across the electric keyboard like puppies headed for a bowl of kibble. The women listened, amazed yet again, as what sounded like a command performance floated effortlessly from the compact instrument. The third time Pinky repeated the measure, though, Jack waved a hand and motioned for him to stop.

"Girls? You missed your cue again."

"We did? Sorry." Meg flushed and shrugged. "I get so wrapped up in his playing I forget to sing," she explained, flashing Pinky a self-conscious smile. "You're so *good*!"

The little man grinned. "I am, ain't I?" he said with a straight face, then flexed his hands dramatically before returning them to the keyboard for a few pounding measures of "Angel of Music," from *Phantom of the Opera*.

Across the aisle, Bo shook his head. "You'll find that when

humility was handed out, Pinky was in the Men's Room."

Immediately, Pinky struck a chord and began to sing. "Oh, Lord, it's hard to be humble..."

The women laughed as Jack gave his long-time buddy an affectionate swat. "You are pure swine, Brown—a ham from cradle to grave."

"Sooo-eeeee!" called Graham.

This time, it was Jack who shook his head. "All right, I'm guessin' we've done as much as we can in here; y'all are gettin' goofy. Let's take a break and pray it all comes together onstage."

As he ambled down the narrow corridor toward the bunks, Pinky and Willard packed up their instruments while the girls flexed and stretched.

"I think I'm gonna try and catch forty blinks," said Sue. "Anybody else?"

As Meg and C. J. nodded, Hayley slid into a seat behind Amanda. and leaned against the window. "Nah, I think I'm just gonna sit here and watch the world go by for a bit." She wiggled her fingers at the others' retreating backs, then used them to wiggle the headrest in front of her. "You're awfully quiet up there, Soccer Mom. Everything okay?"

"Nothing a good, old-fashioned ice bath wouldn't help," Amanda muttered.

Hayley rose and leaned over the top of the seat. "Another hot flash? Feeling a little volcanic?"

"You don't know the half of it." Amanda turned to whisper the details of her encounter with Graham into Hayley's ear, mindful of Willard's presence just a few seats back. "Do not—I repeat, do *not*—leave me alone with that man!" she admonished.

"Oh, honey, I've known Graham for years," Hayley assured

her friend. "I promise you're safe with him. He's all bark and no bite."

"Hah!" Amanda snorted. "What if *I* bite *him*?"

A moment later, Meg ambled back up and plopped into a corner seat with a book. "Not sleepy," she shrugged. Before she could get settled in and begin to read, though, Pinky appeared with a big mug in one hand.

"Thought you might like some hot tea," he said, handing it over. "Rehearsin' is tough on tonsils if you ain't used to it."

"And I'm surely not! How thoughtful of you!" Meg glowed at this unexpected gesture of kindness.

Pinky dipped his head shyly. "Did anyone ever tell you, you look a little like Pamela Anderson?"

♪

Up in the driver's seat, Amanda having abandoned her for a shower, Hayley was thrilled when her cell phone rang, sparing any further overheard conversation between Meg and company.

"Hayley? Cal Taylor. Is my cousin Willard behavin' himself?"

"Actually, as we speak, he and Pinky are acting like a couple of banty roosters, makin' a move on one of my girlfriends!"

"Some things never change," Cal laughed. "Is this friend one of your new back-up singers? Terrible news about that run-in your girls had with the chicken truck."

"Yeah, but I've survived worse surprises. It's actually kind of fun having my best friends bail me out."

"Fun's one thing; business is something else," Cal said, his tone suddenly a tad less amiable. "Can these women sing? I'm not payin' you for a slumber party."

Hayley turned the remark she wanted to make into a cough. "Yes, they *can* sing—quite well, in fact. I'd hardly risk my reputation on amateurs, Cal."

"Well, according to Tipsy, they *are* amateurs, and that's what worries me. I want to get what I'm paying for on this tour."

Hayley's voice hardened and she blinked back tears of fury that suddenly sprang forth. "The only thing *you're* paying for is me—and I *always* deliver, Cal. The rest of it's between me and Tipsy."

Realizing he might have pushed one button too many, Cal changed the subject. "Look, don't expect a big crowd in Easley. It's been raining all day, and the fairground is one big mud puddle. Oh, yeah, and there's a little change in the line-up."

"What kind of change?"

Cal hesitated briefly. "I owed a local promoter a favor, and he called it in. His boy's band thinks they're the next Dukes of Drive. I told 'em they could open for me."

"*Two* opening acts?" Hayley questioned.

"No, y'all are gonna be the closing act now."

"My contract says I'm your *opening* act."

"Your contract also says union singers," Cal returned.

Hayley was silent as she tried to rein in her rage. "I'll let you get away with this tonight, but we'll be talking after the show."

"I'm just hoping there'll *be* a show. This ain't the Ted Mack Amateur Hour. If I don't get professionals, *you* don't get paid."

As Hayley clicked off her phone, a roar of thunder shook the bus and huge rain drops pelted the windows.

"Oh, great," Meg moaned. "My second time on stage, and I'm gonna get electrocuted!"

As Pinky chuckled, and Jack emerged from the bunk area,

Hayley stood and put her hands on her hips. "I just got off the phone with Cal."

Jack lifted his eyebrows. "And?"

"A local band is opening for him tonight."

"*What*?" Jack's face turned as dark as the sky.

Hayley glanced past him to see the entire entourage trouping forth. "Meet me in the back in a minute," she muttered, and moved out of the way as Fred reclaimed his place behind the wheel. "Since it's rainin', I'm gonna drive y'all up to the main entrance so you won't have to walk so far," Fred said as he cranked up the bus and began backing up.

"Thank you! You're a sweetheart!" hollered C.J. as she bent to peer out a window.

As Fred maneuvered around vehicles, trees, traffic cones, and pedestrians, Hayley filled Jack in on her conversation with Cal; Pinky and Meg were quiet, waiting to hear the outcome of Cal's last-minute change, while everyone else was chattering and laughing and eyeing the main entrance coming into view.

"Scoot over, C. J.! I want to see if our name's in lights!" Sue said, elbowing her way toward a window.

As Fred negotiated a tight turn, sure enough, there was a marquee at the fairground entrance—not in lights, but in big, black plastic letters: "*Cal Taylor's Retro Rodeo Tour, Featuring the Piedmont Pickers, the Bailey Mountain Cloggers, and Hallie Swift.*"

"What idiot doesn't know how to spell your name?" C. J. fumed.

"And where's *our* name?" Sue protested.

"Heads will roll!" Amanda bellowed. "Where's your cell phone, Hayley? Call Flopsy and make him fix this! Hayley?" She looked around, realizing the woman in question was missing.

Jack appeared just then, with Hayley right behind him. He rubbed a hand over his face.. "Okay, look, there's been a change of plans. For whatever reason, Cal has booked a local band to open for him tonight. We'll be closing instead, so you have a couple of extra hours to entertain yourselves, or relax, or watch the show. Make sure you're backstage and ready to go no later than 8:30. I suspect the dressing room's in that building over there." He pointed a finger to the northeast.

"Can't we get the bus any closer?" Meg looked dolefully out at the hundred yards to the gate and the hard-packed dirt that stood a good two inches under water. "We don't have umbrellas!"

"You won't melt, princess," Bo assured her.

"Forget the dressing room," Hayley ordered. You guys get on out of here and we girls will dress on the bus. Maybe the rain will let up before long. We'll see you backstage."

An hour and a half later, Hayley and her Hot Flashes stood dripping on the concrete floor of the fairgrounds dressing room, sequins soggy and hairdos at half-mast.

"Well, well," sneered a curvaceous, perfectly coiffed brunette in gold lamé. "If it ain't 'Hallie and Her Wet Noodles.'" Her companions—equally glamorous—tittered.

Amanda caught a glimpse of herself in a mirror. "Whoa! I look like something the wolverines dragged in!"

The brunette harrumphed. "You don't look like a professional *singer*, for sure!" Her eyes narrowed. "By the way, if I find out you housefraus are getting paid scale, I'll file a grievance with the union faster than you can say 'fraud!'"

"They're not getting paid at *all*, Darlene," Hayley countered. "They're doing this out of the goodness of their hearts—a concept about which *you* know nothing!"

Strains of Western swing music interrupted the impending catfight. "C'mon, girls, that's our cue," said the brunette. "Good luck, *Hallie*, and remember—you get what you pay for! No *wonder* Cal changed the line-up: better to have amateurs than *has-beens*."

"Let it go, let it go." C. J. placed a restraining hand on Hayley's shoulder as Cal's backup singers shoved past. "They're just trying to get you all riled up."

"It worked!" Hayley growled.

"Do we need to call Flopsy?" Sue suggested.

Hayley pressed her hands to her temples and slowly exhaled. "I think Cal's hoping this will make y'all quit and go home so *his* singers can back me up. It's all about that bottom line with him."

"That's really rotten," said Sue.

"They'll have to drag my cold, dead body off the stage," Meg muttered.

"And who cares if we don't go on first?" C. J. declared. "They're just saving the best for last!"

Amanda burst out laughing. "C. J., do you *ever* put down your pom-poms?"

"I can't help it," the former cheerleader protested. "Mama always told me to make the best of a situation!"

"Hmm. The best of *this* situation would be to pound those bi—girls—into the mud, sing our hearts out, then stand on stage basking in a standing ovation," said Meg.

"I agree with you—and how often does *that* happen?" Amanda exclaimed. "Surely that's a good omen!"

CHAPTER TEN
If It's Tuesday, This Must Be Lawrenceville

Fred looked at the GPS; another half-hour and the bus would be in Lawrenceville, Georgia. "*Hallelujah!*" he thought. The show in Easley and the one after that had not gone well. Although the last few shows had been okay, the mood on the bus was glum. Bo, C.J., and Willard had crawled off to sleep, Jack and Hayley were on their cell phones—he with Tipsy, she with Keith, Amanda was in her bunk writing postcards to her children, and Sue and Graham were in the midst of a lackluster game of gin rummy. Only Pinky looked happy, Fred observed, and he suspected he knew why: for the last hundred miles or so, Meg Dorris had been cuddled up next to him—sharing her life story, he presumed, from the tidbits he'd overheard. The bus driver glanced in his rearview mirror again, grinning as Pinky hung on the buxom blonde's every word.

"Now you understand why it's so important to me to do this tour." Meg sighed, twisting a strand of hair around her finger. "Everybody else had a future, and *I* had a baby." She looked around the bus and shrugged. "But I have to say, being on the road isn't anything at all like I expected."

Pinky looked distressed. "Aren't you havin' fun?"

"Well, yeah, I guess. It's just a lot more work—and a lot less glamour—than I imagined. If I play my cards right, though," she whispered, "I'm hoping the eventual payoff will be Jack Bisbee."

"As . . . as your road manager?"

"As my knight in shining armor!"

Pinky's face looked like a two-year-old's who'd just lost his lollipop. "You got a thing for Jack? I didn't know that." He took a moment to phrase his next comment. "I . . . I think you're too special for Jack. He'd never appreciate you the way I—I mean, the way you deserve."

Oblivious to the smitten musician's reaction to her revelation, Meg gazed out the window. "This has given me a whole new respect for Hayley, though, now I've seen what this life is like." She turned back to face the fretful Pinky. "I can't imagine doing this for thirty-five years and staying sane!"

"You think these guys are sane?" Fred interjected, overhearing the last remark. "Uh-oh. Another week or two, and you'll be as crazy as the rest of us!"

Meg straightened her legs and stretched. "Aw, it hasn't been so bad—except for Easley. And I guess last night's show could have been better."

"Oh, Lord, don't nobody ever say the word 'Easley' in my presence again!" Willard ambled out of the bunk area and eased down into a seat, a Styrofoam cup of coffee in his hands. "That was, by far, the all-time worst show I have ever been a part of. And I have been a part of some doozies!" He shook his head at the memory. "Cal will never let me live it down. And *you*, missy," he added, lifting his cup toward Meg, "you're lucky it was your first show and they figured you were too green to be held accountable!"

Stung, Meg shrank back against her seat as Pinky bristled. "Willard, that show was nobody's fault and you know it. Anybody woulda missed a beat after their amp blew up! And if you'd looked at *me* once in a while instead of that cute thing in the front row, you'd have known I was trying to slow down the tempo and save the song!"

Willard guffawed. "Save the *song*? I wasn't worried about the dang song! I was worried about whether anyone would ever let us on a stage again!" He kept shaking his head at the memory. "Man, I hope that guy from Tugalo Records wasn't in the audience. He still hasn't called Jack back, you know."

"Did they ever find out who pulled the plug on Darlene's mic during their set?" Meg asked. "I think she thought *I* did it, and sabotaged my amp out of spite."

"That gal was madder'n a wet, settin' hen!" Graham cackled as he threw down his hand in defeat to Sue's final rummy and gave her a thumbs up. "I heard her backstage tearin' into ol' Cal like a wildcat. She went off on you Hot Flashes for everything from bad hairdos to bribery!"

Willard grinned, then took a cautious sip of coffee. "I think Bisbee knows what happened, but he ain't talking."

"Maybe *I* could get it out of him," Meg offered, and Pinky's face went traumatized toddler again.

"You don't know Jack," he warned. "He's not a talker—he likes to keep things to himself." Eager to change the subject, he turned back to Willard. "So what exactly did Jack and Hayley say to Cal after the show?"

"Show?" Graham snorted. "You mean that stinking three-song sampler?" He stood up and swung his arms around to rev up some circulation. "Although I'm thankful Jack stepped in and called it quits when he did—'cause we were on a suicide cruise, for sure."

"Yeah, plus fifty people sittin' in the pourin' rain is not what I call a fan base," observed Willard. "I never seen ol' Cal so mad." He leaned back. "First, Jack told him he was wearin' too much hair dye. Then Hayley said—and I quote: 'If you ever change this lineup again, you lowlife howlin' hyena, I'll tell your wife Darlene's doin' a lot more than *backin' you up* on this tour!'"

Graham slapped his knee and hooted. Pinky and Meg chuckled, and even Sue giggled.

"Musta worked; we been openin' every night since!" Pinky noted.

Willard tilted his coffee to swirl the remaining contents. "Yeah, but I heard Cal tell Jack, one more screw-up, and the Hot Flashes are out. Now don't take that personal, girls," he added, seeing the look of dismay on the faces around him. "My cousin can be a pain in the butt when it comes to business, but I don't know that he wants to tangle with Hayley Swift."

Seeing Meg's gloomy face, Pinky reached over to give her hand a squeeze as Willard rose to get more coffee. "We've done five shows since then, with no major disasters. We're on a roll now, shug."

Meg attempted a smile. "I hope so. It *is* a lot of work, but

I'm really starting to enjoy this, more than anybody knows." She sighed. "I think I'm gonna go take a shower while the bathroom's free. Thanks, Pinky; I like talking to you. You're a good listener."

Pinky's ears flamed. "Shore 'nuff, Miss Meg. Any time." He stood and, as she walked away, Pinky saw Fred wagging his tongue at him in the rearview mirror.

"Oh, kiss my keyboard!" Pinky growled.

Fred grinned and eased the bus off the interstate and on to the Lawrenceville exit ramp. "I love this job!" he declared, and began whistling "The Wheels on the Bus".

"You know, you don't have to wait 'til we circle back to South Carolina; why don't you fly down to Florida this weekend?" It was hard for Hayley to admit she missed her newly rekindled old flame as much as she did.

On the other end of the cell phone, Keith Parker sighed. "Tempting, but no can do. I'm covering for someone else. I'm sorry I haven't been able to catch any of the shows yet."

Hayley snorted. "Count your blessings. Hey, I need to ask you something." She checked to make sure the door to her compartment was completely closed, then lowered her voice. "Have you noticed anything odd about Sue's behavior recently?"

"What do you mean by 'odd?' Sue's always been a little different."

"True, bless her heart. But she seems...I don't know, agitated? Stressed? I mean, for sure, the last couple of weeks have been challenging, and we're all at that 'middle-aged crazy' point, but Sue's saying and doing things that are just, well, weird. I'm a little concerned."

"Are y'all living off junk food? If she's potassium-deficient, that could trigger some problems. So could insomnia, or a urinary tract infection."

"I don't know, this is more like we tell her something, and she says she doesn't remember. Or she'll tell *us* something—fifteen times!" Hayley felt the bus come to a stop, and glanced out the window to see what was up. A banner declaring "Gwinnett County Fair, Welcome to Lawrenceville, GA" billowed in the breeze. "C.J. said it makes her think of how Louise was, when she first got Alzheimer's. She said she used to repeat things, and get distracted, and just generally seem out of the loop."

"Whoa. Alzheimer's? I mean, early onset does happen, but it's not that common. Is there any dementia in Sue's family?"

"I don't know—and I don't know if I could tactfully ask that question! Maybe it's not Alzheimer's," Hayley retracted, "but something's definitely not right. She gets confused. A *lot*."

"Honey, there's a big difference between confusion and dementia. It's certainly *possible* to have Alzheimer's at our age, but it's very rare—less than five per cent of the population. More likely, it's just the change in routine, a urinary tract infection like I said, or even dehydration. Is she drinking enough water?"

"*I* don't know what Sue drinks! I think you need to come make a house call."

"To Sue, or to you?" Keith teased, and Hayley's annoyance dissipated into a smile. "It could be a hearing problem, too," Keith added. "Dealing with all those mikes and amplifiers after living in solitude is probably taking a toll on Sue's ears."

There was a beep in Hayley's own ear. "I have a call coming in, Keith, and I need to take it. Bubba and I have been playing phone tag all day. Can I call you later?"

"Nope, sorry. I'm headed to the hospital. I'll catch up with you soon, though. Bye. Miss you."

"Miss you back." Hayley clicked the disconnect button on her cell phone and the voice of Bubba Troutt hollering at his girlfriend reverberated in her ear. "Hey! Quit yellin' at Suzette and tell me what's goin' on."

"Well, *finally*! SUZETTE! I SAID TO TURN DOWN THAT INFERNAL MUSIC!"

Flinching at the bellowing voice, Hayley held the phone away from her ear for a few seconds, then moved it back. "Is that my gospel version of 'White Christmas'? It's a hundred degrees! Why on earth are you listening to Christmas music?"

"Suzette says it's mental conditioning: if you think cool, you'll *be* cool. All I know is I'm sick of that song—no offense. But that ain't why I called. Listen here, me and her saw that psycho Rhett Wilson at the Dollar Tree in Donelson Plaza today, and he was wearin' a 'Cal Taylor Retro Rodeo Tour' t-shirt. Could he have gotten that on eBay? 'Cause I thought the only place y'all are sellin' those shirts is at your concerts."

Hayley felt the blood drain from her face. "I-I thought so, too, but I'll check with Fred to make sure. Thanks for the heads-up, Bubba; I'll tell Jack." She put her hand to her head and tried to will away the queasiness brought on by the mention of Rhett Wilson's name. "H-how's the pool?"

"Blue as can be—I'll send you a picture."

Hayley gave a weak laugh. "You do that. Listen, I gotta run. Keep me posted—and keep the bills paid!" She snapped the phone shut, took a deep breath, and opened her door just in time to see Sue exit the bathroom, her hair matted with thick, purple goo.

"Hey, is that a new conditioner you're using? How long does it have to stay in? I should try to work in a treatment if I have time."

Sue gave her a blank stare. "Treatment? I just washed my hair, that's all. I forgot my blow dryer, though—left it in the closet."

Hayley pointed at her friend's head. "But you still have goop all over your head!"

Sue reached up. "Oh, good grief! How silly of me!" She turned and went back to the bathroom. "Guess I'll have to do one more rinse before I can dry."

Hayley made a mental note to describe this incident to Keith next time they spoke, then she moved up the corridor to C.J.'s bunk and pulled back the curtain. "Rise and shine, buttercup! Call time's in half an hour."

C.J. rolled over, her face creased by the pillow she'd been curled against for the past two hours. "I can't get ready in thirty minutes!" she complained. "Why didn't you wake me up earlier? And look at you—you're already dressed! Is everybody dressed! I told you to get me up at five!"

Hayley took a step back. "'Scuse me for being nice! You seemed really tired and I thought I was doing you a favor."

Jack Bisbee's wide shoulders suddenly shadowed the hall. "What's all the commotion?"

C. J. sat up, crossed her arms, and glared at him. "The commotion is that there's no way I can be onstage in thirty minutes, ready to sing. Hayley forgot to wake me up."

Hayley gave Jack an imploring look, and he nodded imperceptibly. "Hayley, you and the other gals go on to the dressing room. Me and C.J.'ll be along momentarily."

As the others gathered their possessions and left the bus, Jack took a deep breath, then sat on the bunk across from C. J. and looked at her. "*Are* you just tired, or is there something going on I need to know about? You've been awfully touchy lately."

"What's *that* supposed to mean?"

Jack rubbed a hand over his face and stood up wearily. "I don't have time for this, C. J.. Get your butt outta that bunk and be onstage in twenty-five minutes." He whipped the divider curtain closed behind him and C.J. heard the hydraulic door hiss open and close. She tiptoed out to the lounge area to watch Jack through the window, then stomped up and down the aisle, screaming with every step.

As she made a third pass, Graham stepped out of the bathroom. "Feel better? Sorry for intrudin' on your tantrum; if you'll step aside, I'll be on my way." C. J. moved between two of the seats to let him by, but he turned at the door and winked. "I've seen a lot better hissy-fits, by the way. I'll be glad to give you some tips if you wanna *really* let loose next time."

She screeched and looked around for something to hurl at the grinning fiddler. Somebody's pillow was the closest available choice; it sailed through the air, only to be caught in one hand by Graham. "You need to work on your aim," he said, tossing the pillow back and scoring a direct hit to C.J.'s head. As she burst into tears,

Graham stepped off the bus, his deep laugh spilling into the evening air.

♪

The members of Road Kill stood onstage, tuning and adjusting their instruments as Hayley and the Hot Flashes—minus C.J.—took their mikes in hand for a sound check.

Amanda nudged Hayley. "What the heck's up with C.J.?"

"Beats me. She's been cranky all week."

"Must be that time of the month," Bo joked as he walked past with an amplifier.

Amanda rolled her eyes. "Why is it every time we women get ticked off, you think it's 'that time of the month'? Aren't we ever allowed to just have a bad day?"

Bo set down the amp and raised his hands in surrender. "Sorry! No offense!"

"Plenty taken!" Amanda grumbled. "What if every time a *man* did something stupid we asked if you were having a testosterone surge? How would that make you feel?"

Bo smirked. "Honey, my testosterone surges every fifteen minutes—just like every other red-blooded male's on this planet. Did you skip Biology that day?" The other men onstage guffawed.

As Amanda scowled, Hayley came to her rescue. "You're saying testosterone is responsible for every stupid thing you've ever done?" she accused.

"Pretty much!" every one of the men responded, and then it was the girls' turn to crack up.

"Well, at least you're honest!" Meg said.

Jack's whistle cut their laughter short. "Listen up. The guy from Tugalo Records'll be here tonight, so keep it tight. And this is a long shot—but Tim McGraw may be with him. They're good buddies, and Tim's scoping for a new opening act."

Amanda and Meg shrieked. "Oh, he is so *hot!*" Meg swooned.

"Can we meet him?" Amanda begged.

Jack grinned. "Shake those tail feathers like you did *last* night, and McGraw'll be asking to meet *you!*"

Amanda pranced around her mike stand. "That ostrich feather skirt just flat out inspires me!"

Willard hooted. "I suspect it's inspiring a lot of *other* folks, too!"

Amanda blushed scarlet as Meg teased, "Who knew a middle-aged mom could cut loose like that?"

A frazzled, frowning C.J. suddenly stepped out of the wings, bringing conversation to a halt.

"Glad you could join us," said Jack, unable to keep the sarcasm out of his voice. Glancing around the stage, he rolled his eyes and sighed. "Oh for Pete's sake. Now Sue's gone AWOL. Where the heck did *she* go?"

Pinky nodded toward the bleachers. "Last time I saw her, she was headed out toward the midway. Said something about cotton candy."

Jack erupted. "I swear, this is like tryin' to herd cats. Bo, go find Sue right now. I'm warning y'all: tonight's performance is critical. Now get off the stage and stay in the dressing rooms until show time! If I see *anybody* in the hallway, I'm dockin' *everybody's* pay— and I'm serious as a heart attack! *Capice?*"

Heads nodded as bodies exited the stage in contrite silence.

Jack continued to mutter. "Grownups actin' like three-year-olds, people cryin' an' whinin', people hittin' on each other . . . I might as well be runnin' a flippin' preschool!"

It was ten minutes past show time. Cal stood in the wings gesturing impatiently to his watch as Jack, across the stage, looked at his own watch for the umpteenth time. Hayley's shirt was soaked with nervous perspiration. C.J. stared daggers at everyone.

"So what's the plan? Do we wait for Bo and Sue, or not?" Hayley whispered.

Jack gave her a tight smile. "Cain't do a show without a drummer, darlin'. How's your juggling?" he asked, peering out past the curtain again.

"They're here!" Willard called out in a hoarse whisper. Jack started to lash out at Sue as she took her place in the line-up, but stopped when he noted her dazed expression. He looked at Bo, who shook his head and mouthed, "Tell ya later."

"Okay, folks. Show time," Jack said as he lifted the strap of his guitar over his head. Pinky took the stage with a "Yeehah!" and a wave and, seconds later, launched into the opening bars of "Sister Serenade." As the cheers and applause crescendoed, Hayley allowed herself the first deep breath of the past hour. She put on a practiced smile and held it in place as she strode onstage. *Capacity crowd*, she assessed—*pumped up and ready for a good time*. She scanned the first few rows, looking for Jack's contact from Tugalo Records—and for Tim McGraw, if she was being honest with herself—and spotted them both in the third row, just off dead center. For a split second,

Hayley thought she saw Rhett Wilson, too, and her blood ran cold. A second glance proved it was not her worst nightmare, but simply a dark-haired young man with a greasy mustache and bad haircut. She breathed a silent prayer: *Lord, keep us safe and give us a good show.*

They sailed through "Sister Serenade" and "Love Me, Love Me Not." But two measures into "Rodeo Be-Bop," everything fell apart. It began when Graham turned white, then green, mouthed 'Help!' to Pinky, then fled the stage holding his stomach—his fiddle flung to the floor. Moments later, Amanda's microphone developed a feedback squeal and Sue sang the rest of the song with her fingers in her ears. Meg, embarrassed, and trying to be heroic for Jack, kept glaring at Sue until, finally, Sue stuck out her tongue at Meg and stomped off stage in the middle of "Mister Cool." As she left, she tripped over the power cord to Pinky's keyboard and yanked it loose, leaving the band with no melody accompaniment for almost a full minute while a scarlet-eared Pinky scrambled to reconnect the plug. The killing blow came, however, as Pinky settled back into the chorus; in the middle of an inspired riff, one of Bo's drumsticks went rogue and sailed out into the audience, hitting Tim McGraw square in the face.

Amid the raucous whoops and swelling murmur of the crowd, Hayley had attempted to end the set with some shred of poise, but Cal Taylor's band suddenly converged on the stage from all directions and she found herself shoved into the wings. Jack Bisbee's hands propelled her into the green room, where everyone else had gathered, then slammed the door behind her. The look on his face was murderous. "What the *hell* just happened out there?"

Hayley sank wearily into a chair and crossed her arms over

her face. "It was nothing any one person did, it was just . . . the absolute worst pile-up of fluky disasters I've ever seen in my life and . . ." Suddenly her urge to burst into tears morphed into an absurd desire to giggle uncontrollably. "It actually was pretty hilarious." She peeked out from under one elbow, trying to decide if Jack might see even the tiniest bit of humor in the situation. Given the expression on his face, she guessed not.

"Oh yeah, it was a real scream. We'll be lucky if McGraw doesn't sue us, Cal's as much as told us we're off the tour, and Road Kill can, for sure, kiss any deal with Tugalo Records goodbye."

Sue, who'd been standing quietly behind Hayley's chair, suddenly grew agitated and began twisting her hair. "It was my fault, wasn't it? I'm so sorry, I didn't mean to mess everything up. What can I do to fix it?" She burst into tears.

C. J. ran to wrap her arms around Sue. "Oh, it wasn't your fault, sweetie. It was just a bad night."

"It was *not* just a bad night, and it wasn't a 'pile-up of fluky disasters;' it was people out of their element!'" Jack countered, tossing a look of irritation at Hayley and pointing an accusatory finger in Sue's face. "And, yes, you *did* start the wrecker ball rolling when you decided to stroll out onto the midway ten minutes before the show. This ain't kindergarten, lady; we're supposed to be *pros!*"

C. J. pulled her friend to her chest and turned her away, as if to shield her from Jack's attack. "Lay off her. There's a lot you don't understand."

"I understand you chose to have a first-class temper tantrum after I left the bus."

Before C.J. could respond, a moan rose from the corner of

the room. All eyes turned to stare at Graham, who lay on the floor pale and sweating as he held a cold can of ginger ale to his forehead.

C. J.'s eyes narrowed. "Gee, Jack. Wonder who told you *that*?"

"Leave him out of this. He's the only one here with a legitimate excuse for screwing up." Graham moaned again.

"What's wrong with you, Graham?" Meg asked.

"I don't know, but I think I'm dying—and I'll be glad to go. I puked my guts up just before we went onstage."

C. J. blanched, let go of Sue to fling a hand over her own mouth, and bolted for the door.

Meg stepped forward and placed a restraining hand on Jack's arm. "We've had several perfect shows, Jack, with not one missed cue. Doesn't that count for something?"

"'Fraid not," Jack snarled. "In this business, you're only as good as your last performance."

"And the great Jack Bisbee has *never* made a mistake?" Hayley fired back, and their eyes locked—steel blue against emerald green.

"Don't go there. You know I have."

"Yes, you certainly have. But somebody gave *you* another chance, or you wouldn't be here right now."

His anger turning physical, Jack grabbed a folding chair and sent it flying just as Cal Taylor opened the door and strutted in, full of himself and grinning ear to ear.

"Good job, guys! My band missed a major chord change just now, but thanks to you, nobody noticed because they're still laughing about Bo's flying drumstick! You know what? I think I'll give you a *bonus* instead of firing you. It's been a helluva night for everybody!" He paused to listen. "Hear that? That's my third encore! Ka-ching, ka-ching!" He gave a salute and backed out of the doorway.

Sue, now recomposed, waggled a finger at Jack. "See? It *is* like kindergarten. We just got a second chance!"

Jack swore. "Nobody talk to me the rest of the night," he spat, and stomped out of the room.

"Okay, then! Who wants to go ride the Tilt-a-Whirl?" Sue asked in a cheery voice, and the spent group laughed in spite of themselves.

"You know what?" chuckled Bo. "That is the best idea I've heard all day. Count me in, Suzy-Q!"

"Me, too," announced Willard. "I love the Tilt-a-Whirl!"

"I'll tag along, but I'm not gonna ride," said C. J., from the doorway. "My stomach's doing its own tilt-a-whirls. I hope Graham's not contagious!"

As the others headed for the door, Hayley stood and shook her head. "I'll catch up with you guys later. I have some things I need to take care of—and one of us needs to stay here and make sure Graham doesn't die."

On cue, the dying man moaned pitifully.

As the entourage headed down the hall, Meg stopped abruptly. "Oops! Need to make a pit stop. Don't wait on me, though; I'll find you," she said, stepping into the restroom. A few seconds later, she opened the door to make sure the coast was clear, then turned to race in the direction Jack had gone a few moments earlier. She spied him outside, a hundred yards ahead, on his way to the bus.

"Wait up!" she called, but Jack kept walking. Bending to remove her platform heels, she hiked her dress and took off running. Out of breath and sweating in the humid air, she finally caught up with him and reached to put a hand on his shoulder. "Jack! Slow down! Let me buy you a drink somewhere."

He slung her hand away and kept walking. "Give it up, Meg."

"Hey, it's hot, I'm thirsty, I thought you might be, too. I'm just trying to be nice."

Jack stopped and sighed, lifting his face to the sky. "Then be nice by leaving me alone." There was a sound and they both turned to see Pinky carrying a load of equipment toward the bus. "Leave Amanda's mike and amp in the dressing room, will you?" Jack called out. "I want to take a look at it."

"You got it, boss," Pinky answered as he glanced at Meg.

When Pinky returned from the bus a minute later, he saw Meg still standing where Jack had left her, tears trickling down her face. "I'm thirsty," he said, as he walked up, took out a handkerchief, and gently wiped her cheeks. "I'm no Jack Bisbee, but if you'll let me, I'd love to buy you a drink—something tall and cold, with an umbrella in it and a cherry on top. You don't even have to be nice to me. Just keep me company."

Meg's lips puckered up in a prelude to more tears, but she managed a small smile. "I would love to have a drink with you," she said, finally. "Thank you."

Hayley stood backstage watching Cal Taylor sign autographs. He was slick, and he could work a crowd, but he was a mediocre musician, at best, and suddenly, Hayley was flooded with pangs of jealousy. She knew, given the chance, that she, too, could have crowds eating out of her hand again. Maybe Tipsy was right. Maybe it was time to consider someone else's material. She'd been blessed with two gifts: a knack for songwriting and an amazing set of vocal chords. But staying at the top had taken its toll on her creativity. Even with publicists, producers, label execs, and Bubba, time that should have been devoted to writing got sucked up in maintaining the Hayley Swift persona.

Was it the grueling grind that killed off the muse, or did it dry up and die on its own? She'd been afraid to test that. She pondered the songs Tipsy had pitched to her—songs she'd cast aside only to hear them rocket up the charts on the lips of other artists. She gazed out again at Cal's exuberant face and the clamoring crowd. She'd wasted a lot of years on pride. She wasn't young anymore, but neither were her fellow Gen Xers who just might be getting tired of cookie-cutter pop tarts. There was always room on the charts for excellence. *So who says the new and improved Hayley Swift has to write her own songs?* As Cal posed for yet another picture, Hayley slipped out of the wings and back to the green room, in search of Jack. She was not disappointed. He was there, sprawled in the middle of the floor, sifting through the pieces of what used to be Amanda's amplifier.

"May I come in?" she asked tentatively. "It's after midnight, so technically, the 'no talking to you tonight' rule no longer applies."

Jack grunted. "It's a free country."

"You know, grumpy doesn't suit you," Hayley teased. "I like you much better when you're happy."

Jack shot her a withering look. "I haven't had much to be

happy *about* the last few hours, have I?"

Hayley lugged a chair over to the pile of electrical parts. "Oh, get over it. You overreacted, and you know it."

"I do know it," he admitted, "but put yourself in my shoes: tonight was the chance for me to catch that last break before I'm too damn old to pluck a guitar. It's been a great ride, Hayley, but I'd like to *lead* the parade for a change, instead of bringin' up the rear."

"I know what you mean, buddy. I don't know which is worse—to have had it and lost it, or to never have had it at all."

Jack snorted in derision. "That's a no-brainer! At least you've *had* it." He took a deep breath. "So what's up with Sue?"

Hayley shifted in her chair. "I wish I knew; I'm worried about her. Something's definitely not right; she drifts off into space, says weird things that don't make any sense, she doesn't recognize people sometimes—and I've never known Sue to be temperamental."

"Did you ask Doctor Boy about it?"

"I have. But he's not willing to make a phone diagnosis for a patient he hasn't examined, and besides, he thinks *all* my girlfriends are a little off center."

Jack chuckled. "I think I'm hangin' with him on that one. Though I'll have to say, tonight aside, they've been troupers. They've got talent, Hayley—they're holding their own—but I don't know if they can handle another six weeks of this. Listen," he continued, "since we're having this little 'quiet time,' I have something I'd like to share with you."

"Tight-lipped Bisbee? Sharing with moi? Do tell!"

"Shut up." Jack reached behind him for his acoustic guitar. "I've never asked you to do this before, but will you listen to a song

I wrote and give me your honest opinion? I'm pitching it to Kenny Chesney when we play Newnan. He's there the day after we are."

Hayley nodded. "Of course! I'm flattered."

He began to strum the guitar, tentatively at first, then confidently, then passionately. And then he was singing, rich and full, the bluesy melody and melancholy lyrics fusing into an anguished tale of lost love. The honesty in his voice raked her heart, and she was moved to tears.

When the song was over, they both sat silent. Finally Hayley spoke. "Kenny Chesney can't have that song."

Jack stared at Hayley. "Why not? What do I need to change?"

"Not one word." She smiled. "Kenny can't have it, because it's mine. *I* want to sing your song, Jack."

There was another silence, this one uncomfortable, as they tried to read each other's mind. Jack spoke first. "Hayley, nothing personal, but—,"

"It's *very* personal, Jack. This is the song Tipsy told me to find—ten *years* ago. I know I don't bring much to the table right now, but I can sing this song the way you want it to be sung!"

Jack was quiet for a moment. "So you wanna use my song as your crutch for a comeback? What if you tank, Hayley? What if you fall flat on your lovely face? There goes *my* thirty-five-year shot at overnight success."

"Gee, don't hold back, buddy." Hayley tried valiantly to hold back tears. She swallowed, hard. "You're right, of course. But Chesney—or anybody else, for that matter—doesn't know you like I do, or *care* like I do."

"You care about me?"

Caught off guard by his bluntness, Hayley colored, but recovered quickly. "Of course I care. I care because my bank account is empty, and so is yours. We have a chance to do something about that, if we'll trust each other."

Jack rolled his eyes. "Last time I trusted you, I lost five thousand dollars in a dot com disaster."

"You only lost five??" Hayley shrieked, and smacked him. "I lost *fifteen*, you cad!" She was quiet for a moment, then looked her long-time friend straight in the eye. "Look. If I have to sing somebody else's song, I'd like for it to be yours."

"Why?"

"Because you're my best bud and I want us to share this experience."

"Bullfeathers. You want it because you're desperate and greedy and you know it's gonna be a monster hit."

She shrugged. "That, too."

"It'll cost you."

"How much?"

"I get to sing harmony."

"Are you serious?"

"As a heart attack."

They sat assessing each other, the years of struggling and suffering to get to their respective places in the world weighing heavy against this new horizon.

She hesitated. "You want equal billing? A duo?"

"Nope. Equal royalties. I don't want the fame, just the fortune."

"Gold-digger!"

"Diva!"

"Deal."

"Done."

Slightly stunned at what had just transpired, they sat for a moment then got to their feet, and Jack bent to put his guitar in its case. "Think we should celebrate?"

"Absolutely!" Hayley grinned. "Let's load this mess on the bus and go find the Tilt-a-Whirl!"

CHAPTER ELEVEN
Stop the Bus, I Want to Get Off!

"I bought you a present."

Meg's eyes widened in surprise as Pinky handed her a small package. It was late afternoon and they were seated at a rest stop picnic table on I-75, near Lake City, Florida, en route to their next gig. The other band members were stretching their legs or buying snacks from the vending machines.

Pinky thrust the gift in her face. "Go on, open it!"

"Why did you buy me a present?"

"You'll see."

As she tore off the paper, Meg's expression was confused. "A journal?"

Pinky's ears reddened. "Yep. I've kept one during every road trip since I started in this business, too many years ago to count. I've had a lot of fun, some heartache, and met some real nice folks. Somehow, writing it all down helps me remember I've got a lot to be thankful for."

Tears welled in Meg's eyes. "Pinky, you are such a romantic! *Thank* you—although I'm not sure what I'll have to write about. Nothing very exciting ever happens to me."

Pinky patted her hand. "Doesn't have to be exciting, just tell it like it is. If somebody makes you mad, write it down. If you see a cute little chipmunk and he makes you smile, write it down. If you drink a cup of coffee with some cute, little, bald-headed keyboard player, write it down. If you wonder how it might be to *kiss* that cute, little, bald-headed keyboard player, write that down." He raised his eyebrows. "'Course, it might also be fun to stop wondering and actually *do* it sometime."

Meg leaned to plant a kiss on Pinky's lips.

He blushed all the way down to his toes. "Write down that that was *real* nice!"

A little farther down, Amanda and Graham were strolling away from the vending machines, he with ginger ale and crackers in hand, she with M&Ms and a Coke. As Hayley and Sue approached them, walking in the opposite direction, Hayley stopped.

"You know, y'all might have some regard for other people's *rest*, if not for decency," she complained. "Your giggling kept everybody awake half the night!"

Amanda looked indignant. "For gosh sakes, Hayley, Graham was up sick again all night, and I wasn't feeling so great myself. We were trying to make the best of a crummy situation!"

"It doesn't take a rocket scientist to know if you swap spit with a sick person, you're going to end up in the infirmary yourself," Sue intoned drily.

Graham scowled. "C'mon, now, even *I* resent that. We haven't been 'swappin' spit' or anything *else* we need to apologize for—not that it's anybody's business!"

Hayley raised an eyebrow. "It's my business when it affects

our performance. We can't be at our best if we don't get enough sleep. And as we have already been reminded, this is work—not a slumber party."

Sue stooped to pick a dandelion next to the sidewalk. "Oh, I love slumber parties! I remember on my twelfth birthday, my mama gave me a surprise one. She made me a coconut cake with pink icing, and we all took turns painting each other's toenails. Do you remember that?"

Tension momentarily diffused, Hayley smiled. "I do. We must have played the soundtrack from "Raiders of the Lost Ark" a thousand times! Remember? Your daddy came upstairs and hollered if he heard "Raiders March" one more time, he was gonna throw that cassette on the grill with the hot dogs!"

Amanda's gasp interrupted everyone's laughter. "Birthday! Oh, Lord, have mercy! What's today's date?"

Hayley looked at her cell phone and then at Amanda's stricken face. "September 19th. Why? What's the matter?"

Amanda's face paled and she burst into tears. "I don't believe this. I'm the world's worst mother! Today is the twins' birthday!" she wailed. "My babies are twelve years old today, and I completely forgot! How is that possible? Oh, my gosh, I have to go home! I have to go home *right now*!"

Hayley and Sue stood in stunned silence as Amanda sprinted toward the bus, with Graham on her heels. "Did I say something wrong?" Sue asked, a pained look on her face. "I didn't mean to! What did I say?"

Hayley squeezed Sue's hand and shook her head. "Not a thing, sweetie. Amanda just forgot something." She studied her friend's anxious face. "Are you okay?"

Sue looked straight into Hayley's eyes for a moment and then, as tears began to well, averted her eyes to the grass. "I don't know. I think . . . maybe . . . there's something wrong with me. The things I mean to say aren't the things that come out of my mouth, and, well, I've always been a scatterbrain . . ." she shrugged and attempted a smile, "but lately I feel just . . . lost." She sighed deeply and looked back up into Hayley's eyes. "Why can I remember what happened when I was twelve, but I can't remember if I ate breakfast this morning. Did I?"

Hayley managed to laugh even as tears began to trickle down her own cheeks. "You sure did, girlfriend—a big ol' Western omelet . . . with grits *and* hash browns!" She touched Sue's cheek. "Have you talked to a doctor?"

Sue shook her head and peered down at the grass again. "I thought it would go away. I was hoping this trip would clear my head. Sometimes I think being alone all these years after Bill's death has turned me into a hermit, and all I really need is to get out more—you know, be adventurous." She gave a wry laugh. "Now that I'm living the wild life, though, it's scaring me to death."

Hayley threw her arms around her oldest and dearest friend and hugged her close. "Would it be okay if we talked to Keith about this?"

Sue nodded. "I really like Keith. Did he ask you to the prom?"

Hayley paused, wondering if Sue was reminiscing or confused. "He did," she said. "Keith asked me to the prom. And we went, remember? All of us were there. You and Bill won the "Walk Like an Egyptian" dance contest!"

Sue shook her head. "I don't remember. But Keith's a nice guy. Hey, isn't that C.J. over there?" she interjected suddenly, her attention redirected to the edge of the parking lot. "Why is she bending over that bush?"

"Oh, good grief!" Hayley moaned. "Maybe there *is* a stomach bug going around. C.J.! Are you OK?" she yelled, as she and Sue hurried across the picnic area.

C.J. was leaning forward, with her head down and her hands on her knees. "Oh, kill me, I'm dying." Her face, devoid of color, shimmered with a sheen of perspiration. She wiped her mouth on the back of her hand. "Can you help me back to the bus?"

"Of course!" Hayley reached an arm around and, gently, helped her straighten up. "How long have you been sick? We should have quarantined Graham! We're all gonna be sick before this is over with. Do you want a ginger ale?" She moved around, trying to shield C. J.'s face from the blazing Florida sun.

"No! I want to be in my bed—back home! I want to stop throwing up! I'm sorry, Hayley. I know I've been a pain lately, but I swear, I've had PMS for a month. Ouch, Sue! Watch your elbow! My boobs feel like somebody pummeled them with a tire iron."

Hayley gave a commiserating hug. "I'm not looking forward to hot flashes, but I have to say, after forty years, I am *more* than ready to bid farewell to PMS! You think you're about to start your period?"

C. J. blew out an exasperated breath. "Your guess is as good as mine. These days, I never know if it's going to show up or not. I've learned to travel with tampons wherever I go. I've got 'em stashed in my purse, in the glove compartment of my car, even inside Mama's bathroom at the nursing home!"

Hayley chuckled. "I'll bet that's made for some interesting conversation among Louise's nursing aides! Come on, honey, let's get you back on the bus."

Sue reached to take C.J.'s hand into her own. "You'll feel better in a minute," she comforted, then stopped to gaze across the picnic area again. "Oh, my goodness, look at that! That girl looks like she's ready to have a baby any minute and she doesn't look old enough to even have a driver's license." She gave a mournful sigh. "I wish Bill and I could have had a baby. He would have been such a good daddy."

All eyes turned to a very pregnant young girl who stood fanning herself under a tree, then Hayley looked at C. J., and C. J. looked at Hayley, then C. J. blanched and felt her knees buckle as a wave of shock hit her. Nausea. Breast tenderness. Mood swings. No periods in...a while. *No! Surely not!* she thought as she felt herself sinking to the ground.

♪

The scene on the bus could only be described as chaotic: part psych ward, part infirmary, part war room. Amanda sat in her bunk, sobbing into a cell phone and repeating a litany of self-incriminating apologies to her husband. "Please come get me right now, and bring the twins! I miss y'all so much! You must think I'm awful. I'm so selfish! Why didn't you remind me about the twins' birthday when we talked? Your mother is right, I don't deserve you! Has she given all my clothes to Goodwill yet?"

Meanwhile, the sound of C.J. retching in the bathroom echoed through the back half of the bus while Sue paced up and down the center aisle, singing the chorus to "Sister Serenade" over and over again. Bo exchanged insults with his ex-wife via cell phone while Meg and Pinky cuddled together in a corner, oblivious to it all.

As they rolled down the highway, Fred kept glancing up into the rearview mirror. "I want hazard pay, Bisbee!" he yelled when he finally spotted the road manager. "This is way above and beyond the call of *any* duty!"

"Just shut up and get us to Ocala," Jack growled, as Hayley plopped into the seat beside him.

"Houston, we have a problem," she intoned in newscaster

mode, "several of them, in fact. We've got germs, hormones, unpaid child support, maternal angst, possible brain damage, and maybe a few more surprises! Do you still carry that .22? You could shoot us, and put us all out of our misery."

Jack gave her a bleak look. "Don't think I haven't considered it—several hundred miles back."

Hayley grinned before turning serious. "All kidding aside, what are we gonna do? You think there's any way we can pull off a show tomorrow tonight?"

Meg, inadvertently eavesdropping, pulled away from Pinky long enough to respond, "I'm in! Nothin' wrong with me! And Pinky knows the harmony on every song in our set. Bo and Willard could sing backup if Amanda and C.J. are sick."

"I need a career change," Jack groused, ignoring them all. "My mom always said the music business would make me crazy." He pointed an index finger at his temple and jerked his head. "BANG! It's official! I'm crazy!"

"Actually, Meg's got a point," Willard mused. "It wouldn't be hard for me 'n' Drummer Boy to rework those harmonies. But I'm goin' on record *right now*: I ain't wearin' pink Spandex for nobody!"

Bo, finally off the phone, cackled. "Ooh, let's call Flopsy and see if he has any outfits to show off chest hair!"

"You don't *have* any chest hair; it's all hangin' down your back in a pigtail!" taunted Fred with an accompanying blast of the horn.

Jack stood up. "How 'bout everybody go read a book? I need some time to think. Not you, Fred," he added, and got another honk in response. The others—amazingly—followed orders and headed toward their bunks, but Hayley failed to move. Jack stared down at her. "Well?"

"Even me?"

"Especially you!"

"Who died and left you boss?"

"*Flopsy*, that's who! You got a problem with that?'

"No, sir!" she said tartly as she stood up and stomped away.

♪

An hour later, as Fred pulled into the parking lot of the Ocala Hilton, Jack started banging on walls and clapping his hands to rouse the crew. "All hands on deck," he ordered, then waited at the front of the bus while everyone gathered. "I have an announcement," he said, when all were present. "The Orange Blossom Opry's about a half hour from here. Call time's not until tomorrow afternoon at 4 so, as of this moment, you are officially off duty for the next 21 hours. I want you to get your stuff, get off this bus, get well, get drunk, get down, get funky, get whatever, just stay out of my face. Dinner's on me—so is breakfast and lunch tomorrow—but I don't wanna see you, I don't wanna talk to you, I don't wanna hear from you. Fred, find a drugstore and some Lysol and wipe down this bus from top to bottom. That is all."

"I'll go get the Lysol for you, Fred," C. J. offered. "I need to find a drugstore, anyway."

"Me, too! I need to buy the twins a birthday present," Amanda said, then let loose another wail. "What kind of mother buys her children a birthday present on the spur of the moment at a drugstore?" She burst into fresh tears.

"Plenty, I'm sure," Fred said kindly. "I saw a sign for CVS on the way in. Let me unload the bags and we'll zip back over there." He pushed the button to open the door and climbed down the stairs.

As the others went to gather their belongings, Jack joined Fred outside the bus. "Here," he said, handing Fred a credit card. "Check us in. Put me on the floor farthest away from the rest of y'all, and make sure there's a 'Do Not Disturb' sign on my door." He turned as his band members approached to claim their bags. "Bo, Willard, y'all get the girls' luggage, too. Graham, you keep an eye on Sue. Don't let her out of your sight, you hear?"

Graham cocked an eyebrow. "Did you forget I'm sick?"

Jack cocked one back. "Did you forget I'm boss?"

Trumped, the fiddler's face turned sullen. "How could I?" he retorted, then bent to grab his suitcase and Sue's. "Miss Sue, what's your pleasure?," he called out as she exited the bus and he walked up to join her. "There's a Cracker Barrel across the street; we can treat ourselves to an apple dumplin', we can go to CVS with C. J. and Amanda, or we can go pile up on a big, comfy bed inside this fine hotel and watch a movie."

Sue gave Graham a playful smack. "Mister Frazier, what is it about you and married women? My husband would murder you if he heard you talking that way!"

"I thought you were a widow!"

Sue looked confused. "Well . . . my husband's name is still Bill."

Now Graham looked confused. "Uh, let's go with the apple dumplin's—with ice cream on top. Ice cream always makes everything better. I hope," he muttered.

♪

C.J. wandered the aisles not finding what she was looking for, then approached the pharmacy counter and spied exactly what she wanted. Overwhelmed by a torrent of emotions, she stood, frozen. *There's no way! Pete and I are so careful! Our system has worked for years; why would it fail now? Is this God's idea of a joke? I'm fifty-three years old, for heaven's sake!* She was startled out of her fog when Amanda appeared at her elbow.

"Hey, come look at this," she commanded, dragging C. J.

to the toy aisle. "If *you* were a terrible mother, would you choose tacky t-shirts or cheap imported toys for your children's birthday? You know, the birthday you completely *forgot*, because you were living out a thirty-five-year-old fantasy about being a rock star? Well, country star," she amended.

C. J. stood numbly. "I don't know. I can't imagine *forgetting* my child's birthday." Seeing the wounded expression on her friend's face, C. J. grimaced. "Sorry. I didn't mean that like it sounded." She patted Amanda's arm. "T-shirts, I guess—and some candy. I don't know. Sorry, hon, I'm totally preoccupied. I've got to go back over here and look for something."

As C. J. steered herself back toward the pharmacy counter, stopping en route to take a can of Lysol disinfectant off a shelf, she felt a slight twinge of guilt at abandoning her friend, but reasoned that her own potential life crisis outranked Amanda's. *Let's see . . . in twelve years, I'll be . . . oh, heaven help me! . . . I'll be on Social Security! Pete promised me a convertible at sixty-five; wonder if they make a convertible minivan?*

"Can I help you?" an older woman—65? C.J. wondered?—asked gruffly.

"I . . . I need one of those," she said, pointing behind the counter.

"One of those what?"

"One of those boxes, there."

The woman turned to look at the shelf behind her. "I got lots of boxes, hon. Could you be more specific? Yeast infection? Hemorrhoids? Condoms?"

C. J. recoiled. "Get a microphone, why don't you?!"

Amanda appeared again. "What are you doing?" she whispered. She dodged the elbow C. J. jabbed at her, dumped an armload of guilt gifts on the counter, and started digging in her purse for her wallet.

The clerk sighed. "Ma'am? What it'll be? I got customers here!"

"Oh, go ahead and ring her up. I'm still thinking," C. J. growled.

As the clerk began her beep-and-bag-it routine, Amanda turned to give her friend a smile. She was horrified when C. J. burst into tears.

"What'd I do?" Amanda yelped.

"Oh, Amanda, I'm here for a pregnancy test!" she wailed.

"A *what?* Are you kidding? Does Pete know?"

C. J. gave her friend a look somewhere between bemusement and incredulity. "Of *course* he doesn't! I don't know myself! That's why I'm here! I don't know if I'm menopausal or pregnant!"

"I don't, either," barked the clerk, "but I *do* know you're holding up traffic! Will there be anything *else*, ladies?"

Amanda rolled her eyes. "Can you add a pregnancy test to my order, please?"

"Do you still want condoms?" the woman asked, lifting a box off the shelf.

"NO!" the friends shouted in unison.

Meg emerged from the bathroom, one towel wrapped around her head, another around her body. Pinky was coming to her room in ten minutes. Anxiety, eagerness, and uncertainty pulsed through her body. Who would have guessed she'd prefer a chubby little bald guy to handsome Jack Bisbee? But Pinky Brown made her feel like the most important woman in the world. He knew her—warts and all—better than anyone on earth, after only two weeks. And he still wanted her. Last night, he'd invited her to spend Thanksgiving in Tennessee with his family. Instantly, she'd resolved to quit smoking, lose twenty pounds, stop biting her nails, and maintain her new and improved outlook on life; being with Pinky made it easy. As she rifled through her suitcase for her most flattering outfit, her cell phone rang.

"Hello?"

"Hey, Mom. It's Alice."

Meg felt her stomach tense. "Oh! Alice! Hello, sweetheart! How are you? *Where* are you? Did you get the tickets I sent?"

"Yes, I got them. Thank you. But I can't come to Newnan."

Meg was disappointed, but not surprised. "That's okay. It was a long shot; I was just hoping to see you."

"Well, that's actually why I called. Don't you have a show in Weirsdale tomorrow night?"

"Yes, why?

"Well, I'm just up the road, in Gainesville. I drove a friend down to pick up a car he bought on eBay, and I have a few days off. Can we get together? Where are you now?"

Meg's first reaction was annoyance at having her evening with Pinky spoiled, then she realized this was a perfect opportunity for Alice to see her in a new role—as a success, as somebody people depended on, as somebody someone loved. And it was a perfect opportunity for her daughter to meet the first man who had ever treated her mother like she was somebody special. "Your timing is perfect. Come have dinner and spend the night with me!"

They agreed to meet in the lobby two hours later, and as Meg disconnected, she whispered a prayer. "Thank you, God. I know my life is my own fault, but thank you for making it better."

CHAPTER TWELVE
The Best Laid Plans of Mice and (Wo)Men

The frosty air of the hotel lobby was a welcome reprieve from the cloying humidity. As C.J. and Amanda headed toward the elevator with their drugstore purchases, the silver doors parted to reveal Graham Frazier. "Well, hey, there! Looks like you got your shopping done. Do we need to make a run to the post office?"

Amanda stared at Graham. "Huh?"

"Remember? World's worst mom? Last-minute gift shopping? Express mail?"

She waved a hand and laughed. "Oh, *that*. No, everything's fine. I just got off the phone with Tom and he covered for me; I should have known he would. He called to tell me the twins loved the camera drones 'we' bought them. Problem solved, crisis averted, Mommy hat stored in the closet for a few more weeks."

At the word "mommy," C. J. made a guttural sound and laid a hand across her heart. Amanda turned to offer a supportive smile, but ended up noticing her friend's fingernails. Their chipped polish and ragged cuticles led her to examine her own less-than-pristine manicure.

"You women change moods faster than a pit crew changes tires," Graham complained as he scratched his head in exasperation.

"Part of that whole mystique thing, darlin'," Amanda teased. "Listen, I've had a brilliant idea."

Graham perked up. "Oh, yeah? I've just escorted Sue safely to her room, and she's probably gonna take a sugar-coma nap after all the dessert we ate. If I'm not goin' to the post office, then I'm headed to the bar with nothin' but time. Whad'ya have in mind?"

"Girl time," Amanda said, deflating his hopeful face. She thrust her shopping bags at C. J. "It's been a rough couple of days, and we ladies need some pampering. Go up and take a hot bath," she instructed C. J. "I'm going to see if Fred will take me back to the drugstore." She grabbed Graham by the arm and pulled him toward the door. "Come on, hot stuff; you're coming with me."

"Baby, weren't you just *at* the drugstore?"

C. J. gave another growl as she stepped into the elevator.

"Don't say 'baby!'" Amanda ordered, "and don't ask questions!" She paused and scanned the parking lot when they got outside. "Hmm. I don't see the bus. Guess we'll have to walk, but it's not that far."

"I think we'd have a lot more fun in the bar," Graham protested, dragging his feet, but Amanda maneuvered him toward the sidewalk and kept him moving at a brisk pace.

They entered the drugstore and Amanda made a beeline for the beauty products aisle. "Get a buggy," she decreed. Graham did as told while Amanda inspected the shelves like a general surveying his troops. An assortment of lotions, crèmes, gels, and tools soon filled the cart.

"Sugar, you cain't get no more beautiful," Graham protested as he took inventory of the selections. "Why are women so afraid to be themselves? There's nothin' wrong with lookin' like you've lived a little. You've *earned* those laugh lines; why not celebrate 'em?"

Amanda chuckled and, in spite of her resolve to keep Graham at arm's length, kissed him on the cheek. "You are such a snake-oil salesman, but you are definitely balm for a middle-aged lady's soul!"

Graham slid his arms around her waist. "I'm serious. Older women are sexy as all get-out! You know who you are, you know what you want, you know what's important, and you're not afraid to speak your mind. Don't you realize what an incredible woman you are?"

She threw her head back and laughed full and deep. "Mr. Frazier, you do know how to make a girl feel good. If I weren't a happily married woman, I'd be tempted to throw myself at you right here in the shampoo aisle!"

"I won't tell if you won't!" he said, pulling her close.

She smacked his arms and extracted herself from his grasp. "Believe me, there's a clerk over there who'd broadcast it across five counties. Besides, flattery's better than fooling around any day of the week—you've made my year!"

Graham sighed. "It may be better for *you*; I can't say the same for me. But I meant every word, Amanda." He tilted her chin to allow a direct gaze into her eyes. "You been playin' that 'happily married' card ever since Columbia. You tryin' to convince me or yourself?"

She considered his point. "I *am* happily married but, for

sure, my life's duller than it used to be. I got a dream job after college, traveled the world, lived the high life—then I met Tom and that life lost its appeal. When my twins were born, I thought I'd reached nirvana." She smiled. "I wouldn't trade my life now for the world, but there *are* days I stand in my laundry room and wonder what happened to the woman who knew all the best restaurants in Paris."

"Wasn't that what 'Women's Lib' was about, proving you could have it all?" Graham chided.

"*That* was a big, fat lie. You can *have* it all, but then you're too worn out to enjoy it! At some point, a woman simply has to make choices."

"Are you regretting yours?"

Amanda draped herself over the handle of the shopping cart and studied the floor. "Not regretting, just re-evaluating. This tour is the first time I've focused on *me* in twelve years. I kind of like it!" She lifted her head in time to catch Graham's slow grin.

"I kind of like it, too."

"You are *hopeless*!" Amanda scolded. "Come on, I'm in the middle of an emergency rescue mission." She pushed the cart to the register, where the clerk who'd waited on her earlier looked up and grinned.

"Ain't *you* a purty thing!"

Amanda turned and put a hand over whatever Graham was about to say. "Outside!" she ordered, and to her amazement, he complied.

♪

Bo Whitfield took a swig from his bottle of beer and gave Willard Taylor a nudge. "I'd like me a long, tall drink of that," he said as he ogled the voluptuous redheaded cocktail waitress strutting away from their table.

"After that phone call on the bus today, I'd think your thirst for redheads would be purty well quenched. Do I gather that Ex-Wife Number Two is still tryin' to take you to the cleaners?"

Bo grunted. "Are you kiddin? I'll be lucky if I'm left with a coat hanger! Why do women have to be so gol-durned vindictive?"

"Well, now," said Fred, who had completed his assigned tasks, found a parking spot for the bus, and was relaxing with the boys in the hotel bar, "they tend to get that way when they've caught you arm in arm with a neighbor lady!"

"Aw, I was just teachin' her how to play a paradiddle," Bo growled. "She wanted a drum lesson! And now I'm livin' in a rathole while my ex spends my hard-earned money on her new boyfriend. Wanna hear the latest?"

"NO! Willard and Fred responded simultaneously.

"Reckon Jack'll join us for dinner?" Fred mused, changing the subject. "There's a rib-eye buffet here tonight that sounds pretty good."

"*I* ain't gonna be the one to knock on his door!" Willard said, leaning back in his chair.

"Me, neither," agreed Bo. "Bisbee's been a pure pain in the butt the last few days."

Fred shook his head. "Don't y'all realize the poor man's in love, and doesn't know it?"

"*Jack?*" Bo and Willard yelped in unison.

"Yep, workin' in close quarters with Hayley again is about to kill him."

"Aw, there ain't nuthin' goin' on with Jack and Hayley. How many times have we heard them both say that?" Willard countered.

"Exactly my point," Fred affirmed.

"Nah, that relationship is strictly business," Bo said, shaking his head.

Fred took the last swallow of his drink. "Well, I'm just tellin' ya, one of these days, Jack and Hayley will figure out it *ain't* just business. I'm stayin' outta their way until they *do*, but it's gonna happen—trust me. When you've been in the music business as long as I have, you know things."

Bo signaled the redhead for another round then turned to give Fred an amused look. "You ain't *in* the music business, Fred—you're a bus driver!"

"Yeah, well, without me, you and your drums'd be sittin' in Nashville instead of out here on the road, so what's your point?" Before Bo could respond, Fred pointed to the lobby. "Hey, there's Graham!" He waved, and Graham waved in response, joining them after seeing Amanda to the elevator.

"Well, well," taunted Willard. "Thought you took *Sue* to get ice cream. You double-dippin', my man?"

"For sure, any man'd be a fool to turn down Amanda Brooks for an afternoon delight!" said Bo.

Graham shot the drummer a fierce look. "You make a crack like that again and I'll punch you in the face. Amanda's a class act."

"Not *too* classy, if she's hangin' with you!"

Willard raised his hands. "Girls, girls, there's enough cat-fighting on this tour already. Draw your claws in and simmer down. Where you been, boy?"

Graham plopped into a chair and kicked at Bo's outstretched leg. "I got Sue settled in, and was on my way in here, but got shanghaied into being a 'Spa Night' fairy. Man, am I glad I'm not a woman!" He shook his head. "I never seen so many 'Age-Defying' prod-

Jayne Jaudon Ferrer

ucts and potions!"

"Is that age defying or age *denying*?" chuckled Bo.

Graham raised his arms over his head and stretched. "Big waste of money, if you ask me. I *like* mature women."

"You like women *period*," Willard corrected.

"I'll drink to *that*!" Graham acknowledged as the waitress arrived and delivered another round.

Four floors above the bar, Jack Bisbee lay stretched out on his queen-sized bed and let out a tormented sigh. He glanced at the clock for the fifteenth time in the second half hour of a nap that wasn't happening. Once again, the image of Hayley's face crept, unbidden, into his mind. *'Kenny Chesney can't have that song; it's mine.'* As if caught in an endless loop, the image of Hayley's eager green eyes and elated expression flashed repeatedly in his brain. *'It's mine . . . it's mine . . . you're mine . . . you're mine.'* Suddenly she was leaning forward . . . smiling . . . her soft lips melting into his. He moaned . . . then bolted upright.

"Dang it, Hayley, get out of my head!" He ran his hands through his hair and groaned in agony. "Pull yourself together, Bisbee. This is business; don't make it personal." He shifted to sit cross-legged in the middle of the mattress.

"On the one hand," he said, addressing his image in the mirror across from the bed, "this could be the biggest break you've ever had. Chesney could take this ballad platinum. Can he sing it the way I want him to? Probably—and he's a headliner. On the other hand, Hayley not only wants to sing my song, she wants me to sing it *with* her. What kind of idiot would pass up an offer like that?"

He glanced at the non-descript floral print on the wall, then turned back to answer the man in the mirror. "One who needs to pay the bills. One whose best shot at a record deal went up in flames in Lawrenceville." He flopped backwards onto the bed, emitted a growl of frustration, then sat up again and studied the reflection of the undeniably middle-aged man staring back at him. *Thirty-five years, buddy . . . thirty-five years of hearing your songs performed almost the way you'd have sung them . . . But if my song goes down with my best friend, can we get through that? How do we rescue each other if we're both drowning? . . . I'll be scrapin' Road Kill off the pavement and she'll get stuck playing house with Doctor Boy.*

"Over my dead body!" he heard himself say as he lobbed a pillow at the mirror. He slumped as the realization hit him. "Hayley Swift, I *am* in love with you!"

To: sistersera@hayleyswift.com
From: tennesseetroutt@hayleyswift.com
Subject: I Do Not Get Paid Enough for This!!!

Dear AWOL Employer: Did you fall off the bus, or what? I've left you 14 messages! Are all the cell towers below the Mason-Dixon broke down? CODE RED! Rhett Wilson has gone missing! His parole officer called Tipsy to tell him he didn't check in yesterday, and when the police went to his apartment, he wasn't there. His car was gone and neighbors said they hadn't seen him in a couple of days. We've already notified security at the Orange Blossom

Opry and the police in Weirsdale and Ocala, but you need to be careful. I gave the police chiefs down there your cell number. Of course, you're not ANSWERING it, so I'm not sure why I bothered.

P.S.: Doctor Boy's in a snit because Tipsy called him trying to get hold of you and when he found out what was goin' on, he started to come after you but Tipsy told him to stay put and not get in the way, so HE called me to complain and then TIPSY called me to complain, and now they're both mad and worried sick and driving ME crazy. WOULD YOU PLEASE ANSWER YOUR DANG PHONE?????

P.S.S. Suzette thinks you take me for granted and says I should get a raise. I don't think you take me for granted, but how 'bout a raise anyway? You're startin' to be high maintenance! CALL ME!!!!!!!

Bubba

To: tennesseetroutt@hayleyswift.com
From: sistersera@hayleyswift.com
Subject: RE: I Do Not Get Paid Enough for This!!!

WHAT?????? I knew that creep would try something weird; I tried to TELL y'all that but nobody would listen to me!!!!! Sorry you haven't been able to reach me; I didn't realize I left my phone on the bus till a little while ago. Everyone's on stress overload and we took a break to try and calm down. We're in Ocala tonight, heading down to Weirsdale tomorrow afternoon. Does Jack know about this? I'm SCARED, Bubba! Wilson is a complete FREAK! I'm trying to call you, but you're not answering your phone and Tipsy's not, either. WHY DO ANY OF US HAVE CELL PHONES???????? I'm not calling Keith, though—and don't let him come down here! Wilson is crazy; there's no telling what he might do. Just make sure every policeman in Florida knows what he looks like!!

P.S. Suzette has *way* too much time on her hands.

To: sistersera@hayleyswift.com
From: tennesseetroutt@hayleyswift.com
Subject: RE: RE: I Do Not Get Paid Enough for This!!!

Jack ain't answerin' HIS phone, either—OR his email! WHAT IS WRONG WITH YOU PEOPLE?????????? It's the COMMUNICATION AGE!!!!!!

To: tennesseetroutt@hayleyswift.com
From: sistersera@hayleyswift.com
Subject: RE: RE: RE: I Do Not Get Paid Enough for This!!!

He probably turned his phone off; he threatened bodily harm to anyone who tried to talk to him and we're all convinced he means it. I'm not about to violate his 'Do Not Disturb' command, so keep trying to reach him. Call the hotel and ask for his room. He probably won't answer, but I'd rather YOU get yelled at than me. That's why you get paid the big bucks! (By the way, if we all live through this, the bucks WILL get bigger, I promise. I truly don't know what I'd do without you, Bubba. THANK YOU!!!!!! I don't say that enough.)

Hayley heard a knock on her door as she pressed "Send" and jumped. "Who is it?" she gasped.

"It's me," came Amanda's voice, "host of Magical Makeovers! Come on down to my room and BYOT!"

"BYOT?" Hayley questioned as she opened the door.

"Yeah, bring your own towel. Come on!"

"Hold on," Hayley said, pulling Amanda into the room and locking the door behind her. "I need to tell you what's going on."

Ten minutes later, Hayley and the Hot Flashes, minus Meg, temporarily put their troubles behind them in Room 247, giggling like teenagers as they examined the multitude of beauty products splayed across one bed.

Twenty minutes later, said products were slathered on the various body parts for which they were intended. Sue eyed her now-blue face in the mirror. "Where's Meg? And why does C. J. keep going into the bathroom?"

"Meg's out with Pinky and Alice, hon," Amanda answered, "and C. J. apparently has temporary overactive bladder syndrome. Hey, who's ready for room service?"

"Isn't it wonderful that Alice got in touch with Meg?" C.J. called en route to said bathroom, her fourth visit in as many minutes. "I hope they can come to some kind of understanding. A mother and daughter shouldn't be estranged. That's one thing Mama's Alzheimer's has taught me: you never know when you'll lose someone you love."

Sue stood up. "C. J., get *out* of the bathroom. I need to use it!" She took a few steps in that direction, but Amanda steered her toward a menu by the phone.

"Who's hungry? Cheeseburgers? Fries? Pizza? All of the above? And chocolate! We can't forget chocolate! I swear, who knew menopause could make you so hungry? It's like being pregnant all over again!"

"*WHICH I AM!*" squealed C. J., rushing out of the bathroom with a tiny stick in her hand. "It's blue! It's blue!" she shrieked, leaping up and down.

Hayley and Amanda shrieked in stereo and clambered to hug their friend. Tears mixed with creams mixed with kisses mixed with hair until all three were a multi-colored mess.

Sue, puzzled, looked in the mirror and touched her face. "Isn't it supposed to be blue? It doesn't turn white until it dries."

C. J. collapsed on the now product-less bed, face flushed and arms outstretched. "Ladies, I hereby resign from The Hot Flashes because I am officially no longer eligible! I have to stop shaking my booty and start *knitting* one! Oh, my golly, is this really *happening*??!!"

"Is *what* happening?" Sue began pacing. "Why is everyone yelling, and I need to go to the bathroom and . . . I don't know how to knit!" She started to cry.

"Oh, honey, you don't have to knit and the bathroom's all yours," C. J. soothed, getting up to give Sue a hug. "We do have some exciting news, though. I'm going to have a baby!"

Sue clapped her hands. "Oh, that's wonderful! Oh, C.J., can Bill and I give you a baby shower? He loves babies. Who's the father? I hope it's not that cowboy that's always asking me questions about Amanda!"

"Pete, Sue!" C.J. chuckled. "Pete's the father. That's my husband; remember him?"

"Does he know yet?" Hayley asked, then remembering the blue stick, looked sheepish. "I guess not!"

While C. J. was offering Hayley a closer look at the substantiating evidence, Amanda cornered Sue on her way to the bathroom. "What exactly did that cowboy ask you about me?" she whispered.

But Hayley heard and turned to face Amanda. "Look here. You need to tell us straight up—are you involved with Graham, or not?"

Instantly, the atmosphere in the room tensed. "How can you even *ask* me that, Hayley? I'm *married*!"

"Well, then, *act* like it! You've been flirting with Graham from day one."

Amanda bristled. "I'll have you know I take my marriage vows very seriously, but I don't think a little harmless flirting ever hurt anybody. After being Susie Homemaker all these years, it's quite nice to be appreciated for more than my ability to cook dinner for a change!"

"Are you saying you think Tom doesn't appreciate you, Amanda?" C. J. asked. "Did you forget that, thanks to him, the twins didn't know you forgot their birthday?"

"Gee, thanks," Amanda snapped. "Twist that knife in *deep*, girlfriend." She stomped across the room and crossed her arms. "Look. As much as I love my family, I miss adreneline! I miss romance! For heaven's sake, I would never cheat on my husband, but it feels good to have somebody notice if my hair looks nice, or I say something clever." Tears welled in her eyes. "I promise you, nothing has happened between Graham and me, and nothing *will*. But I've enjoyed these last two weeks, and I'm not going to apologize for that!"

"This from the woman who was a basket case two hours after the bus left her front yard," C. J. teased. "And thanks for reminding me I'm about to return to eighteen years of indentured servitude—with a child who'll grow up mistaking me for its grandma!"

CHAPTER THIRTEEN
Breakfast at the OK Corral

"*OUCH!*" Bo roared, as steaming, hot coffee missed his cup and splashed his blue-jeaned thigh.

"Oops." The curvaceous, redheaded waitress affected an insincere smile. "Guess I'm a little 'distracted' this morning."

Bo winced and fanned his leg. "Come on, darlin', don't be like that. I told you you'll have my full attention tonight. I promise."

"Umm-hmm. You're just one big promise after another, aren't you?" she said sourly.

Willard chuckled. "Don't take it personal, ma'am. He's a drummer; their minds sort of wander."

"His can wander wherever it wants to as long as it doesn't bring him to *my* door again," the waitress snapped, as she stalked away.

Fred sighed. "Thanks a lot, Bo. There goes our only hope for a fresh pot of coffee! I see we're off to a great start this mornin', as usual. Speaking of which, anybody heard from the boss?" He scanned the restaurant.

Bo nodded toward the door. "There's the man himself, front and center."

Jack spotted them and waved. "Good mornin', reprobates! How's the food? I'm famished!"

Willard, Fred, and Bo eyed each other warily. In all their years traveling together as Road Kill, they could count on one hand the times Jack Bisbee had eaten breakfast.

"Who are you, and what have you done with Biz-Boy?" Willard demanded.

Jack grinned. "It's amazing what a little peace and quiet—and a good night's sleep—will do for a man. What are y'all up to today?"

"Hadn't really thought about it," said Willard. "You hear anything from Cal last night—or the guy from Tugalo Records?"

Jack clapped Willard on the back. "Come on, now! It's too early in the day to talk business. Can't a man bond with his buddies? I've been rough on you guys the last few days; we're due for some fun. When's the last time you boys went fishin'?"

"Been a while," Bo admitted.

"What about that amp we gotta fix, and all them guitar strings we gotta replace?" Willard asked.

"Plenty of time for that later. Wonder where we can round up some poles and bait?"

The men were deep in debate over the best way to catch bass when C. J., Amanda, and Sue shuffled in from the lobby. Graham tagged along behind. "Mornin', everybody!" he greeted. "Are we all rested up and happy?"

"As bird dogs on a duck hunt!" Jack pronounced with a jovial salute.

Graham looked to Willard for an explanation of their formerly foul-tempered leader's adjustment in attitude, but only got a "Beats me!" face and a shrug.

Sue took a seat next to Bo and patted his leg. "How about you? Are you a happy bird dog this morning?"

"More like a sad tomcat," Fred quipped. The men guffawed as Bo flashed a sarcastic expression.

"Oh, look, there's Meg!" Sue waved as Pinky, Meg, and a young brunette woman walked in the dining area. "Meg, *you* look happy. And you're so pretty in that outfit!"

"Ain't she, though?" Pinky pulled out a chair for Meg, then turned. "And, gentlemen, this other pretty lady is Meg's daughter, Miss Alice Dorris."

Jack rose to extend a hand. "Nice to meet you, Alice. I'm Jack Bisbee. You live in this area?"

Alice smiled shyly and dipped her head in acknowledgement as Pinky settled both ladies into chairs, then went off in search of orange juice. "Nice to meet you, too. No, actually I live in Macon, Georgia. I drove down here with a friend on an errand, and decided it was a good opportunity to catch up with Mom."

C. J. gave Alice a big squeeze. "It's wonderful to see you again, honey; it's been ages! You need to come back to Skerry and visit. I still make those cinnamon rolls you used to love."

"Mmmm." Alice closed her eyes in rapt remembrance. "I may take you up on that!"

"I invited both Alice and Pinky to come to Skerry for the Pig Pickin' Festival," Meg volunteered. "That's our town's biggest event all year," she explained to the other band members.

"One *no* one should miss," Amanda interjected. "All other events pale in comparison!"

Graham draped an arm around her shoulders. "I wanna come. Think I can pick a pig as good as I can pick a fiddle?"

Amanda laughed and pinched his chin. "Probably. Your talents seem to know no end, Mr. Frazier!"

"*MOM*!"

Suddenly, a tornado of small human limbs whirled across the room, encircled Amanda's hips. and shoved Graham aside in the process. As the Brooks twins clamored to embrace their mother, she beamed down at them, then looked up to meet the cool gaze of her husband. "Tom! *Hi!*" she squealed, dipping one shoulder to displace Graham's arm.

For a moment, no one moved, then Jack reached to offer his hand and broke the awkward silence. "Jack Bisbee, sir. Hayley's road manager. Very nice to meet you. Your wife's got quite a set of pipes. We've enjoyed her company."

Tom Brooks returned Jack's handshake but his eyes were fixed on Graham. "Looks like she's been enjoying yours, too."

"Yup, we're just one big, happy family!" said Bo as he leaned his head back to make a face at Graham.

"I see that," said Tom. "Sorry to barge in and interrupt, but I wanted to surprise my wife. Last I heard, she was miserable." He gave her a flat look. "Guess she got over it. Come on, kids, let's go."

"Daddy, I don't want to get back in the car," Diana whined. "You said we could go swimming!"

Tommy echoed his sister's dismay. "I want to ride the bus and see where Mom's been sleeping!"

Tom gave a tight smile. "Well, that *would* be interesting," he said, his sarcasm lost on the child. "Hon, why don't you and I go take a look at where you've been sleeping? Have a seat, kids, and maybe Mr. Jack will order you some breakfast." He turned and walked toward the lobby.

Amanda followed her husband in uncharacteristic silence as Jack ushered the children to a table. Graham strode over to join them.

"You look a little flushed, Romeo. I think you might need to go lie down," Jack suggested.

"Naw, I'm fine, but thanks. Won't be the first time I played second fiddle to a husband." He grinned at his joke as he pulled out a chair and sat down . "If I get a cup of coffee and some eggs in me, I'll be fine."

"Frazier, I swear, you're a plum idiot. Sorry, kids," he countered, remembering his audience. "That wasn't a nice thing for me to say." He turned back to Graham and lowered his voice. "I could care less about how you feel *or* whether you've been fed; I want you out of the way! Go to your room and stay there till I tell you to come out!"

Bo snickered behind his hand and Jack jabbed a finger at him. "And you go *with* him! I don't know what happened between you and that waitress last night, but as long as you're at this table, we're likely to die from starvation!"

The castouts got up and trudged away like whipped dogs with their tails between their legs. The remaining group sat silent until Diana finally spoke up. "Can we have something to eat, please? Daddy only let us stop to go to the bathroom. He wanted to get here early, to surprise Mom!"

"Oh, he did that! *Surprise, surprise!*" Willard intoned in his best Gomer Pyle voice.

"It's good when children come check on their mama," Pinky said, lifting a juice glass in the twins' honor, then turning to wink and grin at Alice.

As soon as the redheaded waitress noticed Bo missing at the table, she materialized with a fresh pot of coffee, a fresh pitcher of juice, a basket of hot muffins, and a jar of orange blossom honey. "I heard little missy say she was hungry. Darlin', whatchu want?" she asked Diana.

"So, boss," Fred quizzed as the waitress moved around the table taking orders, "are we still up for catchin' some bass?"

Jack looked at his watch. "Unfortunately, we may need to rethink that plan now. It's after nine." He scratched his temple. "Has anybody seen Hayley this morning? She's usually up by now." He stood and put his napkin on the table, then headed toward the lobby. "I'm gonna go check on her; order me a Western omelet," he called over his shoulder, "with a side of blueberry pancakes!"

Tommy smacked his lips. "I love blueberry pancakes!" He turned to Sue, sitting at the table next to him. "How 'bout you? Do *you* like blueberry pancakes?"

"I'll *say* I do!" Sue clapped her hands together, then threw her arms in the air. "WHOOPEE! Blueberry pancakes for everybody! On the house!"

♪

As he reached the lobby, Jack spotted Hayley browsing a brochure rack. "Mornin' sunshine," he said as he walked up and poked her in the back. "How'd ya sleep?"

The woman spun around, her expression changing from surprised to coy when she saw Jack's handsome face. "Like a charm. Thanks for asking."

Jack leapt back. "Excuse me! I'm *so* sorry, I—I thought you were someone else. You're a dead ringer for ... "

"Hayley Swift? I should *hope* so. I spend a *fortune* to look like this. And I believe you're Jack Bisbee, her road manager." She held out a pale, perfectly manicured hand. "Deena Pomeroy, president of the Valdosta chapter of the Hayley Swift Fan Club. It is *such* a pleasure to meet you! Let's see ... if you're here, Hayley must not be far behind. Am I right?" She tossed back her head and laughed. "What a bizarre coincidence! My husband will be *thrilled*. We're both simply *mad* about Hayley! In fact, we have front row seats to see her tonight. Listen, Jack," the woman cooed, pressing close and patting his chest. "It would mean *so* much if Hayley would dedicate a song to us. We're on our honeymoon, you know. Maybe we could come up on stage? Would you ask her? *Please?*" she begged, her face mere inches from Jack's. "For a couple of newlyweds?"

Unnerved, Jack wrenched himself out of Deena's grasp and took two steps back. "Well, we play a pretty tight show, Mrs. .. uh ... ma'am." He shook his head. "You look *so* much like her, I can't get over it! Um ... I really can't promise a song—sorry—but how about an autographed photo? Here's my card; send me your home address and we'll get one right out to you."

Deena frowned. "I don't think you understand, Jack. I'm not only the Valdosta fan club president, I'm the Georgia *state* fan club president. I have *stacks* of Hayley's autographed photos. I send *out* Hayley's autographed photos. I would think I deserve this after my loyalty all these years."

When Jack failed to respond—because he had no idea what to say—she stomped a spike heel and almost went sprawling. In spite of his best effort, Jack's amusement showed and Deena fumed.

"Listen here! It's not like your precious Hayley is a household name these days! If it weren't for devoted fans like me, she'd be playing loser gigs in Podunk USA. Oh, wait; she *is*." She put her hands on her hips. "I hate to tell you this, but thirty-seven percent of our members recently surveyed indicated they do *not* plan to renew their fan club membership. Process *that*!" she challenged, jabbing a scarlet-tipped finger at Jack's solar plexus.

Jack crossed his arms over his chest and struggled to control his temper. He closed his eyes, drew a deep breath, then exhaled. "Ma'am," he continued, the tone of his voice significantly calmer, "when you get to hear the world premiere of Hayley's next number one song tonight, it's gonna knock those fake eyelashes right off your face. I hope you enjoy it."

Deena lifted her nose in the air. "We're obviously done here. Excuse me, I think I hear my husband calling."

Jack watched as Deena teetered away, then he walked to the house phone and dialed the number of Hayley's room. "You awake?" he asked, when she picked up.

"That depends. Are you in a better mood?"

"I'm in a fabulous mood."

"Why? Did everybody quit?"

"Ever the optimist," Jack chuckled. "No, we're all down here eating breakfast and wondering where *you* are. If you hurry, you can beat Amanda's kids to the last pancake."

"The twins are here? And Tom? I'll bet Amanda's over the moon!"

Jack snorted. "More like over Tom's knee. He walked in and caught her mid-clutch with Graham a little while ago. They've gone out to the bus to 'talk.'"

Hayley sighed. "For the record, Amanda swears her relationship with Graham is purely flirtation—and I believe her."

"Good, 'cause she may need your help convincing her husband."

"Listen, have you talked to Bubba or Tipsy?"

"Not recently. Guess I need to turn my phone back on, huh?"

"'Fraid so. Then you know nothing about Rhett Wilson being unaccounted for?"

"WHAT??"

"Yeah, according to Bubba, he's been missing for several days."

"Do they know where he is?"

"Not a clue, but Bubba says they've alerted the venue staff and the police here and in Weirsdale."

"There's another weirdo on the loose, too; I just encountered her in the lobby."

"Who?"

"Deena Pom-a something. She looks *just* like you, Hayley. It was crazy!"

Hayley giggled. "Oh, that's my infamous Valdosta fan club president. She's definitely a little different, but she's harmless. Obnoxious, but harmless. She drives Tipsy bonkers, but she's a great promoter. Is she here for the show tonight?"

"Mm-hmm. And she wants you to dedicate a song to her and her new husband."

"She got *married*? "

"Mm-hmm, and she wants your wedding gift to be a song dedicated and sung to them while they're onstage."

"Sounds like her," Hayley chuckled. "Sure, why not? Might

as well make *somebody* happy on this tour. Speaking of which, what's got you in such a 'fabulous' mood this morning?"

This time, Jack chuckled. "You'll have to come join me to find out."

"Okay, order me some French toast. I'll be there as soon as I get the last traces of 'Spa Night' off my face. My pores are so tight, you could bounce a quarter off me!"

Jack had just swallowed the last bite of his Western omelet and sighed in complete gratification when Hayley entered the restaurant with Bo and Graham demurely trailing behind.

"Hi, guys!" she called to the twins, heading straight for them.

"Have you seen our mom or dad?" Diana asked. "They've been gone a long time and I wanna go swimming!"

C. J. stood up. "Tell ya what. Let's go up to my room and watch cartoons until your food digests." As she gathered a twin in each arm and led them toward the elevator, Bo and Graham slid into the vacated chairs. Jack was not amused.

"I thought I told you two to stay in your room."

"Give it up, Bisbee. I'm a grown man! I need protein," Graham complained. "I ain't gonna make any waves."

The redheaded waitress was on break, so the previously marked men were able to place orders immediately. They ate heartily as Fred and Willard chatted with Pinky, Meg, Alice, and Sue. At the other end of the table, Hayley savored her breakfast while Jack looked on.

"This is really good. Want a bite?" she offered.

Jack eyed her remaining slice of thick, golden toast topped with a pool of maple syrup and a delicate sprinkling of powdered sugar. "Maybe two!" He grinned and leaned forward to let her slide her fork into his mouth.

"My, my. What a cozy scene."

At the familiar voice in an unexpected setting, Hayley started and whirled around, almost stabbing Jack in the cheek as the fork went with her. "Keith! What are you doing here?"

"Well, nobody's been able to get hold of you people since yesterday and there's an APB out for Rhett Wilson. I was worried!"

Jack stood and extended a hand. "You must be Doctor Boy. Jack Bisbee."

Keith took the hand but the expression on his face was less than cordial. "Most people call me Keith."

"Quite a house call," Jack observed. Took you what, six, seven hours to get down here?"

"Wasn't counting. Just trying to get here and make sure everyone was okay."

"No need to worry; everything's fine," Jack assured as he sat back down.

Keith frowned. "Really. Then you weren't concerned that Rhett Wilson checked in at this hotel last night, shortly after you did?" Hayley gasped and sank back into her chair, hand across her mouth, as Jack's eyes widened in surprise and Sue and Meg sat speechless. "The tip-off came when he used his credit card to check in. The Metropolitan Nashville police had the account flagged, so Visa called them when the charge came through."

Hayley took a shaky breath. "Don't blame Jack; he didn't know anything about this until a few minutes ago. Bubba emailed me about it last night, but I didn't tell anyone except Amanda."

Meg shot Hayley an incredulous look and she gave an apologetic shrug.

"Bubba assured me the police had a handle on it."

"Come on, Miss Independence." Keith sighed, and held out his hand. "I told Tipsy when I found you, I wouldn't let you out of my sight. And you don't need to be out here in the open."

"Now, hold on, hold on," Jack said, placing one hand firmly on Hayley's shoulder while using the other to redirect her hand from its path toward Keith's. "From a safety standpoint, I think Hayley's better off staying with a group, where we can all keep an eye out. Fred, Bo, how 'bout you boys head out to the bus and make sure everything is locked up and looks like it ought to."

"Yes, sir," they said and rose to leave.

"Keith, have you had breakfast?" Meg asked.

"Had some coffee a few miles back."

Jack pointed to a chair. "Well, have a seat there next to Miss Alice and let's think this thing through while you ingest a little protein." He turned to grin at a scowling Graham, and motioned to their server.

Not happy, but definitely hungry, Keith did as he was told as the waitress brought him a cup, filled it with hot coffee, took his order, then proceeded to make her way around the table, filling cups as she went. "Alice Dorris. Wasn't expecting to see *you* here," Keith greeted as he leaned to kiss her cheek. "'Bout didn't recognize you. What's it been, fifteen years?"

"At least." She smiled. "How's life in Skerry?"

"Scary," Keith answered, invoking the corny joke they'd routinely shared back in her childhood days.

Alice grinned. "Still taking temps and bandaging booboos?"

"Pretty much. Skerry's not exactly a hot bed of exotic epidemics. What are you up to these days?"

"Dealing with some exotic epidemics, actually. I work for Doctors Without Borders."

"No kidding! That's awesome. I didn't realize you went into health care."

Alice shook her head. "Oh, I'm not a medical professional, I'm their communications director. You know, public relations, grant-writing, that sort of thing."

Meg beamed. "I'm so proud of her! She's really made something of herself."

"Sounds like it—and she certainly grew *up*!" Keith observed, reaching to tug a strand of Alice's hair. He winked at her, then turned back to the matter at hand. "Look, I need to call Tipsy and give him an update. If you'll let Hayley take me to her room to do that, I promise we'll come back. I don't know that I agree with your safety in numbers theory, but I suppose a public place does offer a certain amount of protection."

"*Let* Hayley take you up?" the woman in question bristled. "What is this, the middle ages? I don't need either *one* of you giving me permission to do *anything*! Come on, girls, channel your inner She-Ra and let's go figure out how to deal with Hordak and Rhett Wilson and anybody else who gets in our way!" She lifted Jack's hand off her shoulder, dropped it, and stood up to leave.

"Don't be stupid, Hayley," he warned.

"Hey, now, let's be nice," Keith chided as he stood and took Hayley by the arm.

She jerked it away and gave an exasperated sigh. "Would you two stop it? I am perfectly capable of looking after myself!"

"Hayley! How'd you beat us in here? We just passed you in

the parking lot!" All heads turned to see Amanda and Tom walk in the entrance to the restaurant.

"What are you talking about?" Hayley asked. "I haven't been outside since we got here last night."

"I know who you saw," said Jack, rising, "and I'm gonna go find her and see if she knows anything about this Wilson dude."

He had only taken a few steps when Graham shouted, "There he is! There's Wilson!" and bolted out of his seat as Rhett Wilson and Deena Pomeroy walked in together through the hotel lobby door. Hayley screamed, Sue screamed, Alice screamed, Amanda screamed, Keith whirled around and took a step as Jack turned to sprint back across the dining room. The two men collided, both went sprawling and, from there, pure chaos ensued. Meg leaped over a chair—which hit the table and sent coffee sloshing everywhere— and tackled Deena as Pinky yelled, "That's my girl!" Willard threw his arms around Sue to sit her down, Amanda jumped over Keith and Jack to grab Hayley and drag her away from the maelstrom, and Alice, thoroughly confused but completely dazzled by her mom's bravado, got up and walked over to stand next to the spot on the floor where Meg had the petite brunette straddled upside down and backwards like an unlucky calf at a rodeo.

"Look in her purse," Meg told her daughter. "See if she has a gun."

Eyes wide, Alice did as she was told and pulled out a small black pistol.

"A .22. Figures, you wuss!" Meg snarled at the back of Deena's head as Alice gingerly handed the weapon to her mother.

After the turmoil of the last few seconds, there was a sudden, deafening silence as everyone remained transfixed in either fear or astonishment. Then Pinky yelled, "Wait! Don't nobody move! I done lost a contact!" He fell to his knees behind the table and began feeling around on the floor.

"Pinky, your timin' sucks, man!" Graham hollered from the lobby. He was breathing hard and grinning, with his boot pressed firmly in Rhett Wilson's back, when the crunch of Tom Brooks' fist against his face sent him stumbling backwards. As he hit the tile and slid, he heard Fred cackle.

"Jack *told* ya to stay in your room!" the bus driver chortled.

Having returned from the bus to find utter pandemonium in the lobby, Fred and Bo now looked for a way to join in the action. They found it where Graham's boot had been. When Tom sent the fiddler sprawling, Jack—having disentangled himself from Keith—went crawling across the floor to grab Rhett Wilson and try to hold him down where Graham had had him. The red-faced, enraged man was writhing like a worm and just as Jack thought, for sure, he was going to lose him, Fred and Bo dove like pelicans after a mullet. The three of them had just clamped down the man's thrashing arms and legs when, suddenly, Keith loomed over them and shouted, "The jig is up, Wilson! You have the right to remain silent!"

A group of Japanese businessmen emerged from the lobby elevator just in time to hear Keith's outburst. As one, they whipped out their cell phones and began snapping pictures, murmuring excitedly.

From his perch atop Rhett's outstretched, twitching right leg, Jack stared up at Keith. "Sorry to disappoint you, Doc, but the Miranda bit doesn't happen until the cops arrive."

"Can't I make a citizen's arrest? That's my girlfriend he's going after!"

"*Your* girlfriend? I thought she was *my* girlfriend!"

Keith made a face. "Guess that explains why I arrived to find her cozied up to *you*!"

"What can I say?" Jack flashed a dazzling smile up at Keith then down at Rhett as he shifted his position on top of his squirming, sputtering quarry. "I'm a cozy kinda guy."

A few feet away, Deena Pomeroy struggled to free herself from Meg's vise-like grip. "Get off me, you Heffalump! And let my husband go, you oaf!" she hurled at Jack. "You forget who you're dealing with! I'm the Georgia State Pre—"

"Oh, can it, sister! Nobody cares," Meg interrupted. Still straddled atop the infuriated woman, she twisted Deena's arm a little harder, then turned to beam at Alice, who beamed back as she perched demurely on Deena's calves.

"I know exactly who I'm dealing with," Jack disputed. "Two raving maniacs!" He spotted Amanda pulling Hayley by the hand as they tried to inch discreetly along the edge of the dining room wall toward an escape. "Tom, go find the manager and call 911."

"Why *were* you 'cozied up,' Jack?" asked Rhett with a contemptuous smile. "You and Keith both know Miss Swift is saving herself for me."

"That should go over well with your new wife," Jack drawled. "Mrs. Wilson, did you know your beloved here still carries a torch for Hayley?"

"We both do. I *told* you that. Two's company, three's a party!" Deena twisted her head and caught a glimpse of Hayley against the wall. She mimicked a sexy bite.

Hayley closed her eyes and sank toward the floor. "I think I'm gonna be sick."

Tom, en route back from the registration desk, rushed to help Amanda as she struggled to keep Hayley upright. "Come on, ladies, let's get out of here," he said, hoisting Hayley in his arms and nodding to his wife to head toward the elevator.

As they made their way through the crush of bodies that now filled the hotel lobby, Graham looked up from the floor, where he still lay, and blew a kiss as Amanda passed by.

"Seriously, Graham? Give it a *rest*!" Amanda snapped as she stepped—none too carefully—over him.

♪

Moments later, sirens were screaming everywhere and uniformed officers appeared from all directions. As several policemen dashed in, handcuffs at the ready, Willard realized Sue was becoming increasingly agitated. "Miss Sue, it's a beautiful day outside and it's gettin' a little crowded in here. Would you like to take a walk?"

Sue smiled at him as tears began to well in her eyes. "I would like that very much," she said in a tremulous whisper. "These people are scaring me."

As they exited out the side door, on the other side of the room, Rhett was protesting loudly. "This is ridiculous, officers. I'm no threat to Hayley Swift! I *adore* her!"

"He's been in therapy!" Deena screeched. "His doctor *sent* him here for the concert tonight! *He has a note*!"

Keith guffawed. "Lady, I'm a doctor. We don't write prescriptions for concerts."

A sheriff's deputy tapped Jack on the shoulder, indicating he would take over from there. As Jack, Fred, and Bo clambered up and stepped out of the way, the officer clamped a pair of handcuffs around Rhett Wilson's wrists and helped him to his feet. Jack looked down his nose at the incensed, untidy man.

"You may not be a threat, you demented weasel, but you were told a month ago to stay away from Hayley."

"And I have!" Rhett protested. "My therapist cured me! He told me to find a substitute for Hayley, and I *did*!" He twisted a shoulder in Deena's direction. "That's my blushing bride over there, under that . . . that *Amazon*!"

"She's blushing, all right," Meg chuckled as a female officer helped her to stand, then bent down to handcuff the seething, disheveled Deena before assisting her in getting up. "Her face is so red, I think her head's about to explode!"

Pinky, contact located and held firmly between thumb and forefinger of his right hand, embraced Meg with his left arm and kissed her full on the lips. "I knew you were wonderful, but I didn't know you were Wonder Woman! You put Lynda Carter to *shame*, darlin'!"

As Rhett and Deena were escorted to a squad car, the hotel manager—conspicuously absent until now—launched into immediate damage control. "It's all over, folks. We're back to business as usual. Just a little misunderstanding, a simple mix-up . . . don't give it another thought." He moved officiously among the crowd of police officers, musicians, Japanese businessmen, stunned restaurant patrons, and confused newcomers with a broad, reassuring smile. Simultaneously, through a series of scowls, glares, grimaces, and intense furrowing of eyebrows, he communicated silently, in no uncertain terms, that any staff members who valued his or her job had better get it in gear. "Here we go, have a seat, everybody relax . . . fresh-made muffins on the way and on the house!" he cooed as tension began to give way to Monday-morning quarterbacking and anyone who had witnessed the events of the last ten minutes began comparing notes with their neighbors.

Back in the lobby, Pinky, Meg, and Alice were headed toward the elevator when a camera light suddenly flashed in their faces. One of the Japanese businessmen bowed deeply. " *"Wandāuman. Wandāman. Arigato! Arigato!"* he said with a merry laugh, then waved goodbye as he hurried to join his tour group in the dining room.

Meanwhile, at the registration desk, Bo was relaying his version of the drama to a wide-eyed, twenty-something registration clerk who had fled the scene as soon as Meg charged at Deena. "Yeah, my black belt reputation is legendary back home," Bo was bragging. "That dude knew better'n to mess with me."

Overhearing that line from his position at the other end of the counter, Jack coughed. "You're a legend all right—in your own mind. Find Fred and y'all go gas up the bus, Grasshopper. It's time to get outta Dodge."

Bo winked a farewell to the registration clerk and turned his attention to his boss. "You want us to get the bait now or on the way to the lake?"

"Say what?"

Bo gave a longsuffering sigh. "The bait. You said we were goin' fishin'!"

Jack dropped his head then lifted it toward the ceiling. "How long, oh, Lord? How long?" he quoted from Job. "Bo, the window of opportunity for fishin' unfortunately slammed shut some time ago. Go gas up the bus. I'm gonna check on Hayley."

In the corner of the lobby, Keith's ears perked at the sound of Hayley's name. He suddenly shook hands with the deputy he'd befriended and sprinted toward the elevator, shooting his rival a dark look as he passed.

Jack's look of consternation suddenly morphed into a daredevil grin. "Race ya!" he challenged as he sped toward the stairwell. Three flights and moments later, he knocked on Hayley's door, and she let him in. He was relaying Rhett Wilson's "concert therapy" alibi when there was a rap on the door.

"I'll get it," Jack said innocently, and opened it with a grin. "Oh, look, it's Doctor Parker."

Keith made a face. "That elevator moves like a dead slug."

"Do tell," Jack said airily, as the doctor moved past him.

"Hayley, are you okay?"

The singer lay propped on a pile of pillows on the queen-sized bed, a cold rag folded on her forehead. "I'm fine, now it's all over," she said, attempting to smile. Keith lifted a wrist to feel her pulse, then pulled a stethoscope from the pocket of his sport coat and sat on the bed beside her.

"You carry that thing everywhere you go?" Jack asked.

"I *am* a doctor. And look!" Keith pulled his smart phone from a pocket and waved it in the air. "Here's something else I carry everywhere I go: a communication device—so people can *reach* me if there's an *emergency*."

"Knock it off, boys," Hayley chided. "I'm not up for this."

"No, you're not," agreed Keith as he finished listening to her heart and slid his stethoscope back into his jacket pocket. He nodded toward the door. "You should leave, Jack; Hayley needs to rest. I'll stay with her—and she really shouldn't perform tonight."

"Sorry, Doc. As they say, 'the show must go on.'" Jack looked past the doctor to the patient. "And we still need to talk beforehand,

Hayley." He checked his watch. "I'll bring you a salad around three, okay?"

She nodded.

"Don't stay too long, Doctor Boy. Patient needs her rest." Jack gave a sarcastic smile, then left.

As soon as they were alone, Keith turned his attention back to Hayley. "This isn't the time to get into it, but I'm not sure that man understands the seriousness of this situation. Because of his negligence, you could be dead, sweetheart!"

Hayley repositioned her pillows and struggled into a more upright position. "'That man' has saved my butt more times than I can count. I trust him with my life." She repositioned the rag on her forehead. "He wasn't negligent; he had no idea that maniac was on the loose. And they don't want to kill me, they . . . well, I'm not sure *what* they want to do to me, and I'd just as soon not think about it. Trust me, it's fine. Jack and I go back a long way, Keith."

"So do we."

"*Touché*. But this is different. Jack and I have a connection you don't understand."

Keith gave a sad smile. "Is that what it's called now? I saw you 'connecting' this morning when I got here and, I admit, I was... surprised." He sighed heavily and stood. "I have to wonder if Jack's not simply a convenient habit you indulge in when you're on the road, Hayley. Contrary to what that psychotic woman said, there's not room in a relationship for three."

She shuddered. "Thanks for *that* image. Look, I am so grateful for your concern, and it was incredible of you to race down here and make sure I was okay, but I need to focus on my work now. For the first time in a *very* long time, I have some momentum building.

Plus people are depending on me for paychecks. I just don't have time for ... "

"For me? Look, have I somehow misread everything that's happened over these last couple of weeks?"

Hayley looked pained. "No, of course not. I've loved spending time with you again. It's just ... all this ... the timing ... "

Keith grunted. "Ah, yes, the timing. That seems to be an ongoing issue between us. I thought, perhaps, this time we could make it work." He kicked at the carpet with the toe of his shoe. "I'm a pretty patient guy, Hayley, but don't take me for granted. I won't wait forever and I'm not willing to wait in the wings while you figure out how Jack Bisbee fits into the equation."

"Gaaaaahhhh!" Hayley flung the rag across the room and flopped face down in a pillow. "Why does life have to be so complicated?!"

"It's not that complicated," Keith said quietly. "I love you; do you love me?"

"Since I was fourteen!" came the voice from the pillow.

"Well, then, I think it's time we stop leading separate lives and start figuring out how to make music and medicine mix." When there was no answer, Keith walked over and picked up the discarded washrag. "See you soon," he said as he tossed it into the bathroom on his way out the door.

Hayley grabbed her cell phone as soon as he was gone. She pressed two buttons and waited. "Tips! Yes ... I'm fine ... it's over, he's in custody ... Now, hold on! Nobody intentionally ... I've been ... okay, okay, I'll never forget my phone anywhere ever again ... *okay!* Can we change the subject? ... Look, you know that 'songwriter high horse' you're always fussing at me about? Guess what? I've put it out to pasture. I've found a killer song . . . no, I didn't write it, Jack did—and I've asked him to record it with me. He doesn't know it yet, but we're singing it at the show tonight. I'll let you know how it goes . . . I will . . . absolutely . . . Love you back. Oh! And ask Bubba if my pool is still blue!"

♪

"I don't know about this," Jack grumbled. "We haven't even practiced. That's nuts."

"That's 'organic,'" Hayley teased as she did one last side stretch then straightened her rhinestone-studded tunic. She reached to adjust the collar of Jack's jacket and rested her wrists on his shoulder. "Look, I want this to be . . . spontaneous," she said finally, her brain searching for the right word.

"Yeah, well, that word is usually partnered with 'combustion;' be careful what you ask for!"

Hayley gave him a soft smack on the cheek. "Since when did you become such a coward? How many times have I heard you—in the middle of a set—take your guitar places Road Kill had *never* been before, with poor Graham and Pinky trying their best to hang on for the ride?"

Jack chuckled. "That's different."

She stared him down, nose to nose. "I don't see how."

"Well, first off, a screaming guitar is a whole different animal from a vocal ballad. The high pitch, see, gives it a . . . "

Hayley's fingers pressed against his lips and put an end to an explanation she wasn't interested in hearing. "Just go with your gut. And trust me."

They stood staring into each other's eyes. "With my life, girl—though only God knows why," Jack sighed, and shook his head.

It was a phenomenal show from the start, with one surprise after another. First, Sue said she wasn't up to performing, so Pinky had to handle her harmonies—which he did masterfully and which added a whole new depth to the background vocals. Then, after a rousing six-minute cover of "Thank God I'm a Country Boy" that ended with everyone in the place stomping and clapping and cheering, "country boy" Pinky came out from behind the keyboard and declared his undying love for Meg. The audience went wild, from somewhere, Bo and Graham pulled out several bottles of champagne and started popping corks, and even Cal Taylor's catty bimbos applauded. But when Jack and Hayley strolled onstage, there was absolute silence, as if every person there knew something unforgettable was about to happen—and it did. As the two distinct voices danced delicately through the plaintive melody of Jack's first verse, then melded like sugar and hot tea in the soaring refrain, suddenly the silence erupted into cheers and whistles and applause and people were on their feet again—enthralled, in tears, in love with this man and woman who were turning words and music into magic. It was a night no one would ever forget.

CHAPTER FOURTEEN
Obstacles in Mirror Are Closer Than They Appear

I wish this bus would stop so I could get off; I want to go home! I don't even know who some of these people are. I love singing with the girls, but I don't remember why we're singing in so many different pla-ces. Ooh, there's an IHOP sign! I hop for pancakes, Bill always used to say. I miss Bill. I know he's not here, but I don't remember why. C. J. looks really pretty today. There's something's wrong with her, I think, but I keep forgetting what. This is so nice, to be in a car with a bathroom. How handy! The driver—Ted?— Flopsy?—keeps taking me for ice cream. I don't really like ice cream all that much, but I don't want to hurt his feelings. SPEED LIMIT 70. Oh, goodness, that's too fast! Everything is too fast—except me. I think I'm very slow. I wonder if it's time for lunch.

"Why? Are you hungry? Me, too!" Willard, sitting across from Sue, patted her knee.

She blinked. "What?"

Willard smiled. "You asked if it's time for lunch. Don't worry, we'll stop pretty soon. Fred's tryin' to make tracks, but he won't let us starve. And no matter where we are, he always seems to know the best greasy spoons!"

Sue wrinkled her nose. "That doesn't sound very appetizing. I'd rather eat a pancake than a greasy spoon."

Willard laughed. "Guess I would, too, now that you mention it." He turned his attention back to the table where Bo and Graham were teaching Amanda's twins to play Texas Hold 'Em. Though they were only playing for M&Ms, it was obvious Tommy had a bright future ahead of him as a gambler.

It was the morning after the Orange Blossom Opry show, but the bus was headed back to Skerry instead of the next scheduled show in Newnan, Georgia. The Hot Flashes' fifteen minutes of fame was officially ended, Hayley and Jack were trying to sort out what happened onstage the night before, and they were all trying to process the changes wrought in the past two weeks

C. J. sighed as she stared out a window. "I have to admit, I'm kind of glad it's over."

"Me, too," said Meg, who was seated beside her, "but I hate things ended the way they did." She blushed. "Well, not *all* things!" she giggled and wiggled her left hand—which sported a sparkling diamond engagement ring—in the air.

C. J. threw her arms around her friend. "I'm so happy for you, Meg! Pinky proposing to you on bended knee—right there in front of everybody onstage—was one of the most romantic moments I've ever witnessed! You must be on cloud nine."

"I'm higher than that, girl! I never *dreamed* any man could make me feel so wanted—especially one with such a cute, little, bald head!" Meg sighed. "I know there are a lot of loose ends to tie up, but I feel like I can face anything with Pinky beside me."

C. J. pulled her knees up to her chest and wrapped her arms around them. "I wish we'd known last night would be our last chance to sing together, though. Maybe we could have persuaded Sue to go on with us after all. It was lucky Keith agreed to stay over and keep her company."

"I don't think *Keith* felt especially lucky," Fred the bus driver interjected, his eyes connecting with C. J.'s in the rearview mirror. "Watching the woman you've been in love with since high school pour out heart and soul to another man—in front of a live audience—prob'ly didn't rank in the top best moments of his life!"

"It did get a little awkward," C. J. agreed. "And I can't blame Keith for taking off in the middle of the song; that had to be hard to watch. Poor guy! And if they record that duet and it gets the response that it did last night, he won't be able to listen to a country station for months!" She smiled. "Isn't it ironic the song that's gonna put Hayley back on the charts got her fired from the Retro Rodeo tour? I couldn't believe how the crowd reacted when she and Jack started singing together!"

Fred laughed. "Me, neither. I thought ol' Cal's toupee was gonna pop right off his head, he was so mad—especially after that fifth encore. He definitely wasn't the headliner *last* night!"

"And what a bunch of hooey," Meg protested, "to claim he was firing Hayley because that song wasn't on the lineup. Cal just couldn't handle being upstaged!"

C. J. yawned and stretched. "That man's got one expensive ego: I can't believe he's willing to buy out the rest of Hayley's contract just to get rid of her!"

The curtain separating the bunk area from the front of the bus slid open and Pinky appeared, wearing a big grin. "Hey, there, sugar lips!" he said as he strolled up the aisle. "I just talked to my folks, gave 'em the big news, and they can't wait to meet ya." He bent to give his fiancée of fifteen hours a hearty smooch. "I told 'em we'd try to get over there soon."

Meg looked relieved, then nervous. "I'm glad they took it okay. But what if they don't like me, Pinky? And have you talked to Jack about getting some time off so we can have a honeymoon?"

Pinky patted her on the head. "Don't worry about all that, darlin'. Everything's gonna be fine." He pointed a thumb over his shoulder at the bunk area. "If them two cut that record, they'll be busy bein' celebrities for the next few months, so me and the boys can pick up a little studio work and stay put in Nashville—or go on a honeymoon." He chucked Meg under her chin and lifted his eyebrows. "I been on the phone so long, my ears are sore. Wanna come back here an' rub 'em for me?"

As Meg grinned and stood to follow Pinky, Fred honked the horn. "That there is an *ear*-resistible offer!" he whooped and everyone groaned.

Left alone with her thoughts, C. J. settled back to gaze out the window again as the bus thundered up Interstate 95. Foremost on her mind was how she would tell her husband his midlife crisis was imminent and involved diapers! *So, Pete! Remember how you said you can't wait to be a grandpa?...Pete, sweetheart: sit down. I have* *something to tell you...Pete, darling: this is so funny, you won't believe it...Pete, would you like a drink? How 'bout a double?...Pete, how much do you <u>really</u> love me?...Pete, dear, I've been thinking: I'd really rather have a minivan than a convertible for my birthday. They're so much more practical!...Petey, don't you think our life has become a tad dull?...Sweetie Petey, you stud! You are gonna be the envy of every man in Skerry when they hear this!...* With a sound somewhere between a sigh and a snort, C.J. picked up a notepad and a pen, and wrote:

Top Ten Reasons I Should Embrace Being Pregnant at age 53:

1. No iron-poor, tired blood for me!

2. Fuller, thicker, more lustrous hair!

3. Bigger boobs!

4. I can pig out without apology!

5. Vastly improved selection of maternity wear since last pregnancy!

6. Plenty of empty-nester friends to sympathize--and babysit!

7. VIP seating for high school graduation 'cause I'll be in a wheelchair by then!

8. Great excuse to hire a maid!

9. Can say 'no' to chairing all committees for the next five years!

10. Unparalleled example to my adult children of the importance of birth control!

As Tom Brooks' SUV followed along behind the tour bus, Amanda sat with her arms folded across her chest, staring out the window.

"Well, *I'm* certainly not having that talk with Tom, Jr.! That's a father's job; you have the same equipment down there! Besides, I took care of Diana; this time, it's *your* turn." She turned to waggle a finger in her husband's face. "And you better get with the program, now that he's spent the day on the bus with the 'Testosterone Trio!'"

Tom gave her a dark look. "Can we not talk about those musicians and their testosterone? I *know* you say nothing happened, Amanda—and I believe you—but I'm still ticked off!" His foot pressed involuntarily—or not—on the gas pedal, sending their vehicle precariously close to the rear of the bus. As Amanda planted her hands on the dashboard and was about to let loose a squeal of terror, Tom whipped the SUV into the left lane. As they cruised past the shiny pink and black panels of the bus, their son's face suddenly appeared in the window; he grinned gleefully and waved a handful of playing cards. 'I'M WINNING!' he mouthed. Then he turned and sank out of sight.

"Wonderful," Tom observed. "First they seduce my wife; now they're corrupting my children. What colorful essays the kids can write for their next assignment!"

"Oh, lighten up!" Amanda growled. "They have to learn about the real world *sometime*; who better to teach them than seasoned professionals?"

Her sarcasm hung in the air, in an uncomfortable silence, then Tom spoke. "Look, I know you think I'm jealous—and I am! Who wouldn't be? I get *crazy* thinking about you with some other guy! And I know how hard it is to be a full-time mom, even when you're not taken for granted. And you're *not!*" he added quickly. "You had a killer career, and you were good at it. Now you spend all your time taking care of us; that's a far cry from managing million-dollar clients, and I realize that." Tom hesitated, then reached for his wife's hand. "I was thinking, on the drive down here...the kids are past the stage where they need constant supervision, and I can take care of myself—even if I don't act like it sometimes...maybe you should think about going back to work." He shot his wife a quick glance to check her reaction. "Not full time, necessarily," he added, seeing her expression, "but maybe you might like to go back to doing something more stimulating than...I don't know...alphabetizing your spice rack. We'd miss you, but we could handle it."

"Are you nuts?" she accused, snatching back her hand to flail it in the air. "Who would schedule the doctor appointments? Who would *get* to the doctor appointments? Who'd supervise homework? And I want to be home when the kids get off the bus!"

"You *can* be," Tom reasoned. "Make your schedule revolve around whatever you want. Look in the glove box," he gestured. "Yeah, that piece of paper there. Read it and tell me that doesn't make your heart beat a little faster."

Amanda scanned the piece of torn newsprint. *Skerry Chamber of Commerce Director. Immediate hire! Must be self-motivated and able to work with minimum supervision. Must possess exceptional organizational and communication skills. Must be capable of multi-tasking, creative thinking, budgeting, and administrative duties for multiple projects. Will supervise staff of three. Occasional overnight travel required. Flexible hours. Salary negotiable.*

She laid the scrap of paper in her lap and looked at her husband. "Sounds like what moms across the universe do for free every day," she deadpanned. "What's the deal?"

"Peggy resigned last week to elope with some guy she met on the Internet," Tom explained, "but that's a whole other story in itself. Dave Taylor asked me if I could suggest anybody, because they need the job filled ASAP. The Pig Pickin' Festival is only a few weeks away and, of course, that's the Chamber's biggest source of revenue all year." Tom reached across to stroke his wife's cheek. "I thought of you immediately, Amanda. You could do that job in your sleep." He brought his hand back to rest on top of the steering wheel and shrugged. "It's not show business, and it's not anywhere near as glamorous as your former career, but it's a heck of a lot more exciting than scrubbing toilets."

Amanda flashed him a look of mock indignation. "Says *you*! You have no idea how intoxicating those little scrubbing bubbles can be!" Then she sobered. "Tom, everybody in Skerry thinks of me as a housewife. Who would take me seriously?"

"Are you kidding? You're already on half the committees in town, and people are *still* raving about the talent show you orchestrated at church last year. You're always telling me to think outside the box; now it's *your* turn—and I'll do whatever I can to help you." Tom Brooks stretched his right arm across the seat and squeezed his wife's shoulder. "I love you, sweetheart. All I want is for you to be happy."

Tears spilled down Amanda's cheeks as she strained against her seat belt to kiss her husband's cheek. "I don't deserve you."

Tom grinned broadly. "Maybe not, but you're stuck with me, so try to make the best of it." He gave her a hopeful look. "So can I tell Dave Taylor you'll send him your resume?"

"My resume is fifteen years old. Just tell Dave to give me the *job*! He can fabricate my resume later." She fumbled in her purse for a pen and paper. "Have you thought about how we'll manage in the summer, and on school holidays?"

"Yes, I have," Tom announced proudly. "And I have the solution to that—but you have to promise not to become violent." He flinched in anticipation of his wife's reaction. "Mom bought a condo on the beach last week. She's tired of the traffic in Birmingham."

"SHE *WHAT*?"

"It's fifteen minutes from our house," he added, in an attempt to mollify. "And she wants to invite the kids to stay with her as much as possible." Seeing Amanda's dubious expression, he continued. "Look, she may be Monster-In-Law to *you*, but you gotta admit she's the world's best grandmother. In the summer, the twins can stay with her during the week, happy as clams, and you and I can cavort naked through the house every night. Then on weekends, we'll all be together—without Mom, of course."

"Can I have that in writing?"

Tom turned to give her a reproachful look. "I think you owe it to yourself to consider this, Amanda. It doesn't have to be a life-long commitment; let's try it for a few months, then evaluate."

She sat silent for a full thirty seconds, then stretched over to kiss Tom's cheek again. "Thank you, husband. You know, when I married you, I didn't think it would be possible to love you any more than I did at that moment. But I was wrong."

Tom squeezed her shoulder again. "Back at ya, baby doll— wait! What was that?" He released her and moved his hand to the knob on the radio, turning up the volume.

" . . . long overdue for a hit, brought down the house at the Orange Blossom Opry last night and, we're told, almost ignited the stage in the process! Nashville's newest 'It Couple,' Hayley Swift and songwriter Jack Bixbee, will record the new ballad, titled 'Essence,' on a soon-to-be released CD. Of course, we'll be the first to give you all the details of Hayley's romance and return to the charts. We've missed ya, sister! Keep it tuned to Jacksonville's Country 99.1, WQIK!"

"Congratulations, Miss Comeback!" Amanda gushed as Hayley answered the chirp of her cell phone. "The news is all over— what station is this, Tom?— and you haven't even recorded the song yet! That Flopsy's a PR genius!"

Hayley blinked in confusion. "What are you talking about?"

"Some deejay—it's 99.1 FM . . . out of Jacksonville— was bragging that you and Jack brought down the house last night. He's reporting your new CD will be released any day now!"

"You're kidding."

"Yep, you and ol' Jack 'Bixbee,'" Amanda laughed. "Apparently, fact checking isn't an essential step for breaking news."

"Speaking of fact checking, have you convinced Tom he's still your one and only? Everything cool back there in the Lovemobile?"

"Couldn't be better. We've decided y'all can keep the twins

while we drive on up to the Poconos for a second honeymoon! Just remember Diana won't eat peanut butter, and Tommy won't brush his teeth unless you remind him."

"Er, I don't see that happening, but you're *precious* to offer!" Hayley said in her most syrupy Southern twang. "Listen, I gotta get off the phone; Tipsy's supposed to call any sec. We're stopping for lunch soon, so we'll talk then. Bye—and thanks for the heads up about the radio."

"No turning back now, big boy," Hayley warned as she clicked off her phone and turned toward Jack, pulling her legs up under her on the settee. "Guess what? That was Amanda. She said talk about our duet last night is all over the radio. Why didn't you tell me we had a new CD coming out?"

Jack looked perplexed. "*What* are you talking about?"

"Apparently, word on the street is that 'Essence' is my new big hit."

"*Whose* big hit?" he teased. "May I remind you I wrote that song, and sing fifty percent of the vocals? Do I need to make it fifty-one percent, to keep you in line?"

"Sorry. *Our* big hit. But they said *my* name first on the radio—and you don't want to know how they pronounced *yours*."

Jack laughed. "I don't care how they pronounce my name, as long as they play my song."

"*Whose* song?"

He reached out to stroke her hair, catching Hayley off-guard. "*My* song," he murmured softly. "I'm lending it to you for awhile, to see if you'll get off your cute little butt and get back on the charts where you belong."

"You think my butt is cute?" she asked, with an exaggerated fluttering of eyelashes.

"Last time I got a good look at it, it was. They say a man's memory is the first thing to go, but that image is holdin' up pretty well."

"Jack Bisbee!" she scolded. "Are you looking for trouble?"

"Nope." He leaned forward and his face grew serious. "The only thing I'm looking for is a straight answer, 'cause we been dodging this for a while now. Are you ready to quit playin' doctor with ol' what's-his-name and be *my* girl?"

Hayley's expression went somewhere between panic and euphoria.

"That's not a good look for you, darlin'," Jack teased. He waited for a response, but none came. "I'll be danged. I think I can honestly say this is the first time I've ever seen you speechless!"

The mood and the moment ended abruptly when Hayley's cell phone trilled. "*WHAT*?" Jack barked as he grabbed it and punched a key. "Oh, hey, Tips."

"Where's Hayley?"

"She's busy!"

"Well, I need to talk to her. Is this a bad time?"

"Frankly, yes, but what is it?"

"What the *hell* happened last night?" Tipsy thundered. "My phone's been ringin' off the hook all mornin' an' I got e-mails and voice mails and text messages comin' out the wazoo from everybody and his brother! Some legal dweeb's tellin' me Hayley's been fired,

Cal Taylor's accountant wants to know where to wire the contract payoffs, and every trade pub and talk show in town is talkin' about some danged song called 'Sex Sense'! Now I know Hayley needs a hit, but we ain't desperate enough to get pornographic! What are you yahoos up to?"

Jack kissed the top of Hayley's head as she continued to look as if she were either going to confession or going to throw up. "Well, A) it ain't porn, it's a love song; B) it's called 'Essence,' not 'Sex Sense'; C) Cal fired us because we made *him* look like a yahoo last night; D) send *my* piece of that pay-off check to my accountant, and E) you tell *Billboard* and the rest of them rags we'll get back to 'em in 24 hours. Fair enough?"

"I'll tell ya what's fair," Tipsy fired back, "y'all gettin' your free-floatin' fannies back to my office so we can have us a good, old-fashioned set-to. Where're you at?"

"Couple hours outside Skerry. We're spendin' the night there and we'll be in Nashville tomorrow. Why do we need to meet?"

"Because I'm the manager and I said so!" Tipsy fumed. "On second thought," he corrected, his tone turning sarcastic, "Tim Mc-Graw's in Atlanta. He *loved* that drumstick surprise; why don't y'all drop by and steal *his* show, too? I got room in my office for a few more lawyers."

"Aw, now, Tips, this might be a manager's nightmare, but it's a publicist's dream! Just switch hats!" Jack cajoled. "Or are you gettin' too old for this game?"

"TOO OLD? Listen here, you smart-mouthed, prima donna picker! I'll . . . oh, never mind . . . listen, you're start . . . brea. . . JU . . .CALL . . . GET . . . TOWN!"

Jack chuckled as he disconnected and tossed the phone across the room into an open suitcase. He turned to look back at Hayley, who sat motionless with her eyes and mouth closed. "Hey, Snow White! You waitin' for a kiss to wake up?"

Without a word, she opened her eyes, threw her arms around his neck, and planted her lips full on his mouth.

CHAPTER FIFTEEN
Twist & Shout

"Hello?" Hayley was curious as to who might be calling at seven o'clock on a Thursday morning. C. J.'s voice chirped in her ear.

"Hey, there! I finally told Pete our big news last night—after I poured him a third glass of wine and got up my nerve—and, guess what? He took it like a champ! Said this is a chance to fix all the mistakes he made with our first two!"

"You've been home two weeks and you're only *now* telling him you're pregnant?"

"Well, I've been busy. I had to unpack all my stuff, go through the mail that had accumulated, catch up with what the kids have been up to, and I made some cinnamon rolls and mailed them to Alice. But never mind all that," C. J. said eagerly, "gimme the scoop! Have you talked to Keith since you've been back? I saw him downtown yesterday. He looked pitiful."

Hayley sighed. "Don't tell me that. I already feel bad

enough. I *want* to love Keith, C. J., I do! I've *always* loved Keith. But . . . I don't know . . . it's . . . I *don't*, anymore. I don't know when that happened. And I'm so sorry."

"We can't help who we love, honey."

"Can't we?"

"No," C. J. said firmly. "I don't think we can. We can pretend, and be miserable, but we're way too old for games at our age, Hayley. There's nothing to be gained by holding on to something that isn't there. You both deserve better than that." They sat silent for a moment. "So now what?" C. J. asked.

There was another moment of silence then an audible expulsion of air. "I think I love Jack."

More silence. "You *think* you love Jack, or you *know* you love Jack—but aren't ready to admit it?"

"I'm not *supposed* to love Jack; he's my best friend. I don't want to ruin that."

"A lot of people think marrying their best friend works out pretty well."

"Who said anything about marriage?" Hayley shrieked, and C. J. chuckled.

"Sorry, Meg calls daily to update me on her plans. I have matrimony on my mind."

"I really *don't* love Keith! Wow. That's the first time I've admitted that," Hayley mused. "C. J., *I don't love Keith*! I've *always* loved Keith. But I *don't* anymore! I was feeling guilty about Jack because I'm supposed to love Keith, but I don't! So it's *okay* if I love Jack!"

"So, how's it feel to let go of a 30-plus-year-old prom date?" C. J. said, laughing.

Hayley drew in a long breath and exhaled, loudly. "It feels . . . weird. Good, actually . . . a little scary . . . a little sad."

"Could be you never loved him as much as you thought you did. Face it, honey: you had plenty of chances to come back down here and nab him—but you never did. And Keith had those same years. What did *he* do to advance the cause? If he loved you as much as he said he did, why didn't he do something about it ages ago? Ol' 'Bixbee' managed to pull it off in two weeks!"

"You are so rude!" Hayley accused, giggling, then she sobered. "Keith said Jack was just a bad habit."

C. J. gave a snort. "I'd say Keith was the habit. Jack's been a viable part of your life during all those years Keith was only a memory. But I guess you had to be in the same room with both of them to realize that."

Hayley repositioned herself on her mattress and scrunched her pillow up under her head. "You might be right. Thanks, C. J.. I've been beating up on myself ever since we got back, feeling guilty for being so fickle. But the truth is, I guess Keith and I ended the day I stepped onto that bus for Nashville."

"Sugar, you and Keith are the *only* ones who didn't know that," said C. J. gently. "Now, enough regret. Let's talk about Jack, and 'Essence', and what's happening! I want details!"

"Oh, we'll get to that later," Hayley promised, "but, first, tell me about your mama, and Sue. And what's up with Amanda? I haven't heard a word from anybody! Meg's driving us all crazy here with wedding plans; I can't believe she's calling you, too. Bo nicknamed her 'Bridezilla' until he found out she called a plastic surgeon about frown lines; now he's dubbed her 'Botoxica!'"

C.J. giggled. "I can't believe you offered to let her stay with you until the wedding. Hope you won't live to regret that decision!" She took a breath. "Well, everybody misses you like crazy; we can't wait till you come for the Pig Pickin'. Amanda and Tom are great; she adores her new job, and she's still finding things her mother-in-law changed while we were gone. Sue turned in a resignation letter to her school and—here's some *great* news: she and Mama are going to be roomies!"

"What?!"

"Is that not awesome? I wasn't happy about the care Mama was getting at the nursing home, and we're all concerned about Sue needing supervision, so I talked to some private care nurses, then to Sue, and then Sue and I talked to Keith, and everyone agreed moving Mama into Sue's house and hiring a team of part-time caregivers would be the perfect solution."

"Oh, C. J., how wonderful! Does Sue realize what's happening?"

"Actually, she seems to think they're opening a bed and breakfast, but she and Mama always did get along well, so I think this will be good for both of them." C. J. paused. "Hayley, I know I keep saying this, but you have no idea how good it is to have you back in our lives again. And even though there were moments of sheer terror on that tour, that's the most fun I've had in years. Thank you *so much*."

"Oh, stop! You're making me cry! And why are you thanking *me*? *I'm* the one who got rescued! If y'all hadn't dropped everything and turned into Hot Flashes, Cal would have kicked me off the tour . . ."

"Um, he *did*!!"

Hayley grinned. "Yeah, but not before Meg met Pinky,

Amanda got some ego strokes, we got some help for Sue, and you got one last chance to shake your booty before you start *knitting* one!"

"Very funny. For sure, this adventure didn't turn out like anyone planned! Who'd have thought two weeks on the road could bring about so many changes?"

"Tell me about it! Never in a million years would I have imagined Jack and I recording duets together."

"And never in *two* million years would I have imagined I'd be carrying a diaper bag to Wendy's graduation!"

Hayley laughed. "Uh-oh, I hear the band downstairs. Dog-gone it, I haven't even had my coffee yet! We're rehearsing every day this week, getting ready to record the new CD. It's grueling, but Jack is amazing. His tech skills are awesome, his songs are awesome, singing with him is awesome..."

"You sound like you're twelve."

Hayley giggled "I *feel* like I'm twelve. Well, maybe sixteen."

"Listen, you need to remember you're a hero for every woman on earth over the age of forty! You're proving life doesn't *end* at middle age; it just changes. No pun intended!"

"You are a hoot, Celia Jo Fleming! Take care of yourself, sweetie. Bye!"

♪

Four hours later, Jack slid off a stool in Hayley's basement and raised his hand for the band to stop. "Wait. *WAIT*! How many times do I have to say this? You repeat the chorus *after* the bridge, not before. Willard, if you can't keep your eyes on me, I'm sending your Babe du Jour out of the control booth. Now, take it from the top. Ready, Pinky? *PINKY*!"

Pinky reluctantly turned his attention away from Meg, who sat crosslegged in a corner thumbing through the latest issue of *Southern Bride*. "Sorry, Boss. Meg was showin' me a dress."

Bo clanged his cowbell then slammed a pedal against the bass drum. "Whoo-eee, won't you look cute? Not too much cleavage, now; you don't want to embarrass your mama!"

As Graham sawed a sassy riff on his fiddle, Willard made hand signals to his 'Babe du Jour,' who at the moment was showing a much keener interest in the sound engineer than she was in Willard.

"Don't you talk about my mama!" Pinky warned.

Hayley removed her headphones. "Jack, let's take a break. I'm starving."

Meg looked up from the magazine and glanced at her watch. "Y'all had a break an *hour* ago! Time is money, people. Don't forget, Pinky's helping bankroll this CD. He needs a good return on his investment."

Hayley rolled her eyes. "If we give Pinky his money back, will you stop playing guardian of the watchtower?"

Meg stuck out her tongue, then went back to her magazine as Jack shook his head and set his guitar in its stand. "Hayley, are you sure Tipsy can't convince the label to underwrite this project? I don't understand why they'll pay for studio time for 'Essence' but not for the rest of the songs on the CD—especially when they've got pre-orders out the ying-yang."

Hayley shrugged. "Tipsy says we could release 'Essence' as a single and make a killing, but then we'd have played our bargaining chip. This is our chance to get your music out there and heard. Tipsy thinks doing a ten-song CD, in the long run, is a better career move and a smarter business decision."

"Well, remember," Pinky piped up, "my money is tied to

Meg singing backup on them other nine songs. So it's all or nothin' where we're concerned. Nothin' personal, Jack."

"'Course not, Pinky." Jack laid his guitar across his stool and ran a hand through his hair. "I'm with Hayley. Let's take a lunch break. Miss Swift, may I see you upstairs?"

In the kitchen, Bubba Troutt was making chicken salad for the band, while Suzette filed her nails at the bar. As Hayley and Jack emerged from the door to the basement, Suzanne hopped off her stool and pretended to assist Bubba.

"Sit down, Suzette; you're fine," Hayley sighed. "You're the *only* person around here who's not on the payroll." The singer shot her "Man Friday" a look. "She's *not*, is she?"

Bubba pointed the paring knife he was holding. "No, ma'am, she is *not*."

Suzette affected an indignant expression. "I'm going out to the hot tub. Bubba, let me know when lunch is ready and—" she looked pointedly at Hayley— "I'll be glad to help you. No charge." She pulled a beach towel out of a laundry basket sitting on the counter and stalked away.

"Actually, Bubba, could you excuse us, please?" Hayley asked. "Jack and I need to have a few words."

"No problem. I'll go put up the rest of these towels. Lunch is ready," he said, nodding at the counter behind him, "so y'all can just help yourselves. Mail came; it's in the foyer. I've gotta run some errands in a little while. You need anything?"

Hayley gave a grateful smile. "No, thanks, not right now. And why don't you take the night off ? I think I'd like some quiet time—and you've certainly earned some for yourself."

"Will do. Thanks, Boss!" Bubba picked up the laundry basket and headed toward the other end of the house, whistling merrily as he went.

"Two weeks of rehearsal and I don't feel like we've made any progress whatsoever," Jack groused as he climbed onto a bar stool. "We've *got* to get some tracks down. Even though your label's not paying for this CD, they've scheduled the distribution, and Tipsy's got you booked on half a dozen shows in the next few weeks."

"You mean he's got *us* booked," Hayley said as she poured juice into two glasses and brought them over to the breakfast bar. "We're a team now, remember? Where I go, you go, partner."

"Well, I'd like to go OUT of the studio." He took a sip of juice and shook his head. "Being cooped up all day makes me claustrophobic. And these long days are killin' me!"

"Or maybe it's those long nights we spend smooching on my couch."

Jack lifted an eyebrow. "Any time you're ready to relocate to a more comfortable location, you let me know." He pulled her close and they exchanged a lingering kiss.

"Mmmm, you taste good."

Jack looked sheepish. "I stole a piece of pineapple out of Bubba's chicken salad. Hey," he murmured, tickling her face with a strand of her own hair, "unless you're really hungry, I have a suggestion as to how we can spend our lunch break."

"Do you now?" Hayley broke away and wagged a finger. "That's very tempting, but I don't think we dare leave the lunatics to run the asylum."

"You'll be so distracted, you won't have time to worry about it." Jack rose to come after her. He'd taken her hand and was leading her away from the bar when a series of shrieks split the air. They spun around to witness Suzette and Willard's "Babe Du Jour" wrestling beside the pool, which was now covered for the season. Lacquered nails flashed between handfuls of platinum hair.

"Seriously?" Hayley sighed. "A catfight is *just* what we needed to top off the morning. I can't take any more of this, Jack; you've got to tell the boys to leave their toys at home!"

"I get to keep *my* girl handy."

"Yes, but your girl *lives* here—and pays the bills! Therefore *I* get to make the rules!" Hayley scowled and put her hands on her hips. "Go tell Willard to send that bimbo home. I'm gonna go tell Bubba that Suzette needs to go on hiatus for a few days."

"What about Meg?" Jack asked.

"As long as she's got a mike in front of her, she gets to stay." Hayley headed down the hall then turned back to call over her shoulder, "But tell Pinky any mention of the word 'wedding' in the studio from this moment on will increase his investment by five bucks a clip!"

Inside Pinky's vintage Grand Prix, as he and Meg cruised down I-40 east of Nashville, Meg shifted in the bucket seat. "Baby, exactly how many relatives did you say will be at your parents' house this weekend?"

"Well, Mama had seven sisters and one brother, and Daddy had seven brothers and one sister, but two of my uncles and three of my aunts are dead. I have forty-three first cousins and thirty-two second cousins, but twelve live in Arkansas and we don't hear much outta them, which is okay, 'cause they're nothin' but trailer trash. Everybody else lives right close by, so I reckon they'll all be on hand—maybe even some of the thirds and fourths—cousins, I mean. It'll be a right hefty crowd, for sure."

Meg swallowed hard. "I have one relative in the whole world, and that's my daughter Alice. I gotta tell ya, Pinky, I'm terrified! *Promise* you won't leave me alone!"

"Aw, darlin', when you're with the Brown clan, you're *never* alone. But I promise, I'll stick to you like white on rice."

Meg laid her head on his shoulder and Pinky nuzzled it while trying to keep his eyes on the road. With one hand, he reached to stroke her hair. "You know, it means so much to me that you agreed to wait until our wedding night to, well, be together. My daddy told me that's the most special gift a man and woman can give one another." He kissed the top of her head. "The guys have made fun of me for as long as I can remember, but I'll be the one who can look St. Peter in the eye on Judgment Day, knowin' I was true to my intended."

Meg coughed uncomfortably. "Pinky, you *do* remember I've been married before."

Pinky's ears blushed. "Darlin', we're livin' in the future, and the past is behind us. When we say our vows, it's between you and me and it ain't nobody else's business what you did or who you loved before. From that moment on, you'll be Mrs. Pinky Brown, and I will love you till my dying day." He wrapped an arm around her shoulders and squeezed.

"I love you so much, Pinky Brown!" Meg declared and then burst into happy tears.

♪

At exactly six o'clock, Pinky and Meg walked up the wide steps of a weathered antebellum home in Kodak, Tennessee. The home's wide, wraparound porch was filled with tables of food, tow-headed children, and adults of all shapes and sizes. A short, round, elderly woman, who looked exactly like Pinky—but with a head full of bright red curls—threw out her arms in welcome as she masterfully negotiated a walkway full of rocking chairs and children's toys.

"My baby!" she exclaimed, enveloping Pinky in a hug. "How do, Miss Dorris," she added, turning to hug her son's companion, as well. "Welcome! We've heard so much about you and we're tickled to death our Pinky has finally found the right woman." Mrs. Brown led the couple into a gracious, expansive foyer. "Now, dear, your room is at the far end of the hall upstairs. Pinky, you'll be sleeping with the youngsters, down in the basement."

"Yes, ma'am, I'm happy to meet you, too," said Meg. "I don't have much family to speak of."

Pinky winked. "She has family, but don't speak of 'em much."

Several people standing nearby chuckled, and Mrs. Brown smiled. "That's perfectly all right. We *all* have a few family members we'd rather not speak of. In fact, Pinky, Aunt Violet is here, if you catch my drift. Oh, look, here comes Daddy Brown. Now, Meg, he's a pure devil—don't believe a word he says."

Dinner at the Brown home could only be described as unique. A constant stream of relatives circled in and out of the main dining room to inspect Pinky's intended. Some were subtle, others blatant in their curiosity. Meg leaned over to Pinky between courses. "I feel like a calf at auction! How many more people are waiting to check me out?"

Pinky took a gulp of his sweet iced tea. "Oh, we're 'bout half done. Some'll show up for dessert, and the rest'll wander up about the time we finish the dishes."

From the kitchen, a long parade of Browns suddenly filtered

into the dining room, claiming every inch of space. Mrs. Brown clanged a soup pot with a wooden spoon.

"ATTENTION! Y'all listen up! I guess by now, ever'body's met Pinky's Meg, here. On behalf of all of us gathered here, plus the thirty-some odd cousins who couldn't make it, please allow me to officially welcome you to the Brown family, Miss Dorris."

There was applause from around the room, and Meg felt her face and neck heat up. Under the table, Pinky squeezed her hand as his mother continued speaking.

"A few of us have been talkin', and seein' as how Meg don't have much family to speak of..." Mrs. Brown paused to cast a wink in Meg's direction, "we want you to know, we are here to help you however we can. Cousin Bernice has offered to make your weddin' dress, Sister Sarah will cater the reception, and you can get married right here on the lawn—Uncle Moody's a preacher; he'll be glad to do the honors. Cousin Lou Ella sings like a songbird; she's promised to do a rendition of 'O Promise Me' that'll break your heartstrings. And I'll bake the weddin' cake; I know Pinky's partial to coconut icing, and that'll mound up real nice on that top layer. Aunt Pauline has offered y'all her cabin at Dale Hollow Dam for your honeymoon, and Cousin Bert says to help yourself to the fishin' poles and his john boat that are there."

As cheering and thunderous applause filled the dining room, Meg realized perspiration was streaming down her hairline and her breath was coming in shallow gasps. When Pinky looked at her with concern, she managed a small smile and shook her head to indicate she was fine. He squeezed her hand one more time, then stood.

"Y'all are amazing. Thank you so much. I'm overwhelmed and I can see my bride-to-be is, too." He turned to pat Meg's hand, panicking at her pallor. "A man ain't much without his family," he continued, turning back to address the crowd, "and, boy howdy, that makes me quite a man, I must say!" Everyone laughed. "I'll also say me an' my intended are in the middle of a huge music bizness deal, so we ain't really had much chance to firm up our weddin' plans yet, but as soon as we have a chance to talk about all this, we'll get back to ya."

There was dead silence. Then Mrs. Brown smiled. "Pinky, honey, I think you've missed the point. We know y'all are workin' 'round the clock and are plum wore out. You don't *have* to make any plans; it's all taken care of. Just name the date!" She beamed expectantly as her son bent his head and tried to snatch another glance at his bride-to-be.

"Mama, I believe you done hit the nail on the head." Pinky laughed uncomfortably. "We're so tired, we cain't think straight. I 'speck we oughta just go on up to bed. Come on, darlin'," he said as he put a hand under Meg's elbow and helped her to her feet.

Another awkward silence descended, until Mrs. Brown spoke again. "Meg is upstairs, you're in the basement. Remember?"

"Yes ma'am, I do, but thank you for spellin' it out for everybody else." The gentle reprimand generated titters from several around the room, then some began gathering dishes from the table while others closed in around the couple to offer their good wishes. As Pinky gradually steered Meg away from the crush of relatives and toward the foyer, he leaned close to whisper in her ear. "I'll call ya on your cell phone in five minutes. Don't unpack! We're goin' straight to Gatlinburg. There's a weddin' chapel on every corner there, an' I aim to make you Mrs. Pinky Brown within the next 24 hours!"

♪

Light flickered in every room of the house. There were candles on the floor, on the counters, by the bathtub, even out by the pool. Hayley strolled into her closet and selected an emerald silk caftan that perfectly matched her eyes. She checked her makeup and hair in the mirror one last time, then pushed a button on the stereo system. As soft jazz began drifting through the house, the doorbell rang. Hayley opened the door and her heart skipped a beat. Jack Bisbee had never looked better. Standing there in a crisp, white, buttoned-down shirt and a pair of faded jeans, he exuded clean, raw masculinity—and he smelled divine.

"A rose for the lady," he said, bowing as he held out a single red bud. Hayley felt her toes curl as she motioned for him to step inside.

Jack glanced around the house. "You got the fire marshal on standby?"

"Don't you make fun of my attempt at a romantic atmosphere!"

"Are you planning to seduce me?" he asked hopefully.

"I'm not sure," she confessed. "But if I am, I need a drink. How 'bout a glass of wine—or two?"

They walked, arm in arm, to the kitchen, where Jack uncorked a bottle of Merlot waiting on the counter and filled two goblets. "Any of that pineapple left?" he quipped.

"Ever the comedian," Hayley chuckled.

"Not always." He leaned close and kissed the lobe of one ear. "Hayley Swift, you take my breath away."

Hayley choked on the wine she was swallowing. "You seem to have the same effect on me." She pulled away and cleared her throat. "Let's toast. To a beautiful ballad, and a promising future."

"To love—and honesty."

They clinked glasses, sipped, then Jack put down his goblet. "I can't stand this anymore." He drew in a deep breath and looked intently into her eyes. "Hayley, you will always be my best friend, but . . . "

She braced herself, not sure of what was coming, as Jack paused. Had she misread the signals? Assumed too much? She felt her stomach knot and her body flush. Not just flush, *ignite. No! Not now*! she panicked. Surely her first hot flash could not arrive as Jack . . . what? Dumped her? Proposed to her? Maybe it was just the unseasonally warm weather. But she went lightheaded, felt her knees begin to buckle, and she slumped against Jack for support. He interpreted it as a sign to go on, and hugged her close before lifting her face to look in his eyes again.

"But I've finally admitted to myself you are much, much more than that," he said as he stroked her hair. "I love you, Hayley. I think I've loved you for years, but I didn't recognize it until I thought I might lose you to ol' Doctor Boy." He paused again, the look of intensity on his face almost frightening. "I only hope the fierceness of my feelings can make up for the years we've lost, when we were too stupid to see we belong together."

Hayley clutched at him, joy and relief surging through her body as tears welled in her eyes. "Oh, Jack, I love you, too—so much, it terrifies me! You're the only man besides Tipsy and my daddy that I've ever loved enough to trust. So where do we go from here?"

He held her close for a moment, then pulled away to pinch her cheek and lighten the mood. "How 'bout the bedroom?"

She made a face as she reached for a dishtowel on the counter and mopped the sweat off her face. "How about the studio? It's cooler down there."

CHAPTER SIXTEEN
Mood Swings & Brain Lapses & Night Sweats, Oh My!

C. J. flushed the toilet for the umpteenth time that morning, wincing as her arm jostled against a swollen, tender breast. Yet another wave of nausea hit, and she gripped the wall to steady herself. *I can't believe this is happening again. I should be playing tennis, not reviewing LaMaze procedures! Hee-hee-hoo, HEE-HEE-HELL! Deep breath... hold on...it'll pass... oh! What's that heavenly smell? Cinnamon rolls. I forgot! I made cinnamon rolls this morning! Isn't cinnamon good for nausea? Ten steps to the kitchen counter—just ten steps. Come on, old girl! You can do it!*

She tottered to the kitchen, grabbed one of the gooey treats, took an enormous bite, and collapsed in a chair. *Mmm, extra cinnamon is definitely the trick. Okay, inhale, exhale, aaaaah. Much better.* She glanced at the table top, where no fewer than twenty baby product catalogs lay strewn, their pages dog-eared to call attention to items circled in red. Another wave of nausea rose, and she felt fresh tears well as the bite of breakfast pastry threatened to reappear. "It's not fair! This was *not* the plan!" C. J. wailed aloud. "I don't *want* to go to P.T.A. meetings again!"

For several minutes, she sobbed and pounded the table, stopping periodically to hurl a catalog across the room. Then she stopped and wiped her eyes with the back of her hand, as a picture of a chubby-cheeked infant wearing the latest in fashionable fleece sleepwear caught her eye. "Oh, but look at that little angel. Our baby could be blonde like that." C. J. smiled, then glanced at the clock, and suddenly realized she had a doctor's appointment in twenty minutes. She sighed and tried to remember where she'd last seen her car keys. "Oh, baby," she said aloud as she stood and patted her stomach. "What are you getting yourself into?!"

Amanda scowled at the dozen or so people milling around the table in the Chamber conference room. *Why is it so dang hot in here? Am I the only person in the room melting like the Wicked Witch of the West? Of course I am; I'm the only one in here who's over 40!* She felt sweat run down her back. Her blouse felt like a cellophane wrapper, suffocating her torso. She glanced across at the handsome young man seated at the far end of the table, Skerry's new city planner, Gil Gallahan. So far, she'd seen more schmoozing than planning. *And look at the former Miss Skerry over there,* she mused, eyeing the owner of the downtown fitness center. *She can't wait to let him know she was third runner-up in the Miss South Carolina pageant. Could that tiara tattoo on her wrist be any more ridiculous?*

Amanda cleared her throat. "Excuse me, I think we're all here, so let's get this meeting started." Twelve pairs of eyes turned to stare at her. "Thank you. I think the most pressing issue today is resolving the conflict between the start times of the Frog Jumping Contest and the Horseshoe Pitch. We don't want women to have to choose between watching their children or their husbands, so I propose..."

The mayor leaned back in his chair and offered a patronizing smile. "I don't see this as a real problem—certainly not a *pressing* one."

At the door to the conference room, Amanda's assistant waved a hand to try and get her boss's attention, but the city planner beat her to it. "Are there that many families that would be affected, ma'am?"

Ma'am?! "Absolutely!" she responded. "Mine, for example! How can I be there for my children, who haven't missed the Frog Jumping Contest since they were three, and simultaneously watch my husband pitch horseshoes? Can't be done! You're putting us moms in an impossible situation! And we want the Pig Pickin' to encourage family harmony, not create discord!"

The assistant tried again to get her boss's attention, this time running a finger across her throat in a slashing motion, but once again the city planner claimed Amanda's attention with a beguiling smile. "I understand your concern, but I have to say I think the mayor's right—as he usually is." He gave the mayor a wink and a smile. "This really isn't a pressing issue, Ms. Brooks; in fact, it could be a *non*-issue, if we simply cancel the Horseshoe Pitch. Surely that's an event whose time has come and gone."

Around the table, there were a few shrugs, a few heads bobbing in concession, and a few scowls; the Horseshoe Pitch was a long-time Pig Pickin' tradition.

"Mr. Gallahan, Skerry men have a long and glorious history

of horseshoe-pitching competitions; that event is *sacred*. Even the mayor will tell you that. So here's *my* idea ..." She paused to fling her hair away from her face. "Is anyone else hot?" She glared around the room, then refocused her attention on the city planner. "How about *you* enter that contest so you can learn to appreciate it!"

Abandoning discretion, Amanda's assistant now waved both hands in the air and begged, "Excuse me, ma'am, could I see you outside for a moment, please?"

"Can't it wait? We're in the middle of a meeting here."

The mayor coughed to hide his amusement. "Go ahead, Amanda. We've had your input; I can take it from here."

She whirled. "Are you *dismissing* me? I am the *director* of this event!"

At a complete loss as to the best way to proceed at this point, the assistant opted to simply join in the fray. "Ms. Brooks, you've actually already resolved this particular problem. Yesterday, you told me to leave the Frog Jumping Contest at eleven, and move the Horseshoe Pitch to one."

Amanda blinked a few times. "Oh. Well. How about that? Problem solved." She nodded her thanks to the flustered assistant, waved her on her way, then consulted her agenda. "All right then, moving on—we still don't have a cakewalk chairperson."

The games coordinator cleared his throat. "Um . . . actually, we do. You asked me to find someone last week, and I did. I . . . um . . . believe I sent you an e-mail to that effect."

The mayor chuckled. "Amanda, hon, is there anything *else* you've overlooked? Booking the entertainment? Ordering the pigs?"

There were chuckles around the room and the former Miss Skerry leaned toward Gil to observe in a loud whisper, "My mom says when you're middle-aged, you get real forgetful."

"Excuse me, I heard that!" Amanda fumed. "I am *not* forgetful! I am trying to take care of eighty-seven different things at the same time!" Twin streams of perspiration trickled down from behind her ears and met at the tip of her chin. She took a deep breath, weighed the chances of continuing the meeting with any shred of dignity, and gave it up. "This meeting is over!" she abruptly announced, snapping her notebook shut. "You people all have things to do. Stay on task and call me if you need anything."

There was a lot of whispering and a few snickers as the attendees filed out the door in clusters of twos and threes. Gil Gallahan lingered behind. "Sounds like you could use some help," he observed, flashing that trademark smile as he approached Amanda. "Is there anything I can do?"

"Actually, yes." Amanda gave him an equally dazzling smile. "I noticed that you only ordered five porta-potties for this event. We expect several thousand people, so do the math! I want *twenty* Porta-Potties guaranteed by tomorrow. *Deluxe* models!"

As Gallahan scowled and headed out the door, Amanda shouted a P.S. after him. "And if you find out I already ordered them, order more anyway! For once in their lives, maybe women won't have to wait in line to tinkle!"

As soon as the nurse went into Sue's bathroom and closed the door behind her, Sue got up off the sofa, grabbed the clipboard off her coffee table, and began to read.

Patient: 53-year-old Caucasian female

Diagnosis: peri-menopausal/menopausal; early-onset dementia, possible Alzheimer's

Medications: 5 mg Aricept daily; 1 mg Estradiol daily; 5 mg Provera every day; 500 mg Vitamin E daily, 1000 mg calcium daily, .25 mg Halcion as needed

Symptoms include: confusion, disorientation, agitation, depression, repetitive behaviors, distraction, sudden emotional outbursts, mood swings, unexplained anger, aggression, erratic appetite, fatigue, dysmenorrhea, headaches, nocturnal sweats, hot flashes

Good heavens, doesn't every woman my age have these symptoms? I don't feel like I'm falling apart! Well, sometimes I do. That other lady is the sick one; and why do these maids keep writing notes about me? I own this place! I run this establishment! I must not be too crazy or I'd be in a loony bin! I'm going to tell Bill about this when he calls tonight; he'll know what to do. Let's see what they wrote about me yesterday . . .

Observations: Patient was in a generally responsive mood, but resisted medications. When walking patient outdoors, she tried to kick a cat, then stopped abruptly to admire a neighbor's hibiscus. Patient refused to eat Mexican casserole for supper, saying (quote):"Who knows who you might have chopped up and baked in there?"

Oh, please, I was joking! But I'll have to use that line again, because I HATE Mexican casserole. If God had intended me to eat Mexican casserole, I would have been born in Mexico! I'm going to hire some new maids. It's none of their business what I do. They need to just clean the house and stop writing all these notes! Or maybe I should go home. Mama and Daddy must be worried sick about me, and I've learned my lesson. I might even eat Mexican casserole if I could eat it with the Campbell's Soup Girl spoon Santa left in my stocking. I bet it's still right there in Mama's drawer. Uh-oh, here comes the maid. Listen, here! I'm the boss, girlie, and don't you forget it! You'd better make me a peanut butter and honey sandwich for lunch, or you're fired!

♪

Meg stood up and walked around the room, stretched her arms, wiggled her fingers, then returned to her keyboard and began to type in a frenzy:

The virile Viking's red hair flamed in the wind. His muscles rippled as he tied the small dinghy to the ramshackle dock and turned to face his prisoner with a seductive smile. "We shall be safe here." The blushing virgin clutched her shawl closer. "Are you mad? How can I be safe with the very bandit who stole me from my father's castle and holds me against my will, un-chaperoned? Sir, you have ruined my reputation! The prince will never honor my betrothal pledge now!"

The sailor's shirt billowed in the breeze. Tall and majestic as the forested mountains that flanked them, the man threw back his head and laughed.

Meg lifted her hands from the keyboard and clapped in delight, then reached for the tabby cat curled at her feet. "I can't wait to read this chapter to *my* fire-headed Viking," she told the cat. "It's my best one yet! And to think I nearly failed Senior English!"

She put down the cat and stood, stretching first, then revolving slowly to savor the new office Pinky had created especially for her. The cat padded across the floor to find a patch of sunshine as Meg looked around the room and beamed. *I love my writing loft! Buying this old theater was my baby's best idea yet—other than eloping! Pink everywhere I look—wallpaper, flowers, cabinets, candles . . . it absolutely oozes romance—just like me!*

She crossed to the window and waved at Pinky, who was unloading carousel ponies from a rented truck in the parking lot below, then she looked into the cat's green eyes. "My hardworking handsome hero!" she sighed, then she gasped. "That's *it*!" she yelped, causing the cat to leap from her arms. "That's the title of my next book! '*Hardworking Handsome Hero!*'"

Candles flickered and an evening breeze blew ripples across the surface of Hayley's hot tub as Jack, wrapped in a thick terrycloth robe, made his way from the driveway to the patio. The steaming water in the hot tub bubbled and gurgled invitingly. Jack smiled as he knocked twice, then opened the French doors and stepped into Hayley's den where she stood, frowning, by the breakfast bar. He reached to embrace her, then pulled back, surprised by her damp skin.

"You've already been in? I thought you were gonna wait for me."

"I *did* wait."

"But you're wet!"

"Yeah, that's *sweat*. I'm burning up!!"

"Got all hot and bothered just thinkin' about me, huh?"

Hayley rolled her eyes. "This is fever, not lust. I think I'm coming down with something."

"*Well*, then—Doctor Feel-Good, at your service!" He kicked off his sneakers and dramatically peeled off his robe, revealing bright yellow bathing trunks covered in flamingos.

Despite her grumpy mood, Hayley had to laugh. "That is the ugliest bathing suit I have ever seen."

Jack feigned a wounded look. "Aw, now, I paid a lot of money for this! Come on," he urged, moving to slide an arm around her waist. "A few minutes relaxing in that hot water and you'll feel great."

"Hot water is the *last* thing I want to feel!"

"Would you rather go for a walk?" Jack asked, retracting his arm. "It's fairly chilly outside. Or we could go get some ice cream."

"I don't know *what* I want. Just leave me be," Hayley sighed.

Jack scowled. "What in the world is *wrong* with you?"

"I told you, I'm on FIRE!"

"Well, don't waste it!" Jack quipped, trying to lighten the mood. He reached out for her again. "C'mere and let's see what kind of conflagration we can muster up!"

"Don't *touch* me, I mean it!" Hayley grabbed a magazine off the bar and began fanning her face. "I'm, like, a billion degrees here! This *can't* be normal. Are there flames coming out of my head?"

Grumbling, Jack backed away, his hands raised in acquiescence. "I swear, sometimes I think God put women on this earth just to drive men crazy. I'm gonna go over here and sit on the couch. You holler when you flip your switch back to 'civil.'"

"I wish I *could* flip a switch!" she retorted. "I wish I could wave my hand and be standing in a cold shower!"

"Well, here! I can help with *that*!" Without stopping to think, Jack grabbed an open bottle of water sitting on the bar and poured it on Hayley's head. "How's that, 'Mercury Girl'? Feel better?"

Hayley's eyes blazed as she shook her head and shoulders, sending water droplets in all directions. "I can't believe you did that!"

Instantly, Jack looked chagrined. "I can't believe I did, either. I . . . I . . ."

"But you know," Hayley interrupted, a look of surprise on her face, "it actually felt pretty good!" Looking into Jack's doleful, repentant eyes, she began to giggle. "Here. See if it makes *you* feel good!" She grabbed the bottle from Jack's hand and sent the remaining water splashing across his chest.

Erupting in laughter, each attempted to fling the remains of their unexpected water bath onto the other. Dripping and still giggling, Hayley turned to go get towels from the bathroom. As she made her way down the hall, she tripped over a t-shirt lying crumpled on the floor. She picked it up, and her eyes fell on the words 'Hayley & the Hot Flashes.' Is *that* what this is?" she murmured aloud. *Where's my phone? I need girl talk!*

CHAPTER SEVENTEEN
Great Unexpectations

Amanda cradled her cell phone against one ear while stretching off the exam table for her purse. "Wait a minute, Millicent. You've already had the twins for two weeks. I know 'Grandma's Beach House' is big fun, but I miss my children! Well, you shouldn't have made plans for them this weekend without asking me. Hold on, I've got another call coming in. No, never mind. I'll call you back." She pressed a key on the phone. "Hello? No...The purchase order on my desk...What do you mean, you can't find it? It's right there!" *Honestly! Can't a woman go to a doctor's appointment without people calling every five seconds?* she thought to herself. "Look, I'll be back soon, so...no, I...well, you could...maybe if...oh, good grief, just deal with it!"

She disconnected the phone and was contemplating which direction to hurl it when the door opened and a woman wearing a lab coat walked into the exam room. "Hi, I'm Dr. Jan. My nurse tells me you're having some hormonal issues. Been there, know what *that's* like!" She made a face.

Amanda's answer was a snort. "I think life was simpler when women were *dead* by the age of fifty."

"That bad, huh?"

"Are you kidding? I've started fantasizing about yanking out my uterus and beating it to death. And I am so tired of hormone jokes, and smirks, and 'Watch out, she's lethal today!' cracks—and not just from men! You'd think other *women* would be sympathetic. But, noooo, *everybody's* enjoying a laugh at my expense." She rubbed her temples. "I'm telling you, the insanity that's my life these days isn't funny. My last doctor—male—accused me of exaggerating my symptoms. I thought about stabbing him with a tongue depresser!"

Dr. Jan chuckled as she claimed a chair from the corner and sat down. "Duly noted! I'll watch what I say."

Amanda grinned. "So, can you fix me?"

"How do you feel about hormone replacement therapy?"

"I'll try cyanide therapy if you say it'll help!" Amanda cracked, then sobered. "Unfortunately, I don't think taking hormones is an option, given my family history. My mother died of breast cancer, and I have high blood pressure—dual red flags."

The doctor grimaced. "Nope, you're definitely not the ideal candidate for HRT. Have you tried herbal options? Yoga?"

"Actually, chocolate and profanity are my preferred methods of coping, but I'm a Sunday school teacher with two children at home, so mostly I tough it out."

"No pain or irregular bleeding? Nothing that might signal the need for a hysterectomy?"

Amanda looked alarmed. "Hey, I was kidding about getting rid of my plumbing! I just want it to *play* nice."

Dr. Jan laughed. "I understand. But here's the deal: until menstruation stops altogether, you're officially in 'peri-menopause,' which can last for up to ten years. When most women hit the magic age of fifty, though, things start to escalate, so the good news for you is that this should all be behind you fairly soon. In the meantime, though, symptoms can come and go at random, so you have to learn to manage them to maintain your sanity. Let's talk about your lifestyle."

Without any warning whatsoever, Amanda burst into tears. "Oh, let's not!" She gestured toward a box of tissues and the doctor quickly complied. "Dr. Jan, I've made such a mess of things! A few weeks ago, I had the most amazing adventure with my girlfriends. I got to sleep late, pluck my eyebrows and shave my legs without interruption, ponder the universe, enjoy great conversation—and people even cared what I had to *say*—one, in particular." She paused to blow her nose and give the doctor a doleful stare.

"That sounds wonderful!" said Dr. Jan. "So...?"

"So being out in the world again made me believe I was bored staying at home, that I was being taken for granted. So, like an idiot, I came home and got a job. But I *hate* it—hated it after only a week! I can't tell anybody, though—I'm too embarrassed. But now I'm constantly juggling, I'm always frazzled, I only get to see my kids on weekends—*if* I'm lucky—and that's just for ten minutes in the car on the way to a ball game or to church." Two big tears slid down Amanda's cheeks. "This isn't what I envisioned at *all*, but now I'm stuck."

Dr. Jan leaned forward to give Amanda's hand a compassionate squeeze. "Unhappy, maybe, but surely not stuck. Lots of moms work, Amanda. Maybe you don't have the right support system."

Amanda guffawed. "My support system is half my problem! I have the world's best husband, a mother-in-law most women would kill for but who's making me crazy, and girlfriends who tell me I'm brilliant. How can I let them down, after everything they've done to make this work for me?"

"You said you went back to work because you were bored. Did a career outside the home seem more exciting?"

Amanda rolled her eyes. "*Seemed*—definitely past tense! I had a *truly* exciting job before I got married and I guess after being a domestic goddess all these years, I felt like I was missing out. But now I realize how much I *enjoyed* being a stay-at-home mom—all my volunteering, and spending time with my children, and keeping our home running smoothly." She sighed. "I'm still trying to do all of those things, *plus* make this stupid Pig Pickin' happen, and I'm trying to pretend that I'm Superwoman, but the truth is . . ." and, here, she began to sob. "I'm falling apaaaart! My life is a meeeeesss! And it's all my faaaaaaault!"

Dr. Jan proffered a few more tissues from the box on the table beside her. "Does your family need your income?"

Amanda sniffed a few times then shook her head. "Not really. The extra money's nice, of course, but we've survived without it for the past twelve years."

The doctor smiled. "Amanda, peri-menopausal hormone fluctuations may not be the sole source of your problem. Stress can affect the human body in surprising ways." She leaned back and crossed her arms. "You certainly don't have to earn a paycheck to prove you're a smart, talented woman, and there's a fair amount of research that indicates multi-tasking isn't all it's cracked up to be."

Dr. Jan reviewed the notes on the chart in her lap. "You know, there's a *reason* why 'Superwoman' is a myth. What's preventing you from quitting your job and going back to your former 'boring' life?"

"Pride," Amanda readily confessed, "and knowing they will never find a better Pig Pickin' director than me!"

Dr. Jan's hearty guffaw could have been heard across the street. "You may have to choose between your pride and your mental health. Whose happiness matters most—the Chamber of Commerce's or yours?"

Amanda sighed as she let the simple truth of the doctor's words sink into her brain. Dr. Jan rose and patted her patient on the shoulder. "This is easier, Amanda, because you have choices many women don't. Follow your heart—or, to be more blunt, go with your gut." She scribbled some words on a notepad. "In the interim, add some soy products to your diet, and here are some herbal therapies you might want to try." She tore off the sheet and gave it to Amanda. "A massage now and then can work wonders and, of course, exercise always helps." She grinned and cocked her head. "Swearing does seem to help on occasion, and medicating with chocolate is fine—in small doses—but, ultimately, eliminating stress is what will help the most. I want you to go home, think about this, make some decisions, and come back in a month. If you're not feeling better by then, we'll do some blood tests and see if there might be something else going on. Sound good?"

Amanda felt a new crop of tears coming, so she bit her lip and nodded. "My friend said you were the best doctor on the planet," she finally managed. "Thank you so much; I feel better already."

Dr. Jan gave her patient a pat. "What you're going through is very normal. You were smart to seek medical advice, though, and we'll definitely keep an eye on things, but I think you're going to be fine."

"You don't look old enough to be so wise!"

The doctor grinned. "Ha! Pick a number."

"Fifty?

"Higher. Next decade, in fact."

"*No way.* Sixty?"

"Sixty-four, thank you. It helps to have good genes and a husband who keeps me laughing and does my laundry." She smiled warmly. "You'll get through this, Amanda. Menopause won't kill you—although you may *want* it to. A positive attitude is your best defense, so you're in great shape." She walked toward the door and opened it. "See you in a month—and good luck."

When Amanda emerged into the waiting room a few minutes later, she spotted C. J. flipping through a magazine. "Hey, you! Do we have a lunch date I forgot about?"

"No, it's check-up day. I came early so nobody could find me for a few minutes." The two shared a smile reserved for overwhelmed mothers around the world.

"I *love* Dr. Jan! Thanks for the referral. She gave me a cure for everything that's ailing me, *and* assured me I'm not crazy!"

C. J. groaned. "You're lucky your problems are so easily solved. Do you have any idea how many types of *car seats* there are to choose from these days?" She held up an ad. "And now they have *wipe warmers*? Give me a break! Hey, you packin' any chocolate?"

Amanda plundered her purse. "'A positive attitude is the best defense.' That's what Dr. Jan says."

"Easy for *you* to say—and her," C. J. retorted, making a face. "*Y'all* don't have nursing bras in your future! I'm glad you like Jan;

she's super. Now about that chocolate..."

As Amanda produced an Almond Joy and opened the package to share half, she took a closer look at her friend. "Your eyes are as red as mine are; have you been crying, too?" She plopped down into a vacant chair. "What's wrong?"

C. J. waved a hand. "Oh, I'm not upset, I'm mad—so mad I could spit, actually. I came *thisclose* to smacking some pierced, dyed, tattooed panhandler at the Piggly Wiggly before I got here. She had the audacity to ask me how I could, in good conscience, bring an innocent child into 'this war-infested, materialistic world!' I told her there was no conscience involved—just lust and stupidity—but it was absolutely none of her business, either way! Can you believe that? Since when do rank strangers get to voice their opinion about my right to bear children?"

Amanda giggled at her friend's indignant expression. "Did you mow her down with the grocery cart?"

"I thought about it, but decided a neon prison jumpsuit wouldn't be a good maternity look." C. J. brandished a finger. "But that's not the half of it! Last week, Mrs. Hornbuckle accosted me after church, to say—none too discreetly—how *nice* I am to act as a surrogate mother for some poor girl with no ovaries!" She rolled her eyes. "I wanted to *die*! I ended up spending half the Sunday school hour explaining to Reverend Blalock and the entire Senior Adults class that I am most certainly *not* a surrogate mother and that Pete and I *are* in our right minds, despite evidence to the contrary. What is so *wrong* with being pregnant at fifty-three?" she fumed, then held up a hand. "Don't answer that. But why is it anybody's business besides *ours*?"

Amanda hugged her. "It's not. But that's one of the infinite joys of living in a small town. Everybody *makes* it their business."

"Speaking of small town joys, how's the ol' Pig Pickin' coming along?"

Amanda rolled her eyes. "Dr. Jan just witnessed my epiphany. I'm doing such a great job, it's killing me. I'm thinking this may be the only pig I ever pick."

C. J.'s eyes widened. "What? I thought you loved working for the Chamber."

"I thought I did, too—but not more than I love my sanity. I've got some brutal decisions to make. And I think I need to schedule a family meeting."

"Ugh. We're having one of those tonight," C. J. said. "The kids have been so busy since I got home from the tour, we haven't had much time to talk. But I'm getting some strong negative vibes about this baby."

"From Skip?"

"No, he's tickled to death. Jokes about how he'll finally have somebody to play baseball with him." C. J. looked pained. "No, Wendy's the one who's upset. You've never heard so much door-slamming. But she won't talk about it—all she does is glare at me."

Amanda glanced at her watch as her cell phone rang. "Argh. It's Monster-in-Law. I was supposed to call her back." She rose and headed for the door. "Gotta run, girlfriend. Call and let me know how things go."

♪

In the kitchen of her spacious ranch-style home, C. J. gave her legendary homemade spaghetti sauce one more stir then called out, "Dinner's ready!" Pete breezed into the kitchen almost immediately and was pinching his wife's behind when their daughter came through the door.

Wendy gave an exasperated sigh as she slumped into her chair. "Can't you people keep your hands to yourselves? It's bad enough my friends tease me about my wanton parents; now you're telling me I can't have a new car because you have to start another college fund!" She tossed her mane of golden curls and crossed her arms rigidly across her chest. "How selfish can you be? Did it ever cross your mind to use protection? You're always preaching to *us* about safe sex. Well, DUH!"

C. J.'s cheeks flamed as she brought a bowl of spaghetti to the table, and though she was trying not to cry, tears began to well.

Pete pointed a finger at his daughter. "You are way out of line, young lady! Apologize to your mother, right now."

Wendy's eyes were fiery. "Why should I? I'm not the one who got knocked up! Here I am with only a year left in college, and my whole life is turning upside down. I am *not* changing my plans to make your life easier . . . and that baby is *not* sharing my room!"

"Not to worry." Skip Fleming entered the kitchen and wrapped his arms around his mother. He tossed a look of contempt at his older sister before giving C. J. a kiss on her forehead. "Junior can share *my* room. I can't wait for a baby brother to upstage the Drama Queen!" He released his mother and swiped a piece of garlic bread as Pete passed by with the basket. "Oh, man. This smells delicious, Mom."

C. J. sat down and wiped her eyes with a napkin. "Thank you, honey." She turned to her daughter. "Can we please try to keep this civil, Wendy? I'm sorry you feel this way," she began, her voice breaking immediately, "but this baby is coming to us for a reason. He—or she—is a blessing, albeit an unexpected one. Someday, you'll understand that."

"The only thing I understand is that you haven't given a single thought to how this affects the rest of us!"

"Don't include *me* in your temper tantrum, sis," Skip protested with a wave of his salad fork. "I think it's awesome!" He winked at C. J., who smiled in spite of herself. "Mom and Dad are great parents, and this is one lucky baby to have *me* as a big brother!"

Wendy bolted up from the table. "You are such a suck-up! Why don't you tell Mom what you said at *first*, when they dropped this precious little bomb on us?"

Skip reddened and lowered his gaze to his plate. "Uh, that it was really a surprise?"

Wendy cocked her head. "No, actually, I meant the part where you said, 'Man! Hope that doesn't screw up our vacation in Cozumel!'" Pete choked on a mouthful of salad, and even C. J. had to suppress a giggle. "Oh, so it's funny when Skip complains," Wendy glowered, "but if *I* say anything, *I'm* being hateful! Well that's nothing new—he's always been the favorite, and now there'll be another son, another golden boy." She stormed away from the table. "I think I'll move out now, before the Walton Family is reborn right here on Culpepper Drive. *'Good night, Skip-boy!'*" she mimicked over her shoulder. "*Gag, gag, gag!*"

"Come back here!" Pete roared.

Wendy, to her credit, stopped and wheeled, her eyes shooting daggers.

"I'm still waiting for that apology to your mother, and in case you've forgotten, I'm the one *paying* to put you through college. If you want to strike out on your own, I'd be only too happy to accommodate you. Tuition, books, sorority dues, clothes, gas . . . why, I could save a fortune!"

Jayne Jaudon Ferrer

C. J. gestured for her husband to calm down, then gave a weary sigh. "Wendy, I have total strangers badgering me about this pregnancy; I don't need grief from you, too." She ran a hand through her hair. "Your father and I didn't *plan* this baby, but that doesn't mean it's not wanted. If you can't accept a sibling with the love it deserves—if you don't want to be part of this 'new and improved' family—then perhaps you *might* want to think about moving out."

Wendy gasped. "You're kicking me out?? I can't *believe* it!"

"That is not *remotely* what I said," C. J. countered, in a voice thick with emotion. "It would break my heart to see you move out when our family should be closer than ever. But this isn't about making *you* happy, Wendy. It's about accepting change, taking life as it comes, facing unexpected challenges with grace. There's a reason this baby is being born, and it's not your place to condemn it. Your role is to welcome him or her with open arms."

Wendy tossed her head. "Oh, *please*! You act like he's some new messiah! *I'm* not gonna worship him!"

"That's it! Go to your room, right now!" Pete shouted, jumping to his feet and, in the process, sending his chair flying.

Wendy put her hands on her hips and lifted a defiant chin. "I am twenty-one years old. I am *not* going to my room."

Pete strode across the room and grabbed his daughter's purse off the kitchen counter. "You're right, you're not going *anywhere*. Let's see how independent you are without your car keys and cell phone!"

"Those are *mine*! You can't do that!" she shrieked, running toward him.

"Oh, yes, I can. I pay for them!" Pete bellowed, digging in the purse till he retrieved the contraband items. "These are mine till you apologize and learn to show some respect!"

Wendy's scream of outrage reverberated off the walls, and the slam of her bedroom door, shook the house to its foundation. Then all became completely silent but for Pete's labored breathing and Skip's voracious chewing, which halted only long enough for him to say, "Wow, Mom, this really is your best sauce *ever*. Have you considered entering this in a recipe contest?"

C. J. threw a piece of garlic bread at her son, hitting him squarely on the chin. "You really are a suck-up," she declared as she picked up her sweet tea and guzzled it.

CHAPTER EIGHTEEN
Revelations

"See that cardinal over there, Louise?"

"Where?"

Sue pointed across the yard. "By the basket-flower bush. See it?"

Louise stopped rocking and squinted her eyes. "I see him. Look at him, ricocheting around like he's the only redbird ever was. Reminds me of my husband." She resumed her rocking.

"I used to have a husband. What was your husband's name?"

Louise studied the cardinal again while she thought. "I don't remember," she finally admitted. "He was tall. He drove a green Buick, and he loved Kraft Macaroni & Cheese."

Sue sat silent in her rocking chair, pulling at her sleeve. "Something happened to my husband, but I don't remember what. He's been gone a long time, though." She sighed heavily. "I really miss him. Maybe he'll call tonight."

Louise turned toward the sound of a car door closing, then tensed as a woman approached the porch. "Oh, no, here comes that hussy!"

"That's C. J., Louise—Celia Jo, your daughter."

Louise frowned, her lips pressed tight, as C. J. opened the gate to Sue's yard. C.J. wore a black maternity dress decorated with huge, hot pink flowers that accentuated her protruding stomach. She carried a wicker basket and a bunch of bright yellow roses. "Hello, ladies. Fresh flowers and fresh, hot cinnamon rolls, just for you!"

Sue licked her lips and stood up. "Yummy! Let's go see if that maid has some coffee ready."

C. J. planted a kiss on her mother's gray head. "Hi, Mama. That's a pretty dress you're wearing."

Louise stiffened in her rocker and glared at her daughter. "You have no right to talk to me in that dress. Take it off this instant!"

"You don't like it? I thought the pink flowers were fun."

"It's a baby dress."

"You think it's too young for me?"

The older woman reached out and yanked at the dress. "You take it off *right now*! You have no right to wear one of those. Nobody's supposed to know!"

C. J. and Sue exchanged looks of confusion. C. J. patted her mother's face and smiled. "It's okay, Mama. Everybody knows. I'm the town's walking advertisement for safe sex."

Louise's hand slapped her daughter's cheek with a loud smack. "Don't you talk trashy to me, young lady!"

Caught off guard, C. J. gasped and stumbled backwards as tears welled in her eyes. "*Mama!* I'm sorry! I . . . I was just trying to be funny!"

Sue began to pace and twist her hands. "Oh, this is bad. This is very, very bad. Where is the maid? Bill's going to be angry. Oh, this is a bad thing!"

Suddenly, Louise lunged out of her rocking chair and jerked the basket from C. J.'s grasp. "You tramp! I'm not paying to raise that baby. I'm too *old* to have a baby. I've already had two babies, and I don't want any more!" Her face crumpled and she began to sob. "Oh, I wanted my baby! Why didn't they let me keep him?"

Sue paced back and forth across the porch. "MAID! MAID!" she yelled, pounding on the door frame, as Louise moved several feet away, alternately picking at the wicker basket's handle and glaring at C. J. out of the corner of her eye.

A young woman wearing brightly colored scrubs appeared in the doorway, her face full of concern. "Sorry, Sue, I was putting away some clothes. Is everything all right?" She pushed open the screen door, took a step forward, and C. J. came into her view. "Oh, honey, you're *crying*! What's wrong? And what happened to your face!" She rushed to help as C. J. shook her head and sank into the rocker Sue had vacated earlier.

"I . . . I'm not sure *what* happened, Jackie." She raised a trembling hand to her cheek. "I came up on the porch to give Mama a hug and . . . well . . . she slapped me! Something about my dress upset her. She . . . Jackie, she called me a *tramp*!" C. J. buried her face in her hands and sobbed.

The nurse bent to put her arms around C. J. "Oh, honey, she's just having a bad day. Your mama loves you to death. You know what Alzheimer's is like."

"Doesn't make it any easier to hear your mama call you something like that!" C.J. wailed into Jackie's shoulder.

The nurse gave C. J. another quick hug, then turned to reach out for Sue. "Miss Sue, how would you like a cup of tea? Water's already hot." She took Sue's arm and guided her toward the door. "And, Miss Louise, if you'll come back over here and take a seat, I'll bring you a cup, too."

In response, Louise turned and hurled the basket at Jackie, sending cinnamon rolls flying in all directions.

"That was very rude!" Sue scolded, as the nurse opened the screen door and propelled her inside.

Jackie shut the door and started back toward Louise. "Oh, my goodness, Miss Louise, those are homemade cinnamon rolls your daughter brought us. And look at these beautiful yellow roses!" She bent to pick one up, then gently put her arm around Louise and guided her into a rocker. "C. J., did you grow these?" she asked as she held the rose to Louise's nose so she could smell, but Louise pulled her head back and turned to stare across the street at a neighbor's lawn. Jackie gave C. J. an encouraging smile and a nod.

"Um . . . I see they have a new birdbath over there." C. J.'s voice was still wobbly. She cleared her throat and tried to steady it. "How about if we sit here and watch for a while, Mama, to see if any of the birds are taking advantage of it?" She gingerly approached the rocker next to Louise and took a seat. "You want Jackie to go get you that tea she was talking about? Sounded awfully good."

Louise continued to stare at across the way. Then she spoke in an angry, measured voice. "I know you stole my baby. You go get him. *Right now*. I want my baby back. Don't you come back here again without my baby boy."

C. J.'s eyes brimmed again. "What baby is she *talking* about, Jackie? I didn't have a brother."

Jackie made a sympathetic face. "She could be thinking about somebody she knew forty years ago, honey. Some days, she's clear, but other days, she doesn't make a bit of sense." She patted Louise on the back, then bent to pick up the wayward basket. "Listen, I just mopped this porch a little while ago, so I'm invoking the sixty second rule, and dusting off these cinnamon rolls. We're not about to waste these delicious things!" She looked up to see Sue still standing behind the screen door. "Come on back out here, Miss Sue. Let's salvage these goodies C. J. made for us. Couldn't be nothin' on this floor but a little pollen, and if *that* could kill us, we'd all be *long* dead!" She handed the basket to Sue as she emerged from behind the door, then turned back to C. J., who sat slumped, watching Louise pull the petals one by one off the rose Jackie had given her. "I'm so sorry. I know how hard this is for you. My granddaddy has Alzheimer's."

C. J.'s tears fell unchecked, but she nodded. "I'll be okay; thanks. My skin's gotten thicker these last few weeks. You can't believe the things people say when you're pregnant at my age." She made a contrite face. "I sure didn't expect my *mother* to be in that category, but I know she's not herself." She pushed herself, awkwardly, up out of the chair. "I think we'll try this another day," she sighed, giving Louise another kiss on the head. "Bye, Mama, I love you. Sue, I love you, too. And Jackie?" She moved to engulf the nurse in an enthusiastic hug. "I *so* love you. Y'all have a better day."

She walked down the porch steps and opened the gate. As she turned to wave, Louise raised a fist. "You hussy! At least I had a *husband*!"

As C. J. sank into her car and felt tears coming again, her cell phone rang. She would have ignored it, but Hayley's name flashed on the screen. "Hello?" she sniffed.

"Girl! I am officially a hot flasher. Either that, or I'm turning into a supernova. I emailed you last night; why didn't you answer me?"

"I'm sorry. I was having a meltdown of my own." C. J. relayed the details of Wendy's ugly outburst. "She apologized this morning, but Pete is still holding her keys and cell phone hostage. What he doesn't realize is that it might actually be in *everybody's* best interest for Wendy to move out in her current state of mind, but he thinks he's helping." She paused to take a shaky breath. "So Wendy's home doing the laundry, which means we'll all have pink underwear, and I've just been slapped in the face and called a tramp by my loving mother."

"*What?*"

"I have no idea. Something about my maternity dress set her off. Then she insinuated, in a voice loud enough for the next county to hear, that I'm an unwed mother! I'm sure by tonight, all of Skerry will be questioning this baby's parentage—and I'm already the talk of the town."

Hayley chuckled. "Sounds like you need to get out of Dodge again! Why don't you come visit me for a few days? I could use some female companionship."

"Trouble in paradise?" C. J. teased. "How're the recording sessions going? How's Jack? Then let's get back to your hot flashes. We told you, Hayley—when you had one, you'd *know* it."

"Well, y'all had me thinking thirty seconds of extra sweat; this was more like ten minutes of welding torch! Jack's so annoyed with me, I haven't seen him since; I wasn't very nice to him—plus he really wanted to believe my 'glow' was all about him! Oh—and to add insult to injury, this morning I woke up and my *sheets* were soaking wet! I know I'm not ready for Depends yet; what is *that* all about, and what else do I need to know that you haven't yet told me?"

C. J. was out of breath, she was laughing so hard. "You know, I'm hardly the poster child for menopause right now, in my present condition; you should probably get your information from a more reliable source! But, hey, ignore all my other questions for the moment and tell me how Meg is doing."

"Oh, my goodness. Where to start? When she's not reminding us not to waste Pinky's money in the studio or helping him renovate the theatre they bought in Pigeon Forge, she's trying to give Nora Roberts a run for her money."

"Huh?"

"Yes, it seems, when Pinky gave Meg that journal, he unleashed a beast. She's churning out one bodice-ripper after another. Wanna hear the latest title?"

"I'm not sure."

"*Lonely No Moor*—as in, the moors of Scotland. Catchy, huh?"

C. J.'s shriek was so loud, Hayley had to pull the phone away from her ear.

"Oh, *please* tell me it's not about a short, bald piano player who rescues a big-bosomed, bleached blonde damsel in distress!"

"Hey, they say write what you know," Hayley quipped, and C. J. went into another fit of giggles. "Actually, I have no idea," she finally confessed, "and who knows? It might turn out to be a best-seller!"

"Okay, change of subject," C. J. interjected. "Well, sort of. I have guests coming for dinner: Keith and Meg's daughter, Alice."

"Coincidence or are you trying to make a very odd match in between rereading Dr. Spock and preventing World War III in your dining room?"

"No, it's a coincidence. Really!" C. J. protested, even as Hayley's hoot of disbelief came down the line. "Although, despite the age difference, they do seem to have a lot in common. In any case, I'm glad Keith's not sitting around fuming about you and Jack. Anything else you care to tell me about the progress of *that* relationship, by the way? I throw one heck of a bridal shower!"

"For now, we're taking things step by step," Hayley said. "Listen, tell everyone I said hello, and we'll see you soon. Have you learned the new Hot Flash song yet? Don't forget we promised Amanda we'd perform it at the Pig Pickin'. At least now I'll know whereof I sing!"

"I don't know, I'm thinking pink spandex over a four-month bump may be more than our fans bargained for! But maybe they'll be too busy ogling my new and improved bosom to notice. Gotta give those pregnancy hormones credit; they do fill out the ol' Maidenform! Talk to you soon, sweetie. Bye!"

Keith Parker rang the doorbell and smiled broadly when Wendy Fleming opened the door.

"Hi, doc!" she said

"Wow, Wendy! Look at you, all grown up. How's life?"

The young woman sniffed. "A little *confining* the last twenty-four hours. You need to talk to Mom?"

Keith cocked his head. "Um, if I'm not mistaken, I was invited for dinner."

"Who is it, Wendy?" C. J. called out, emerging from the

kitchen with a dish towel in her hand. "Oh, Keith! Hi. Did I say six? I thought I said seven...but who knows? Doesn't matter. Come on in."

Keith stepped into the house and offered his hostess a bottle of wine. "I'm pretty sure you said six, but, either way, I have no life, I'm not on call tonight, and your house always smells way better than mine, so here I am. What's cookin'? The wine's for Pete; I brought you these."

He produced a box of Godiva chocolates, and C. J. pretended to swoon then kissed him on the cheek. "Oh, you fabulous man! Why hasn't somebody snatched you up and given you a houseful of babies?"

Wendy groaned as she headed the opposite direction. "Good grief, Mother. Is that *all* you can think about?"

Keith followed C. J. into the kitchen and perched on a bar stool. "Give me a job. I'm no surgeon, but I can disfigure vegetables with the best of 'em!" he offered, noting the makings for salad spread out across the countertop. "You feeling okay these days? Energy level holding up?"

She gave him a wry smile as she handed over a cucumber and a paring knife. "Why? Do I look a little rough around the edges? I get winded pretty fast, but I try to rest every day. Apparently, it's 'beat up on pregnant, middle-aged moms week' and someone forgot to tell me!" She divulged her various tales of woe to Keith, ending with her mother's disturbing outburst that morning.

"I hate that for you, C. J. It's not uncommon for Alzheimer's patients to be physically aggressive—especially with the people they're closest to."

"But I don't understand what set her off—something about

my maternity dress. She was fixated on babies—said she'd had *two*, and kept referring to one of them as 'him.' Usually I can figure out what she's talking about, but this time, I'm stumped. Maybe she's confusing herself with me; *I* had two babies—up to now! A boy and a girl."

Keith stopped chopping the cucumber. "You don't know, do you? Louise never told you."

C. J. frowned in confusion. "Told me what? What don't I know?"

Keith laid down the paring knife and ran a hand through his hair. "Do you mind if I pour myself a drink? I can't believe I'm the one telling you this. Come sit down."

They moved to the kitchen table and Keith opened the bottle of wine. He poured a glass, took a sip, and cleared his throat. Wendy, headed to the kitchen for a soft drink, saw their serious expressions, and stopped where she was. She stepped quietly out of view and listened.

"First off, I'm telling you this as your friend, but also as a doctor," Keith explained. "And I'm *only* telling you this because you have Healthcare Power of Attorney for your mom, otherwise I'd be violating patient confidentiality." He took a breath. "Louise *did* have two babies, C. J. Right after you left for college, your mother had a miscarriage." Ignoring C. J.'s gasp, Keith continued. "She didn't even know she was pregnant until she wound up in the emergency room. It was early term, but it devastated her and she ended up in a severe depression. Standard treatment at that time to regulate chemical and hormonal imbalances was to administer high doses of some pretty powerful drugs, but because she and your father didn't want it known, instead of keeping her in a treatment center, Dr. Braddock agreed to let her be confined to the house with a nurse for several months." He took a long look at his friend. "Did you know any of this?"

Stunned, C. J. shook her head then took a sip from a bottle of water. "No, none of it! I remember after my freshman year, I went to summer school so I could be near Pete; he was working on his master's. At the end of August, I came home for a few days before fall semester started. Daddy told me Mama was worn out and he was making her spend the week in bed. He'd hired a lady—her name was Hilda—to cook and clean and help out. Daddy assured me she was fine, she'd just been trying to do too much, so I didn't think anything about it. I'd go in and visit with her in the mornings, if she wasn't sleeping, and I think I took a tray in and had dinner with her once or twice. I tried not to bother her otherwise. After I went back to school, Mama called me every Sunday night, like always, so I honestly never even gave it another thought." She slumped in her chair. "How could I have been so oblivious?"

"You were eighteen years old!"

"Still! And why didn't Mama *tell* me? Why didn't Daddy? I could have been there for her! I don't understand." Her face crumpled as tears began to flow.

"I have no idea," Keith admitted with a shrug. "I guess they didn't want you to worry. Remember, depression was still looked on as shameful in those days, as if a person could control it." He smiled. "Not to mention, your mother strikes me as the kind of woman who would be mortified for people to know she was still enjoying an active sex life at her age."

C. J. made a face. "I heard *that*!"

"I only know all this because when Dr. Braddock retired

and I took over his practice, Louise became my patient, and all this was recorded in her medical files. The report said she snapped out of it after a few months and never had any more problems. I watched her for signs of renewed depression for several years, but she seemed perfectly fine until the dementia set in."

C. J. sank back into her chair. "Oh, my poor mama! What must she have gone through?"

Suddenly, Wendy came out of hiding and ran to the kitchen. "Oh, Mom, I'm so sorry," she cried, as she threw her arms around C. J. "I've been so hateful. I never even stopped to think about how you might be feeling about having *your* life turned upside down!"

"Oh, sweetheart, it's okay," C. J. soothed, pulling her daughter close. "Shh, shh."

As the two women cried and comforted each other, Keith excused himself to the porch. A few moments later, Skip pulled his pickup truck into the driveway and sauntered across the lawn.

"Yo, Doc! What's goin' on? I'm headed to the kitchen to grab some iced tea. Want some?"

"Trust me, you don't want to go in there right now, Skipper," Keith warned. "There's enough saltwater flowing to fill a fish tank; Wendy and your mom are having a 'moment.'" At Skip's raised brow, he held up a hand. "Everybody's all right, they can fill you in later, but let's hang out here till the all-clear sounds." He gave the handsome adolescent an assessing glance. "So how's the life of a college man these days?"

"What can I say? I have to beat the girls off with a stick!" Skip bragged as he mounted a porch rail. "Dad's on my case, but I don't see the big deal about making Cs and Ds the first year, do you? Now that I'm a sophomore, if I play my cards right, I'll start for the baseball team next season." He bent to peer through the window, trying to finagle a glimpse into the kitchen. "What's for dinner?"

Keith laughed. "I saw salad in the making; that's all I know." Both men turned their attention to the road as a blue Prius pulled up in front of the house. Noting the female driver's mane of dark, flowing hair, Skip made a noise of approval. "Mmm, who's that?"

"No idea," Keith admitted as he straightened and tried to get a better look. "C. J. didn't mention any other guests; I thought I was it." As a curvaceous brunette slid out of the car, he squinted. "Alice?"

About that time, Pete's Jeep rounded the corner. He honked, waved, parked, then got out in time to give Alice Dorris a warm hug before she walked up the driveway. "Hey, Skipper! Hey, Doc! Glad everybody could make it!" Pete let Alice proceed him up the porch steps. Skip was waiting with a welcoming hand.

"Alice is in town for a few days before she heads off to the rain forest to rid the world of foul disease," Pete explained.

"That sounds fascinatingly gross," said Skip.

"Hey, some people bungee jump for thrills; I give shots to unprotected natives!" Alice quipped and turned to Keith. "Hello, again," she said, extending her hand. "How've you been?"

Keith gave her hand a withering look. "A handshake?" he said, pushing the proffered arm out of the way and giving her a peck on the cheek. "I *have* seen you naked."

As Skip choked and Alice's eyes widened in alarm, he grinned. "Okay, so you were nine at the time. You had a bike wreck while I was doing my residency here. Your mom brought you into the ER to make sure you weren't dead."

"I remember that! I broke my collarbone." She wrinkled her

nose. "Mostly I remember being mad because I couldn't ride my bike the rest of that summer."

Keith grimaced. "Yeah, and I was probably the bad guy who delivered that edict. Sorry! So what brings you to Skerry? And what's this about a rain forest?"

"You remember I told you I work for Doctors Without Borders?"

"Sure, I've been jealous ever since!"

"Well, there's some kind of viral epidemic in Malaysia. It's like flu—primarily affecting the young and the elderly. There's a skeleton crew there now, but we're taking in a full team in a couple of weeks and we'll be there a while. I told Mom I'd come check on the house and pack up some more of her things before I take off. She and Pinky have their hands full with the new venue, so it'll be a while before they can get back over here."

"I've heard of Doctors Without Borders," said Skip, slightly awed by this woman who was obviously as smart as she was beautiful. "It sounds like a really cool organization."

Alice smiled. "It *is* cool—and they offer a lot of internships. You won't get rich, but you'll meet some amazing people. You should think about it."

"*I've* been thinking about it," Keith interjected, "ever since you mentioned it in Florida. The website says they're looking for anesthesiologists and emergency room physicians right now; how about GPs? I'd love the chance to use my skills for a good cause like that, and I'm ready for a change of scenery."

"What? And leave this seaside paradise where everybody knows everything, from your first love to your shoe size? How *could* you?" teased Pete.

"Exactly for the aforementioned reasons!" Keith returned.

"I can put you in touch with the HR manager," Alice offered. "Remind me when I leave tonight and I'll give you her contact info."

Pete reached to pull up his jacket collar. "'Scuse me, this is a lovely conversation, but why are we having it out here in this brisk autumn breeze when we could be inside where it's cozy? Come on, let's see what's cookin'!"

"You mi—" Keith started, then winked at Skip.

"Sure, Dad," agreed the teenager. "Lead the way!"

But all was well when they entered the house, and in less than ten minutes, the entire group was seated around the dining table.

"This tomato and cucumber salad is amazing, C. J!" Alice closed her eyes in pleasure as she took another bite.

"It'd taste better with one of your mama's Big Boys," C. J. sighed. "I have seriously missed Meg's homegrown vegetables these past few weeks. Pigeon Forge is getting itself a world class gardener!"

"I sure didn't inherit her green thumb," Alice admitted. "I can't even keep *silk* plants alive!"

Keith laughed louder than he meant to and, beside him, under the table, Skip gave him a swift kick. "Smooth, man! Ya gotta be smooth," the younger man muttered under his breath.

Noting the doctor's flushed face and her brother's bemused expression, Wendy decided there was mischief afoot. "So, Alice, what does your boyfriend think about you deserting him to rescue germ-laden tribes in the rain forest?" she asked, then kept her eyes on Keith.

"Actually, boyfriends don't fit into my lifestyle very well,"

Alice confided. "I've discovered most men seem to prefer *video* game adventures to the real thing."

"Hey, I resemble that remark!" Pete protested, and everyone laughed.

"Not to mention, on any given Saturday night, I'm more likely found in a village lean-to than the local pub; I'm not a very convenient date."

"Yeah, but what you're doing is so cool," gushed Skip. "I mean, you're, like, really making the world a better place. Most of us only *talk* about doing that."

Alice smiled. "You're sweet but, trust me, I'm no hero. When we run out of coffee or have to slog through the rain for days at a time, I whine as loudly as anybody." She winked at Keith. "I guess I handle the pythons pretty well, though."

Skip sat up so hard he bumped the table and endangered everyone's tea glass. "Pythons?! What do you mean?"

"Well, they usually start with an ankle, so I've learned to wake up if it suddenly feels like my socks are too tight."

The look of horror on Skip's face was so intense that the others burst out laughing. His expression didn't change as he realized the object of his infatuation had just pulled one over on him.

"Careful. Don't lose your smooth," Keith whispered behind a napkin and the teenager grabbed it out of his hand, wadded it up, and threw it at him.

"You want to talk about adventure, then *I'm* your man, Alice!" said Pete. "Tackling fatherhood again at fifty gives 'thrill-seeker' a whole new meaning!"

"That's right," laughed C. J. "Imagine how creative you're going to have to be hunting buffalo out there with all those young whippersnappers!"

Wendy's lip curled as her brain started to bring forth images. "You're not going to start acting like you're all *young* again, are you?"

"Oh, my gosh! That makes me remember when my dad went through his 'mullet' phase when I was in high school," C. J. said with a laugh. "Mama adored Paul McCartney, so Daddy let his hair grow out in back and dyed it jet-black. Then they fell in love with "Miami Vice" and he bought a white blazer and quit wearing socks. It was *so* embarrassing!"

"Sort of as silly as Dad looking at convertibles last week?" Wendy asked pointedly.

C. J. turned to her husband and frowned. "I thought we agreed a convertible was totally out of the question right now."

Pete made a face at his daughter. "Tattletale!" Then he shrugged. "A guy can dream, can't he?" He elbowed Keith. "Bringing home buffaloes is a lot of work; we hunters deserve a little reward, doncha think?"

"At least you have someone to bring those buffalo *home* to, pal," the doctor lamented, taking the conversation in an unexpected direction. "It's hard to keep your provider instincts sharp when all you do is catch and release. I envy you, Pete. I thought I'd be where you are now, with a beautiful wife, great kids, my own La-Z-Boy, and too many bills to pay. I'd give anything to be in your shoes."

"Oh, man, can I fix *that*," Pete offered. "Follow me to my office! Which bills would you like to take over?"

As Keith chuckled, C. J. reached to touch his hand. "I thought you were happy on your own. You seem so content."

"You know, half the town thinks I'm gay."

"They do not," C. J. protested—though she knew tongues did wag on that subject from time to time.

Keith lifted his chin toward Alice. "How about you?" he asked. "You're thirty-five and single; do people assume you're lesbian?"

"Oh, every day," she said merrily. "Sometimes it works to my advantage; Casanovas don't come calling if they think you swing the other way."

Wendy stood and pushed back her chair. "Excuse me, but I have movie plans, and this is *way* more information than I want to know about any of you! Great dinner, Mom. It was nice to meet you, Alice, and to see you again, Doc." She picked up her dishes and headed toward the kitchen.

"Skip, you can be excused, too. Why don't you get started on the dishes?" Pete suggested.

"Heck, no, Pop! Y'all keep talkin'; I'm learning all kinds of things!"

C. J. wiggled her fingers in a farewell. "Exactly the point, sweetheart. Bye!"

"I should probably head home myself," said Alice. She stood. "This has been such a fun evening."

"Oh, wait!" C. J. tried to make a quick exit from her chair, a move that was, unfortunately, no longer possible. "I baked some muffins for you! Let me get them."

"What? No cinnamon rolls?" Keith chided. "You slacker!"

As Pete helped C. J. to her feet, Keith walked Alice to the door. "You don't need to walk me out," she assured him. "There's plenty of light out here. Stay and visit."

Keith met her smile with one of his own. "I wanted to get

that information you promised me."

Alice raised her eyebrows. "You're seriously interested?"

"Absolutely. Along with everyone else, I think *I'm* having a midlife crisis." He paused. "Let's just say I'm ready to explore some new opportunities and meet some new people."

C. J. and Pete joined them at the door with two zip bags of plump, blueberry muffins. "I redirected a few for you, too, Doctor Parker," C. J. said. "Any man desperate enough to envy Pete's life definitely needs some intervention!"

Keith grinned and kissed the top of C. J.'s head, then shook Pete's hand. "Best buffalo I ever ate, buddy."

"Come back next week and I'll teach you how to spear a cable bill!"

There was a flurry of farewells then the guests made their way down the sidewalk to Alice's car. She unlocked the door, opened it, and reached in to retrieve one of her business cards from the side pocket. "Here's the number you need," she said, indicating one in an upper corner. Ask for Gina." She paused. "She's swamped right now, though, so if you aren't ready to act on this right away . . . "

"I am. The sooner, the better."

"Well, I suspect a GP with a geriatric specialty would be a welcome addition to the team." Alice studied him, trying to assess. "I've given out my card before when all a guy wanted was *my* phone number. Not to be presumptuous, but that's not what this is about, is it? That was a nice little speech you gave in there about hearth and home but, frankly, you don't strike me as the recliner type and I am most assuredly not looking for a husband."

Keith gave a wry grin. "Are you kidding? I just woke up after a thirty-five-year bad dream, Alice. Believe me, I need a change of scenery a lot more than I need domestic bliss. Besides," he added, as she stepped into the car. "I'm old enough to be your father."

Alice shot him a look. "You're not, are you? I mean, you *were* there at the right time."

Keith raised both hands. "I wasn't *that* there."

"Just checking." She got in the car, closed the door, cranked the engine, and rolled down the window.

Keith dropped into a kneel that put his head at eye level. "So what if I want to see you again *and* I want to sign on with DWB?"

Alice met his gaze and pursed her lips. "I don't know, Parker. You're a pretty old horse; show me your teeth." Keith obligingly opened his mouth, turning this way and that. "Not too bad," she appraised. "And you *have* already seen me naked; I guess that counts for something!"

Caught off guard once again by her wit, he straightened and she sped off into the night, her laughter cascading down the lane.

CHAPTER NINETEEN
Schemus Interruptus

Hayley woke from a sound sleep at the pounding on her bedroom door. "We're burnin' daylight here!" came Meg's voice. "The band's waitin' to put down the last track. Get a move on!"

With a groan, Hayley slowly crawled out of bed and made her way across the room. She opened the door reluctantly and stared into her friend's impatient face. "Now that you live with Pinky," she grumbled. "can I get my house key back?"

"The door was already open—'cause everybody is here and downstairs in the studio except you and Jack! 'Scuse me for saying so, but you're not setting a very good example," Meg groused. "Plus we told the engineer he'd have all the tracks by noon today—and it's already after nine!"

Hayley sighed. "If I give you back all of Pinky's investment money right now, will you go away and let me go back to bed?"

"Well, I'm sorry, but it's a little annoying that you and Jack are layin' up here canoodling while the rest of us are trying to get this CD finished!"

Hayley eyes widened. "Not that it's any of your business, but there's no canoodling goin' on in *here,* girlfriend; I don't even know where Jack is!"

"Well, you need to find him. The meter's runnin'!"

"Meg, if you say one more word about money, I swear I'm gonna go downstairs and erase every track! Go away—and tell Bubba to bring me some coffee!"

When Hayley walked into her den a half-hour later, pure chaos was waiting. A reporter and photographer from *Billboard* sat on the couch, an hour early for their interview. Two painters, a plumber, and a pest control technician were arguing in the kitchen about who would have access to Bubba first. Bubba, however, was nowhere to be seen, and the phone was ringing off the hook. Willard and Bo were arguing about a chord change, and Suzette and three friends—unannounced and uninvited— had dropped by to use the hot tub, accompanied by Suzette's incessantly yapping Maltipoo.

Jack stomped upstairs from the studio and stood in the doorway, shell-shocked at the commotion before him. He shoved his way toward Hayley and gripped her upper arm. "We're waiting on you!" he snapped. He held onto her and surveyed the room with a dark scowl. "Is this what your life is like all the time? Because my nerves can't take this."

At that precise moment, a flash went off. "'*It' Couple Caught in Domestic Feud*!" the jubilant photographer shouted with glee. In an instant, Jack leaped across the room and his fist sent the man's camera sailing through the air and into the refrigerator before it crashed onto the kitchen floor.

Out of nowhere, Bubba suddenly materialized. "Ooh, you oughtn't have done that, Jack," he chastised. "That punch'll be on the Internet in two minutes."

"No, it won't. That camera is history."

"Yeah, but mine's alive and well!" came a cheerful retort as one of Suzette's friends waved her smart phone in the air. "How much?" she baited. "*Nashville Gab* said they'd pay me five grand for anything I could get. You willin' to top that?"

"Suzette!" Bubba barked. "You know better than to bring unapproved guests over here! I love you, sugar, but you have earned yourself a big time out! Get that fool dog and your girlfriends *outta* here!"

"*All* these people need to get out of here!" Jack growled.

"Yeah, includin' *you*, cowboy," Bubba retorted. "You don't live here, either—so you just became a liability. If that photographer sues Hayley, we may haul *your* butt to court!"

Jack's eyes blazed. "I ain't your *cowboy*, Mary Poppins. If you'd been in here doin' your job instead of struttin' around who knows where, none of this would've happened! It's like a Chinese fire drill in this house! I don't know how Hayley stands it." He turned to Hayley, who stood frozen in disbelief at what was happening around her. "If we're gonna do this thing, this craziness has to stop!"

"If you're gonna do *what* thing?" Bubba challenged. "Nobody does 'things' with Hayley, without me knowin' about it!"

Hayley watched as Jack stepped closer to Bubba. Even though he towered over the little man, Bubba was unfazed. Jack glared and crossed his arms. "'*Scuse* me for not gettin' a permission slip to date your *boss*, Mr. Troutt. I was under the impression Miss Swift ran her *own* life."

Bubba puffed out his chest. "She does. But she hires *me* to run everything else!" He eased a narrow clipboard out of his back pocket. "You see this? It's a list of everyone who's authorized to be on the property today—and, guess what? Your name ain't *on* it! Access denied! Now git your ugly butt off Ms. Swift's premises—and the rest of you go with him!" He wheeled to yank the reporter off the couch then backtracked to shove the workmen out the door. "Everybody means *everybody*!"

As she was being removed from the couch, the wide-eyed reporter clutched at Hayley. "I'm sure we won't sue if you'll give us an exclusive on this!" she whispered excitedly, but before Hayley could respond, Bubba finished pushing the woman out the door and locked it behind her. She banged on the window. "But, wait! We're *supposed* to be here! We're scheduled to do an interview!"

"Come back in an hour when it was *scheduled*!" Bubba yelled and closed the blinds in her face.

Hayley reached up to pat Jack on the chest. "Your butt's not that ugly," she consoled, "but you'd better do as Bubba says. You could stand a little cooling off."

Jack shot her a look of derision. "No, we're going downstairs to finish this track *right* now—but then, trust me, I am *so* out of here. You people are drivin' me nuts! I'm callin' Tipsy and gettin' a road gig."

"Now, wait a minute!" Hayley pouted. "We're supposed to be a team now. Are you gonna take off every time there's a little confusion?"

"*A little confusion*? Is that what you call this? I don't know *what* I'm gonna do—I just know I'm not doin' it in a houseful of lunatics! Now get downstairs!" Jack bellowed. "We have a CD to finish."

♪

A few hours later, Jack stared out the window of Tipsy's office. "You wouldn't have believed it, Tips; it was a zoo."

Despite finding Jack's tale of woe highly amusing, the older man managed a look of sympathy. "You've been in this business long enough to know celebrity life is squirrelly, son. That's part of it. Privacy is a luxury—and it all but disappears once you're at the top of the charts. Y'all haven't even released the "Essence" CD yet; you sure you're ready for this?"

"I'll never be ready to let other people run my life."

Tipsy chuckled softly. "Which is why you're still doing road gigs at your age. I can help you out this time, Jack, but you're gonna have to make peace with this lifestyle. It is what it is."

"Yeah, well, if this is fame, I don't want it."

"Hayley learned to handle fame and you can, too," Tipsy assured him. "There are worse things than being adored, you know."

Jack grunted. "Slidin' down a razor blade into a bucket of alcohol?"

Tipsy flinched. "Ouch! Tell ya what: give me five minutes and I'll pull together a road trip to Memphis. I got a so-called 'hot' band over there you can check out for me." Tipsy rifled through a pile of papers on his desk and reached for his phone. "Bernie can drive up you tomorrow, if you're ready to go."

"How much would I have to pay you to let me leave right now?"

"Just go get us some coffee. It'll calm your nerves *and* mine."

With a growl, Jack turned and strode out the door.

Tipsy had no sooner finished the calls necessary to arrange Jack's trip than the phone rang again. "*WHAT*?" he barked. "Oh. Sorry, Hayley. Hold on, I'm tryin' to do ten things at once. Can I put you on the squawk box?" He pushed a few buttons to activate speaker phone functionality. "Can ya hear me now?"

"Loud and clear, boss. Which do you want first? The good news, or the bad?"

The manager sighed heavily. "I just got Bisbee out of my office. Let's go with the good!"

Hayley took a breath. "Okay, the good news is the engineer has all ten tracks. The bad news is, we'll never be able to perform "Essence" again, because Jack Bisbee is a crotchety old hermit and a control freak who doesn't play well with others."

Jack opened the door, juggling two cups of coffee, just in time to hear Hayley's uncharitable assessment. He stopped when Tipsy held up a shushing finger and motioned for him to stay put. "You're not telling me anything I don't already know, darlin.' Listen, I got a million things on my desk, so I'll make this brief. You two need to work it out, 'cause I just booked you to sing on *New Country Superstar* next week.

"Sounds good to me," Hayley said stubbornly, "but I can't speak for Jack. Nearly four million people watch that show, Tipsy—he couldn't handle ten people in my living room this morning!"

Jack opened his mouth to protest but Tipsy gestured again for him to stay quiet. "Don't be so sure, sweetheart. That kind of exposure will lead to some big bucks, and it's been my experience that money can make people do a lot of things they don't want to. As a star, Jack'll directly benefit from whatever I negotiate. I've got some offers on the table, but it all starts with him singing in that TV studio. How much you think it would take for him to sing to four million people?"

"That's *co-star*, thank you," Hayley reminded him. "Well, my manager always told me to aim high, and I'm thinkin' ratings for *New Country Superstar* will be through the roof—especially if country's new 'it' couple can keep the peace long enough to sing their new three-minute song. How about three thousand...*each*?"

Jack choked on his coffee and Tipsy glared at him. "I taught you well, little girl! But that's not a *completely* unreasonable price; I'll see what I can do. 'Course, with Jack not available to concur, I cain't really seal the deal. I guess I'll try to negotiate ten grand total and let you lovebirds split it fifty-fifty."

Jack could keep silent no longer. He stomped over to lean over the phone. "That's fifty-one/forty-nine, thank you very much. And I want the check made out to *me*."

"BISBEE! You get back here this instant!" Hayley's voice blared through the speaker.

"Not happening! I'm here taking care of unfinished business. Tipsy, any word from the label yet? Do they still just want "Essence," or have you been able to talk them into bankrolling the whole CD?"

The manager shifted uncomfortably under Jack's penetrating gaze. "'Fraid I haven't heard a word, but maybe no news is good news." He pointed an accusing finger at Jack. "In the meantime, it doesn't help that you two aren't speaking! What is the *problem*, children?"

"Don't be pointin' your finger at me!" Jack groused. "Talk to Mercury Girl! She's runnin' a zoo out there. I can't concentrate in that kind of confusion. And *another* thing!" Jack whirled around and jabbed his finger at the phone. "That house ain't big enough for me *and* Bubba. If I come, he goes, and if he stays, I'm gone. If you're ready to have *that* discussion, I'll come back over—as long as *you* answer the door and there aren't fourteen other people in the room. I'll talk, and I'll even listen. But it's gotta be just you and me—and I mean that!"

Hayley's exasperation was audible. "Fine. Try to grow up on the way here." She hung up so fast, the dial tone blared over the speaker.

Jack sighed and rubbed the back of his head. "Well, thanks for the road trip offer, Tipsy, but I guess I'll have to take a rain check; the longer this thing festers, the uglier it's gonna get." He reached in his jeans pocket and pulled out a crumpled piece of paper. "Will you sign my permission slip so Commandant Troutt won't turn me into a toad if I'm not on his dadblame list?"

Two days later, Hayley sat in her kitchen reviewing the *New Country Superstar* contract Tipsy had faxed. "It's only been forty-eight hours since Tipsy dangled this deal in front of us, and here we are signing contracts. Sometimes, the man amazes me. Everything look okay to you?"

Jack nodded and took a sip of his coffee. "I guess so. All those zeroes are *definitely* okay! You're the TV expert, though; everything look kosher to you?"

"Been a loooooong time since my last TV appearance, I'm afraid; I'm hardly an expert anymore!" She flipped through the pages one more time. "Hmm. Tipsy only crossed out every third line; that's a good sign! Here, sign on this page, and initial this one."

Jack obliged, then cocked his head. "Listen."

Hayley straightened. "What?"

"*Nothing.* Isn't it wonderful? Meg and Pinky and the boys headed off to Pigeon Forge, there's not a reporter or photographer in sight, Suzette's still in the dog house, Bubba's off doin' whatever it is he does, and all's right with the world." He sighed contentedly. "This is perfect." He leaned closer, his eyes narrowing to a seductive slit as he cupped Hayley's chin in his hand. "How about a smoo—"

"Mornin'!" sang Bubba as he burst into the room, then stopped and cocked a finger when he saw he'd interrupted something. "Do you have *permission* to do that? Heh-heh-heh!"

Jack sat back and rolled his eyes. "I knew it was too good to last."

Hayley grinned. "Oh, now, just think about your Happy Place," she chided.

"TMI!" Bubba roared, waving his hands in the air as he crossed the room. "I don't wanna hear, I don't wanna know!"

Hayley made a face at him. "Jack's Happy Place is a *closet*, Bubba. I cleaned out that little one in my office." She reached over to ruffle Jack's hair. "We struck a bargain. When it gets crazy here, instead of running away in a huff, 'Jack the Grown-Up' will simply go to his Happy Place and do some deep breathing."

Bubba looked at the pair like they'd suddenly sprouted horns. "Y'all ain't right, but whatever." He pulled his ever-present clipboard out of his pants pocket, glanced at it, then grinned at Jack. "Well, looky here! Your name's at the top of the list this time!" He moved toward the laundry room. "'Scuse me, but there's a lot goin' on around here this afternoon. The painters and the plumber are comin' back to finish what they started when I ran 'em out the other day, and Tipsy's sendin' a runner over to pick up them contracts."

He paused to look up. "You signed 'em, right? Also, your Georgia fan club president is in the neighborhood . . . "

"WHAT?" Jack and Hayley chorused together.

Bubba rolled his eyes. "The *new* one—not that weirdo. She's meetin' that 'Heather Red Hat' lady here; you remember her, the lady who heads up your LaVergne fan club chapter? They were hopin' to get a photo with you and Jack for the next newsletter. That won't be a problem, will it?"

Jack was already on his feet. "Oh, it is definitely time to head to my Happy Place. Why don't you come *with* me?" he said, holding out a hand to Hayley.

"Jack, it's *your* Happy Place. *I'm* happy right here—plus I have work to do."

Jack persisted, pulling her out of her chair and dragging her toward the office. "I can invite guests to my Happy Place. You can be my first! You're even on the list!" he yelled toward Bubba's retreating back.

It was a tight fit, but Jack managed to pull the louvered doors shut and balance on the bar stool that, besides a lap desk, a notebook, and a pen, was the lone furnishing in his "happy place." He pulled Hayley between his knees, locked his arms around her waist, closed his eyes, smiled beatifically, and nuzzled her face.

"Well! This is interesting. What exactly goes on in your Happy Place?" she asked.

Jack's response was a grunt. "I don't know; this was *your* idea. Deep breathing, I think you told Bubba. Or maybe it was 'heavy breathing.'" He kissed her nose. "I vote for number two."

Suddenly Hayley gave a yelp and jumped as a fly swatter snaked through the slats of the louvered door and brushed up against her arm. "Sorry to interrupt," came Bubba's voice, "but Jack forgot to initial one page of the contract, and the runner's here." Three inches of ballpoint pen appeared between two slats, and a sheaf of papers slid through two others. "I didn't hear anything, by the way—not that I was listening. I have no interest in intrudin' on your Happy Place, Jack, so don't go gettin' your panties in a wad."

Jack jerked the pen out of Bubba's fingers and initialed the contract. Then he opened the louvered door and thrust the document at Bubba. "Does the word 'privacy' mean *anything* to you?"

"Do the words 'six thousand dollars' mean anything to *you*? Just takin' care of my employer—which is my *job*, Mr. Bisbee," he said, retreating from the room in a huff.

Jack pulled the closet doors shut again, then pulled Hayley back into his arms. "Guess I'll be changing the name of this little hideaway to my *Almost* Happy Place," he snorted. "Okay, where were we?"

Hayley tilted her head and grinned. "I think you were about to tell me what an incredible woman I am," she prodded.

"Indeed I was. I'm sorry it took me so many years to figure that out." Jack pulled away and looked down into Hayley's eyes. "Can you love a crotchety old hermit who doesn't play well with others?"

Hayley gasped. "You heard me say that? You were in Tipsy's office?"

"From your lips right to this old hermit's ears, darlin'."

"I'm gonna kill him! What else—"

"'Scuse me, again! Sorry!" Dismembered parts of Bubba appeared between the slats as he moved up and down, trying to determine the best place to aim his voice. "The dry cleaner's here. Did you decide which outfit you're wearin' to the Pig Pickin'?"

Jack buried his head in his hands. "She's goin' naked!" he barked. "Go away!"

Bubba wolf-whistled. "Well, now, *that* should perk up attendance! Fine. I'll just pick somethin' out. Y'all carry on."

"Oh, we're carryin' on somethin' fierce in here," Jack sighed. "*Goodbye*, Bubba—and shut the door!" Waiting for the sound that signaled they were alone, Jack exhaled and stood up. "This is completely ridiculous."

"No!" Hayley protested. "You said earlier you wanted to talk to me about something; what is it? If you're worried about the TV show, don't be. There'll only be about two hundred people in the studio audience; focus on them and don't think about who's watching at home."

"I'm not worried about the TV show."

"Are you worried about the CD? You know Tipsy always comes through. We just have to trust that he'll get the label on board."

Jack rolled his eyes—something he noted he was doing with great frequency since making the Swift house an almost daily destination. "I'm not worried about the CD. I'm not worried about *anything*. I'm just tryin' to have a *moment* here, if you'll shut up and listen, because Bubba will undoubtedly be back any second and—"

They heard the door open. "Um, 'scuse me one last time, but the painter accidentally ran into Jack's truck when he was tryin' to back down the driveway. I was tryin' not to come in here again, but we need Jack's driver's license for the accident report. And you should probably know it's only five minutes till the fan club ladies show up." Bubba stood quietly for a moment, then using one finger, slowly slid one louvered door back far enough to peep inside. "Y'all have been in there an awfully long time; how happy do you need to *be*, for heaven's sake?"

Hayley gave Jack a look of defeat. "I'm gonna go check my lipstick."

Jack held her in place. "No, you're not. You *stay*. Right here." He yanked out his wallet, grabbed his license and thrust it through the doors, missing Bubba's nose by mere centimeters. "Here. Now don't come in this room again unless Jesus shows up at the front door with Gabriel and Saint Peter! I need five minutes *alone* with your boss. Got it?"

The two men locked eyes, then Bubba sniffed. "Fine. I'll put the world on hold till you say so." He snatched the license from Jack's fingers and marched away, slamming the door behind him.

Hayley pushed a strand of hair from Jack's flushed forehead and bit her lip in a not-very-successful effort to keep from giggling. "I'm sorry about your truck. And I'm sorry your Happy Place isn't . . . happy."

Jack's s grip nearly crushed her. "Sweetheart, *any* place I'm with you is a Happy Place; that's what I've been trying to tell you." His voice was a fierce whisper. "I love you, Hayley. I am crazy, insane, desperate, stupid in love with you." He found her mouth and kissed her, hard, then kept on kissing as he moved his right arm from her waist to fish around in his shirt pocket with one hand. Still kissing, he used his other arm to grab hold of Hayley's left arm and work his way down to her hand. And, suddenly, there was a two-carat tear-drop diamond ring on Hayley's finger and her finger was in front of her face and they were both shaking and crying and laughing. "Hayley Gayle Swift, will you marry me?"

The office door burst open while Hayley's mouth was still frozen in astonishment. "Okay, *technically*, I ain't in the room; I'm out in the hall. But there's a policeman out here who needs a word with you, Jack, and I get the feelin' he's tired of waitin'. If your five minutes ain't up yet, it needs to be!"

Jack's only response was to raise an eyebrow. "Well?"

Hayley flung her arms around his neck. "YES! YES! YES! YES! YES!"

As they kissed one more time, Bubba stepped deeper into the room and pushed back the closet doors. "Ain't love grand? Come right on in, officer. This is my boss, Miss Hayley Swift, and if I eavesdropped correctly, her new fiancé, Jack Bisbee. You can be the first to say congratulations!"

A short time later, after Jack had followed the policeman outside, signed the incident report and watched his wounded truck get towed away, he came through the poolside French doors, grabbed a Cheerwine out of the refrigerator, and joined Bubba, who stood at the bar folding laundry. "Ms. Poppins, we need to talk."

The little man winced. "Oh, I know what this is about. Move over, little dog, 'cause big dog's movin' in." He sighed and dropped the dishtowel he was folding. "Don't suppose you'd be willin' to be a reference while I'm lookin' for a new job?"

"Hold on," Jack admonished. "Nobody said nothin' about you needin' a new job." He popped open the Cheerwine, took a long swig, and leaned back against the counter. "Hayley depends on you, she trusts you, and that's worth a lot, But this 24/7 thing ain't gonna work if I'm movin' into the equation. Can you do your job livin' someplace else?"

"You're thinkin', where—Timbuktu?"

"No, I own a two-bedroom condo about five miles up the road, with a pool and a clubhouse. It has satellite TV and high-speed wireless Internet, there's a pool table and a gym in the rec room, and all my neighbors are old and deaf." He leaned forward in a conspiratorial pose. "Here's where I'm headed with this: you can live at my place rent-free, work here from nine to five, then GO HOME every night. To *your* home! Well, *my* home, 'cause I'll be movin' into *this* home." Jack cleared his throat and gave Bubba an enthusiastic pat on the back. "Any time Hayley and I are out on the road, you can stay here, of course. And when you're here during the day, doin' whatever it is you do, well, I'll try to stay out of your way. I'll probably set up an office down in the studio and spend most of my time down there working on songs." He straightened and took another swig of soda. "What do you think?" When Bubba didn't answer, Jack rolled his eyes. "Come on, now. I like you, Bubba; I just don't want to find you in my kitchen if I get up for a midnight snack!"

Bubba pursed his lips and tilted his head as he contemplated the offer. "Does your condo allow pets? Like, can I keep Suzette's dog over there?"

"I guess so—but why would you *want* to?"

Bubba shrugged. "We men do lots of things we're not crazy about if it keeps our woman happy."

"Indeed, we do." Jack extended a hand. "Bubba Troutt, you're a wise man. And I like you, I just don't wanna *live* with you."

"I am, indeed, a wise man," Bubba agreed, shaking the extended hand. Then he smiled broadly. "Which is why, if I'm gonna be takin' care of the *both* of you now, I'll be asking for another raise, 'cause I like you, too, Bisbee—but you wear me out!"

♪

"Well, that was fun." Hayley sat in front of a mirror backstage on the set of *New Country Superstar*, removing makeup from her face with cold cream. "Didn't you think so?"

"Mmm," Jack grunted. Squinting in the blinding glare of the lights that surrounded the mirror, he, too, was smearing cream on his face then wiping it off with clumsy, impatient strokes of a tissue. "Are we rich yet? 'Cause if we are, do we have to keep doin' TV shows?"

Hayley laughed. "Yes, silly boy. The richer we are—which we most definitely *aren't*—the more TV shows we have to do. Tipsy will see to that."

Jack snorted. "And here I thought he was on *my* side."

"Oh, quit your fussing and come on." Hayley rose and knocked his shoulder with her hip as she gathered her tote bag and headed toward the dressing room door. "Come on, the limo driver said he'd be waiting out back."

A sleek black Lincoln limousine was waiting at the curb and a light mist was falling. As Hayley and Jack stepped out of the studio onto the sidewalk, the driver sprinted out of the car and ran to open the door.

"Thank you," Hayley said as she ducked into the spacious cab and scooted over for Jack and his guitar to join her.

"My pleasure, ma'am," said the driver as he closed the door behind them.

As the vehicle moved silently through the quiet side streets and quickly made its way onto the lights of Broadway, Jack turned with a smile. "Sure you won't join me and the boys at Tootsie's? We're gonna play all your favorites."

"Is Meg here, too, or did she stay back at the theater?"

Jack nuzzled her neck. "I believe our budding author stayed put to work on her vocabulary words."

Hayley gave him a swat. "Don't be mean. You know, if it's just you guys, I think I'll go home and go to bed. Tell them hey for me, though, and y'all come over tomorrow. I'll make a big pot of chili."

The driver eased the limo gently against the curb and started to get out but Jack held up a hand. "No need," he said, as he opened the door and the lights and music from Tootsie's legendary Orchid Lounge spilled into the interior. "Sleep tight, beautiful," he said as he gave Hayley a parting kiss, then headed inside.

Sitting in the dark stillness, and weary from her long day, as the limo pulled back into Broadway's steady stream of traffic and headed for I-65, Hayley let her head fall back against the seat.

"Would you like some music, ma'am?" the driver asked.

"Oh, thank you, no. If you don't mind, I'm actually enjoying the quiet."

"No problem, ma'am. You rest and I'll wake you when we get to our destination."

"Mmm. Thank you. And thank you again for picking us up. That was very nice of the studio to do that."

"Our pleasure, ma'am. We're happy to be of service."

Hayley heard the door open but it took a moment for her to clear the fog from her brain and resume consciousness. As the limo driver extended his hand to help her out of the car, she blinked a few times and looked around. "Oh," she said. "I think there's been some mistake. This isn't my house." She looked around for a familiar landmark. "I don't know *where* we are."

"But *I* do, and I promise, you'll love it," said a voice that was strangely familiar. Hayley whirled to see Rhett Wilson standing in front of her. He was holding an enormous bouquet of pink roses and wearing a broad smile. "Dearest! How lovely to see you again." He bowed, then stepped forward to place the bouquet in her arms, but she pushed them away.

"Why did you bring me here? Take me home!" she ordered the driver, trying to get back in the car, but he blocked her way. "What are you doing? You need to help me! This man is a maniac!"

Rhett reached out to pull Hayley away from the limo. "Not likely to get much help from him, my love. He's with me." At the look of confusion on her face, he continued. "The TV show didn't provide pick-up service; *I* did. Clever, yes? Well done, Jeremy," he said over his shoulder as he forcibly shoved Hayley up the driveway. "You know what to do next."

The driver reached into the car to retrieve Hayley's tote, met her eyes briefly—apologetically, she thought?—as he handed it to her, then got in the vehicle and backed down the drive. As Hayley watched the taillights diminish into the darkness, the fear gnawing her insides pulsed and grew. "No, wait!" she yelled, breaking away from Rhett and running pointlessly after the limousine that was already nothing but two red dots in the distance.

Suddenly, the fear she felt morphed into anger.

"Why aren't you in jail, you lunatic?" Hayley demanded, turning around and stomping back to where Rhett was standing.

"Friends in high places." He chuckled softly as he bent to retrieve the discarded roses. "As it happens, I have a cousin who's a judge in Marion County—and another one who's a bail bondsman. I left Ocala soon after you did."

"Where's Deena?"

"Oh, she's right inside—and where are my manners, leaving you standing out here in the cold? Do come in. We have some refreshments waiting. I thought you might be hungry after your performance tonight." He tried to take her arm but his hostage jerked away, stumbling on the unfamiliar ground. Rhett caught her elbow and kept her from falling. "I'm only trying to be helpful, Miss Swift; having you hurt yourself is not part of the plan."

She jerked away again. "What *is* the plan? What do you want from me?" Fighting the panic she felt as she looked around and saw nothing but pitch black darkness in every direction, Hayley said a prayer and tried to assess whether defiance or cooperation was her best defense.

"If you'll stop acting like a child and come in the house, we can talk," said Rhett, his tone markedly sharper than it had been initially.

Compliance, Hayley quickly decided—at least for the moment.

She followed Rhett up a walkway and several stairs onto an old-fashioned wooden porch. Deena Pomeroy stood waiting in the doorway.

"Hayley! Hello!," she gushed, stepping aside to let them in.

"Darling, Miss Swift wants to know 'the plan,'" Rhett said, as he gestured for Hayley to sit on a sofa and laid the flowers on a coffee table in front of it.

"Well, you explain it to her, dear. I'll go get our refreshments." Deena disappeared momentarily into the next room and returned with a tray of coffee and a picture-perfect coconut cake. "I know you love coconut cake; I read it in one of your interviews years ago. This is your recipe!" She set the tray on the edge of the coffee table, sliding the roses out of the way. "And I remembering reading somewhere that you like roses. Rhett, you serve the cake while I put these beauties in a vase." She disappeared again as Rhett came and sat next to Hayley, picked up the cake knife, and traced it down her arm and across her lips before slicing a piece of cake.

Hayley took a deep breath and focused very hard on not throwing up.

Deena returned with the vase of roses and placed them on a bookcase at the end of the sofa. She took the piece of cake Rhett offered her then sat in a rocker opposite the sofa.

Rhett took a bite of cake. "Mmmmm. Perfection, darling." He took another bite and turned toward Hayley. "So, since you don't seem at all interested in . . . well, what we *hoped* you'd be interested in . . . "

Hayley closed her eyes and tried to think about happy things. *Summer in the mountains. Harmonizing with Amanda. Cute puppies.*

"We're *very* disappointed about that," Deena interjected, "but it's no fun if everyone's not a willing partner."

Snowcones. Seagulls at the beach. Thanksgiving dinner. Sparklers.

"So we've come up with *another* plan," Rhett continued. "Since your value has significantly increased in recent weeks, we've decided to settle for money instead of love. Who do you think will pay more: Jack or Mr. Mack?"

Hayley stared incredulously at the man next to her. "Are you crazy? Neither *one* of them has any money!"

"Well, perhaps not now," Rhett shrugged, "but they *will*— as soon as your new CD is released.

"That could be months from now! What are you planning to do—hold me hostage here until the royalties start rolling in?"

Rhett smiled patiently. "Oh, we don't want to inconvenience you any longer than we have to, darling. No, I've arranged for Jack—or Mr. Mack, whoever responds first—to get a tidy little loan to get the ball rolling and, after that, they'll be able to make quarterly deposits to our account in the Cayman Islands until the full amount of ransom is paid."

Hayley smirked. "Let me guess. One of your cousins is a loan shark."

"An uncle, actually."

"What if they forget to make the payments?"

"Then Jeremy might show up to offer you a ride again one day."

"Seriously? What do you plan to do, stalk me the rest of your life?"

Rhett shrugged. "What can I say? I adore you. And if I can make money off you, all the better. Speaking of which, while we're waiting to hear from one of your menfolk, I'd like you to do us a favor."

"Not likely!"

He made a face. "Now, don't be like that. Deena spent the best years of her life promoting you. She estimates she's sent out at least ten thousand autographed copies of your picture—"

"Not with *my* autograph!"

"Well, sort of," Deena giggled. "I have a signature stamp! It looks just like you signed it for real. The fans love it!"

Rhett gave an impatient sigh. "The *point* is, my wife has played a pivotal role in your success. Surely you won't begrudge her a little kindness after all she's done for you."

"At the moment, what she seems to have done is marry a madman who keeps interfering in my life and has now committed a FELONY. You're aware, Mr. Wilson, kidnapping will get you six to ten? You don't *have* enough well-placed relatives to weasel out of *this* one."

Rhett bolted stiffly off the sofa, his face contorted in anger. "I've had about enough of your belligerent attitude, Miss Swift. I'll thank you to remember I've tried to be a generous and gracious host, but you are making it very difficult. Just because I admire you does not mean you can abuse me."

As he bent to grab the cake knife and brandish it in Hayley's face, both she and Deena screamed.

"Listen to me! You are going to get up and go downstairs with my wife and you will do exactly what she tells you to and, if you don't, I cannot be responsible for my actions. Is that perfectly clear?"

"It is," Hayley nodded, deeply regretting her change in strategy from compliance to defiance. Bad call. *Bad* call.

"Good." He inhaled deeply, closed his eyes, and exhaled. "Deena, darling, take Miss Swift downstairs while I go try to calm down. I would hate for anything untoward to occur this evening. That is not part of the plan and you know I don't like it when things don't go according to plan."

"I know, Rhett, I know. Please calm down." Deena rose and put her arms around her husband. "Everything will be fine. You go take one of your pills and lie down. I'll take care of Hayley and then we'll all get some sleep."

Against her better judgment, but convinced at this point she was safer with Deena than with Rhett, Hayley followed her lookalike down the stairs.

"I'm so sorry," Deena whispered as she flipped a switch on the wall and fluorescent lighting revealed a credible, if a bit home-spun, recording studio. "Rhett sort of lives in his own world and he doesn't handle things real well when people don't do what he wants them to do." She looked at Hayley. "He really hates it when people call him crazy. Please don't do that. It will make life a lot more pleasant."

"Duly noted," said Hayley, then nodded toward the array of sound equipment and musical instruments sprawled around the finished basement. "What's all this?"

Deena beamed. "Pretty cool, huh?"

Hayley surveyed the computer, digital keyboard, Sabian B8 cymbals, monitor speakers, and Fender bass and guitar. Not top of the line, but sufficient to get the job done; she'd seen worse. "Who sings?"

"Me."

"Are you any good?"

For the first time, Deena's cool façade faltered and a sliver of self-doubt showed through. "I...think so—Rhett says I am. He keeps bringing musician friends over to record with me and wants me to send out some demos. But I'm on the dark side of forty now, I'm not blonde, and, well...country music's in a different place than it was in the '90s when I first wanted to be you."

"Talent trumps age and beauty every time," Hayley said. "Look at Susan Boyle. And Julia Child didn't learn to cook until she was almost forty."

"You're kidding!"

Hayley smiled. "Then there's me: proof positive that gump-tion and a great song can create miracles."

"Oh, you deserve to be back in the spotlight. Your voice is amazing and Jack's song...gosh, it's beautiful." At Hayley's puzzled look, Deena laughed. "I watched you on TV tonight." Suddenly, the woman's eyes welled with tears. "Y'all are good people, Hayley. I'm sorry all this has...gone the way it has."

"Me, too. I liked you a lot better as a fan club president than as a kidnapper." Hayley looked over her shoulder to make sure they were alone, then lowered her voice and continued. "Deena, honey, I'm thinking your husband may not have your best interests at heart. You could go to *jail* for this—and you dang sure can't cut a record behind bars."

Tears were now streaming down Deena's face. "My mama would be so ashamed of me. *None* of this is who I really am, Hayley, I promise. I don't know how I let Rhett talk me into it."

Hayley snorted. "You wouldn't be the first smart woman to fall for a stupid man. Happens on a daily basis, I suspect." She gave a commiserating smile. "Look, is there a bathroom down here? I could use one. Then, how about you play me some of your recordings?"

"Are you serious? You'll really listen?" Deena wiped her face with the back of her hands as her eyes widened in surprise and anticipation.

"Absolutely," Hayley said as she pointed tentatively toward a door that looked like a potential bathroom. At Deena's nod, she moved in that direction. "Queue up your best efforts and we'll take a listen."

As she closed the bathroom door behind her, Hayley flipped the light switch, locked the door, and scrambled in her purse for her cell phone. Turning on the water to mask any unbidden beeps, she punched in 9-1-1, held the phone to her lips and whispered, "Help!

This is Hayley Swift and I've been kidnapped by Rhett Wilson. Call Tipsy—um, Clarence Mack—then use my GPS to find me!" She decreased the volume to zero then set the phone on the vanity while she did what she needed to do—racing through memories of movies she'd seen in which tracing a call seemed to take at least a minute. Who knew about such things? But this was all she could think to do, under the circumstances. She washed and dried her hands, finally disconnected the call, tossed the phone back in her tote bag, and started to unlock the door, then stopped. No point reminding Rhett Wilson she had a cell phone if he hadn't already thought of it: instead of carrying her tote back out into the studio, she put it in the bathtub, behind the shower curtain.

Speak of the devil, there he stood when she opened the door. "Deena said you'd agreed to listen to some tracks. I was hoping you might." He smiled. "Glad to see you're being a little more cooperative. It's definitely in your best interest."

"Well, gee, Rhett, after you reminded me how much work Deena has invested in running my fan club all these years, how could I say no? Besides, I gotta keep an eye out for the competition."

Deena giggled. "Oh, please. I'm no competition for *you*."

"There you go again!" sighed Rhett, turning to glare at her. "Why do you *do* that?"

"Do what?"

"Put yourself down! What happened to my sassy Hayley-Gayley stand-in?" he taunted, strolling over to Hayley and wrapping his arm around her waist. "I don't want some sniveling wannabe; I want the real thing, and if you can't be the real thing, you can take your fake-from-head-to-toe self back to Valdosta."

"You're a pig, Wilson," Hayley spat as she yanked herself

away and started toward Deena, who had her face in her hands and was crying quietly. She'd only taken a step when Rhett reached out to grab her hair and pulled it, hard.

"I don't like being called names," he whispered savagely. As Hayley slapped at his hand to release her hair, he twisted it tighter and she gasped.

"Let her go, Rhett! You're mad at me, not her!" Deena sobbed.

"*You* shut up," Rhett barked at Deena, then he jabbed a finger from his free hand in Hayley's face. "And *you* sit down and listen!" he ordered, then shoved her across the room onto a sofa. She landed on the frame, banging her hip hard enough to make her yelp in pain.

"Now, I know a lot about recording technology," Rhett said as he turned to face the computer screen and began to open files, "but I don't have the industry contacts that you do. I thought, once you hear my little songbird, you might tell me the best place I should send these tracks."

Hip and head throbbing, heart and brain racing, Hayley reined in her urge to lash out. With enormous effort, she managed to sound nonchalant. "Can't do much to help you if I'm holed up in the middle of nowhere."

Her captor turned his head toward her and winked. "A temporary impediment, my dear. By this time tomorrow, I'm sure your gentlemen friends will have made all the necessary arrangements and you'll be back at home in your *own* studio."

"I sincerely hope so." She moved gingerly to one end of the sofa and motioned for Deena to join her. "Crank it up, Colonel

Parker, and let's hear what your girl can do."

♪

"What do you mean she's not home?" Jack squinted across the room at the clock above the bar in Tootsie's. "It's almost 2 AM! She said she was going straight home."

"I know what time it is!" Bubba sputtered. "Why do you think I'm calling you? I'm worried! If she ain't with you, where the heck *is* she?"

"Man, I don't know. The limo from the studio dropped me off here about 9 . . . there's no way to reach anyone at *New Country Superstar* . . . have you called the police?"

"No, I called you first. They're next."

"No, listen, I'll call the cops. You call Tipsy and Meg and see if they've heard from her. Call ya back in five."

"What's up?" Graham and Bo, having seen the scowl on their buddy's face from the dance floor, came up to the table where Jack and Pinky were sitting just as Jack was punching 9-1-1 into his cell phone.

He took a deep breath before answering. "Hayley's missing. I'm gonna take this outside where I can hear."

"9-1-1. What is the nature of your emergency?"

"A missing person. Hayley Swift. Look, it hasn't been very long, but she's not where she's supposed to be. Something's wrong."

"One moment, sir. I'll check our database."

♪

Loud, insistent banging. A hammer? Radiator? Engine? As the fog of sleep receded and Hayley's conscious mind came to, she realized the intrusive sound was someone banging on a door. She looked around at the unfamiliar surroundings, bewildered, until a gruff voice called "Rhett Wilson? We know you're in there. Open the door!"

Hands outstretched before her to prevent encountering obstacles in the dark, she moved awkwardly across the tiny bedroom, unlocked the door, then dashed across the living room to unbolt the front door. A swath of pulsing lights—red, white, and blue—lit up the night and a contingent of uniformed men and women littered the lawn. In their midst, Hayley spotted the face she most wanted to see. "Jack! Oh, Jack!"

She flung herself out the door and shoved past the phalanx of police officers into Jack's waiting arms, sobbing hysterically. As EMTs made their way toward the reunited couple, a sleep-tousled Rhett Wilson took Hayley's place in the doorway. An equally disheveled Deena peered over his shoulder.

"This was *not* part of the plan," Rhett said dully.

CHAPTER TWENTY
Wrap Party

The members of Road Kill—plus Meg Brown—were on a tour bus rolling down I-20 East. Fred glanced up from the driver's seat to survey the motley crew in his rearview mirror. "Two more hours and we'll be in Skerry!"

From his seat by the window, Graham grunted. "Woo-ee. I can hardly contain my excitement at seeing Tom Brooks again."

"And whose fault is that, you 'redneck lothario'?" Pinky teased, then turned to wink at Meg. She looked up from the romance novel she was reading and beamed. "Aw, you read that in my new manuscript!"

"I keep telling you people, it wasn't like that," Graham protested. "I didn't even get a good smooch out of the deal! And my jaw's *still* sore where that man decked me on false pretenses!"

Meg glanced over her reading glasses. "Oh, please, Graham. I'm bettin' there are husbands all over this country who missed their opportunity to take a punch at you! Tom just got lucky."

"Okay, y'all need to hush. I got a new song comin' together here." Willard's face took on a mournful cast as he did a quick tuning of his guitar strings and began to sing.

Oh, our days on the road are ending, my friend;
we're closin' that chapter and door.
Who knows what adventures lie just ahead,
at Pinky's Palace, forevermore."

"How's that strike ya?"

"Dead!" pronounced Bo. "You ever thought of a career in aluminum siding? 'Cause you *shore* ain't gonna make it as a poet!"

"It ain't finished yet," Willard growled. "But *somebody* needs to write a special song for this last gig. Dang, we been on the road together more'n two decades; this is a big change!" He sighed heavily. "I'm a little bummed, this bein' our last road trip."

Bo rolled his eyes. "We ain't dying, Willard. We're givin' up the road to be a house band. We're still gonna be *playin'* together."

"Five days a week and twice on Saturday!" Pinky quipped as he stood up and stretched. "The boys that pick together, stick together!" He leaned against the safety bar at the front of the bus and crossed one foot over the other. "I can't tell y'all how tickled I am that I was able to pull off this deal in Pigeon Forge. Daddy always told me if I put aside at least ten percent of every paycheck I ever got, it'd pay off someday—and he was right! I got my bride at my side," he winked at Meg, "my kinfolk helpin' me run the place, and I've hired the best musicians in the business—who just *happen* to be my best buddies. I'm as happy as a fat, little, bald-headed fella can be!"

"You're gonna make Jeff Bezos look like an underachiever before you're through!" Meg gushed from behind her book.

"You've encouraged me every step of the way, sugar lips!"

"Good gosh a'mighty!" Bo exclaimed. "Willard, start singin' again! I'd rather listen to *your* trash than theirs!"

"You got it," Willard said, and strummed a chord. "I call this one, 'Ode to the Road'."

"I believe the *other* Willie's already got that one locked up!" jeered Fred.

"Shut up, bus boy," Willard said and began to play.

My buds and me are wild and free;
We've roamed this country wide.
But one among us screwed it up—
Went off and took a bride.

As Meg gasped and threw her book aside to lunge for Willard's guitar, the musician scrambled out of the way and continued.

So now we're speedin' on our way,
To one last outdoor gig.
We'll make a memory tonight,
At the pickin' of the pig.
Oh, we're settlin' down in Pigeon Forge;
Our ramblin' days are done.
Pinky's Palace in the gorge
Is where we'll have our fun.
Five nights a week, two matinees;
We're finally off that bus—
A steady paycheck in our hands;
The girls now come to US!

This time, everyone on the bus cheered and clapped, and Fred gave two enthusiastic toots of the horn.

"Whoo-ee!" Pinky whooped. "Now that there is a *song*! How 'bout you sell me the rights to that, Willard? I'll make ya a fair offer and we'll open the show with it every night."

Willard grinned like a chimpanzee. "You really like it?"

"Like it? I love it! It's perfect! And I mean it—I wanna buy it! Think about it and let me know."

"Who'da believed Pinky Brown would turn into a music business mogul?" Graham declared as he laughed and shook his head. "How many of your relatives you got on the payroll now?"

"Thirty-four cousins, two uncles, and three aunts. Mama wouldn't let me hire the trailer trash side of the family," Pinky said with a chuckle. "But y'all remember—I'm the only Brown that can boss you around. Any of my cousins try to act like big shots, you tell me."

"Or me," Meg interjected, "'cause I'm the manager." She shrugged. "'Course I'll be spending most of my time writing. Pinky says we can sell my romance novels in the gift shop."

"That's right, baby doll. And you can autograph 'em after every show." Pinky blew a kiss and Meg pretended to catch it.

Amid the gagging sounds, Meg raised her voice. "Hey, did y'all hear what my pen name's gonna be?" She paused a moment for dramatic effect, smiling beatifically at each band member, then closed her eyes. "Lola Midnight," she whispered.

"She might wanna check out that aluminum siding job, too," Bo cracked in Fred's ear, and the bus driver upset traffic in six lanes as he guffawed and laid into the horn.

♪

A carnival atmosphere filled the streets of downtown Skerry. The town square teemed with festival goers in a tangle of balloons and streamers. The high school band played a Sousa march as Miss Pauline's Dancing Dollies performed on the main stage. The aroma of roast pork, funnel cakes, and cotton candy wafted in the air. The weather gods had smiled on the mid-autumn day; there wasn't a cloud in the sky, and the temperature was Indian summer at its best.

Amanda Brooks, Pig Pickin' Festival Director, surveyed the scene from her perch atop the Chamber of Commerce balcony. She held three clipboards, and sported a bulging fanny pack around her slender waist. The walkie-talkie in her left hand squawked incessantly, but Amanda's expression was giddy. Beside her, as yet unnoticed by the crowd, stood Hayley Swift and Jack Bisbee.

Hayley grinned at her friend in bemusement. "You certainly seem in your element, kiddo. Sure you wanna give this up?"

"Why do you think I'm smilin'?"

"I thought maybe it was because Tipsy offered to take your mother-in-law off your hands for the day."

"No, I considered that a direct gift from God!"

"They make a cute couple, don't they?"

"They do, indeed," Amanda agreed. "I haven't seen Millicent Brooks emote that much in thirteen years! And who knew Tipsy was such a Romeo? Are you sure my children's grandmother is safe with that silver fox?"

Jack trained Amanda's binoculars on the square, trying to locate the couple in question. "Believe me, Tipsy's all charm and no conquest. But to tell you the truth," he said, handing the binoculars to Hayley, "I think he's lonesome. This could be the best thing that happened to either one of them—and to you, too. Of course, that's my unsolicited opinion."

Amanda rolled her eyes. "You're in love. You have no judgment capabilities whatsoever."

Hayley's smile bordered on neon. "Are we that obvious?"

"Well, if I hadn't seen it on your faces, that two-ton rock on your left hand would have been a dead giveaway!" Amanda hugged Jack and Hayley simultaneously. "I'm so happy for you. Things have moved right along since our ill-fated tour, haven't they? Thwarted kidnapping, among other things. Sheesh! I'm glad those weirdos are finally out of your life. Hard to believe it hasn't even been two months since we were sitting at the Dairy Dip, ruining your career!"

"*Reviving* my career," Hayley corrected, "and I'm forever grateful to you guys. I am so blessed to be able to keep doing what I love, with people I love!"

"Uh-oh, this is starting to sound like a Hallmark moment. Do I need to go for Kleenex?" Jack mused.

Amanda waved a hand in his face. "Oh, hush. Oh, look! There's C. J.! Y'all go ahead; I'll catch up in a sec. I've got a pie contest to oversee and some frogs to round up. Somebody tipped over the cooler and we've got rogue amphibians hopping everywhere!"

♪

As the sun began to set and a cool breeze blew in from the sea, Hayley and the Hot Flashes gathered on the front steps of the Skerry, South Carolina courthouse. C. J. tugged at the taut pink spandex fabric that silently screamed in agony across her pregnant belly. She grunted, adjusting her outfit for the hundredth time. "It's a good thing my sashaying skills are not as well-known as *yours*, Amanda, because one false move and this dress is a goner! But don't I have a fine-lookin' bosom?" she preened. "Pregnancy does have its assets!"

Meg poked. "Are those *real*?" she teased.

"They'd better be!" C. J. retorted, swatting away Meg's finger. "With the price of formula these days, I'm counting on these girls to *produce*!" She flinched suddenly and grabbed her belly. "Ow! Kicking! Kicking!"

There was a flurry of squeals and flailing hands as Hayley, Amanda, and Meg circled around to feel the source of excitement.

"Gonna be a soccer player!" Amanda predicted. At her words, Hayley suddenly began keening and tears welled in her eyes. "What have you got against soccer?" asked Amanda, a perplexed look on her face.

Hayley tried to smile, but the result was more of a crazed grimace. "It's not that. I'm just thinking about what a miracle this is—*all* of it!" She fanned her hands to try and ward off the tears that were welling. "Having y'all back in my life, everybody embarking on new beginnings . . . This is gonna sound so selfish, but right now I have everything I ever wanted!" She shook her head. "Well, no, that's not completely true. It would have been wonderful to have a child—I'm a little jealous, C. J.," she said, looking at her friend, "but I don't see that happening at this point." Then the tears began to flow in earnest—and not just from Hayley.

"Who needs a child?" Meg announced, attempting to lighten the mood. "You've got *Jack*. Same thing!"

Giggles suddenly replaced the tears as the women regained their composure and began to look around for tissues to dry their eyes and salvage their makeup. "You don't know the half of it," Hayley divulged, and told them the tale of Jack's 'Happy Place.'

"Hey, there's Flopsy!" Amanda interrupted suddenly. "Are we ready to serenade, Sisters?"

"Oh, my gosh, are we singing that? " Meg looked stricken.

"We haven't rehearsed it and I haven't sung it since our last show!"

Amanda cackled. "You know you know that song like the back of your eyelids."

"Of course, you do," agreed C. J., reaching past her belly to give Meg a big hug. "And besides, this might be our last chance to sing it, what with me getting back in the motherhood ring and you starting a new career as an author. It's wonderful to see you finally get what you deserve—and I mean that in the nicest way!" she giggled. "Pinky is the gentleman you've waited for all your life, isn't he?"

"He absolutely is," Meg said, "and it was worth the wait!" Her attention moved from C. J.'s face to over her shoulder. "Ooh, they're motioning for us to come on."

A few minutes later, Hayley and Jack strode onto the main stage amid a swell of cheers and applause. Slowly, a hush fell over the crowd as the haunting opening strains of "Essence" flowed from Jack's guitar, and an almost tangible wave of affection for the hometown girl-made-good—and her hero—enveloped the handsome couple. On the ground behind the stage, Graham chewed on a toothpick and watched with a mix of pleasure and pain as, twenty feet away, Amanda pirouetted in front of her family, her silliness endearing and her affection for her loved ones undeniable. She glowed with the magic of the moment, oblivious to the charm she exuded.

"That is one fine woman," Graham sighed to Bo.

"I'll give you that, but unless you're gunnin' for another smack in the jaw, you…what was it?…'redneck lothario'?…you best let that one go."

Graham caught Tom Brooks' eye and met his gaze. The two men considered each other for several seconds, then nodded slightly in acknowledgment. "And that is one lucky man." The fiddler turned to face the drummer. "You reckon the ladies in Pigeon Forge will truck with two sorry skunks like us?"

Bo kicked the dirt. "Well, if they won't, sounds like Pinky's got plenty of cousins to choose from!" He shook his head. "Can you spell 'gravy train?'"

Graham shrugged. "Yeah, but ya gotta love a man who takes care of his kinfolk." He grinned. "I just hope they don't all look like Pinky! I don't know if I could face that many bald heads and red ears every day!"

As Jack and Hayley bowed again to thunderous applause, the Hot Flashes and Road Kill joined the couple onstage. Hayley moved up to a microphone and waved at the crowd. "How y'all doin' out there?" Whoops and cheers echoed and she waited for the noise to die down. "Some of you know that my band had a close encounter of the wrong kind a couple months back, at the beginning of my Retro Rodeo tour. These fine ladies—my best friends—known here in Skerry as The Girls Next Door—" she had to pause here for more cheers, "—rose to the occasion and saved my neck. They left their families and jobs behind for two weeks to give me the most fun I've had in years, and I'd like to thank them for their loyalty and support." She turned and bowed to the Hot Flashes as the crowd erupted into an avalanche of whistles, shouts, and applause. "One of our group can't be up here tonight," Hayley continued, "so here's a shout out to Sue Campbell. We love you, Sweet Sue--and we love *you*, Louise White!"

The crowd roared as a spotlight scanned the crowd and came to rest on the front row, where Louise and Sue sat on either side of Jackie the nurse. Sue reached for Jackie's arm and tugged on it. "Maid, make them turn off that light! It's too bright!"

Louise squinted her eyes. "Are we in a lineup? I refuse to take a polygraph!"

The spotlight swiveled back to Hayley and, as the audience uproar gradually diminished, she took the microphone off its stand and turned to wink at the three Hot Flashes beside her. "We're gonna do a little song for you right now that we wrote to remind us that it's not age that matters, it's *attitude*!"

A cacophony of catcalls rang out as Bo hollered, "Age only matters if you're a cheese!" and followed up with a rim shot. Instead of dying out, though, the cheers and whoops grew more and more raucous, until Hayley finally shook her head, shrugged, and yelled, "Play it, boys!"

♪

Tom Brooks poured orange juice into a champagne glass as Amanda breezed into their kitchen. She paused long enough to give him a quick smooch before moving on to the refrigerator to collect another platter of fruit. "If that's plain O.J., go take it to C.J."

The affable banker caught another smooch on the rebound as his wife giggled at her unintentional rhyme, then headed back out into the bedlam of gift wrap, bows, and half-eaten brunch food that cluttered the room beyond. C. J.'s baby shower was in full swing as in the den, Tipsy Mack and Millicent Brooks were engrossed in deep conversation with Hayley and Jack, while in the living room, Keith, Alice, Willard, and Pinky listened—with varied facial expressions— as Meg read an excerpt from her hot-off-the-press romance novel. Bo and Graham sat at the dining room table, marveling in turn at the diminutive dimensions of newborn-size disposable diapers, the complexities of a car seat harness, and the disturbing concept of nursing pads.

"I need a refill," Graham determined, heading toward the kitchen with his glass, but he turned to leave when he saw Tom already there.

"Hold up, pal," Tom said. "We need to talk."

"We do?"

"Well, I do. I need to apologize to you for that punch back in Ocala."

Graham instinctively reached up a hand to rub his jaw. "I guess I can see how it looked from your perspective, and I won't insult your intelligence by telling you the thought didn't cross my mind. But Amanda made it clear from the get-go she was a one-man woman."

Tom stood a little taller. "I know that. But I still think I owe you one."

"No, really! One was enough!" Graham raised his hands to block his face, and Tom laughed.

"At ease, at ease. You helped me realize I shouldn't take what I've got for granted, though. How 'bout we declare a truce?" Tom suggested as he extended a hand. "Although, make no mistake, if you ever do more than eyeball my wife, I *will* kill you," he added jovially.

"Fair enough," Graham conceded as he took the proffered hand. "You make sure you take that pretty lady someplace where she can prance around in that pink dress from time to time."

"That's a deal," Tom nodded as he let go of Graham's right hand to take the glass out of his left. "How 'bout a refill?" he offered, gesturing toward the punch bowl on the table.

"Absolutely. Hit me!" Graham said, then ducked and chuckled. "No pun intended."

Tom filled Graham's glass and his own half full of punch then gave a surreptitious look around before backing away from the table to set the glasses down on a counter. Reaching up, he opened the cabinet above it. "You don't strike me as a punch man," he said, taking down a bottle of Bacardi and pouring a healthy dollop into each glass. "Amanda bought this to put on the fruitcakes she's making for Thanksgiving, but I think it deserves better. To your excellent taste in women, sir," said Tom as he lifted his now-full glass.

"And to yours," returned Graham, lifting his own glass to complete the toast. "If she cain't be mine, I'm glad she's yours!"

In the living room, Pete Fleming suddenly whistled through his teeth. "Everybody listen up! I need all the male guests to accompany me on a short errand. C. J., don't look at me in that tone of voice! I promise, we'll be right back. You ladies keep playing with the baby stuff; there's plenty of it!" He opened the front door and started herding. "Come on, fellas, let's go." Tom slipped the bottle of rum up Graham's sleeve as the two of them came out of the kitchen and made their way across the room to follow the rest of the men outside.

Comfortably sprawled in a rocking recliner, C. J. beamed at the women surrounding her. "This is so much fun, Amanda. You are amazing, throwing a baby shower the morning after the Pig Pickin'!"

"Pure ego," Amanda bragged. "Superwoman had to make one last appearance before she permanently hangs up her cape!" She handed the mother-to-be a fresh glass of punch. "I'm just upset we couldn't find the perfect gift for you: I searched *everywhere* for a stroller that converts to a wheelchair!"

The women hooted as Hayley waved a hand. "Honey, has it dawned on you that you can put this baby through college on your

Social Security benefits? Good timing!" Amid another round of laughter, a familiar voice rang out.

"Yoo-hoo! We're here!" All heads turned to see Nurse Jackie enter from the kitchen, with Sue and Louise in tow.

"Oh, hey! We didn't hear you drive up," C. J. apologized as she lumbered out of her seat to kiss her mother.

"I'm not surprised," teased Jackie. "Sounds like a party in here!" She ushered Louise to a chair next to C. J.'s recliner and settled her down. "They're both having a good day," she whispered to C. J. as the guest of honor maneuvered herself back down into a sitting position. "C.J., your mama has a present for you," she said as Louise pulled a package out of the tote bag she was carrying.

"Oh, Mama, thank you!" said C. J. as Louise handed her the package. She tore off the wrapping to reveal a satin-covered baby book. "It's beautiful!" she squeaked, her throat clogged with emotion.

Louise reached out to cup her daughter's face between both her wrinkled hands. "I want you to write down every moment in this baby's life, so you won't ever forget. I'm sorry I never took the time to keep a baby book; memories are as precious as love and friends, and I never expected to lose mine. Write down your memories, sweetheart, so you can remember this baby forever."

Saltwater flowed like a fountain as the friends exchanged hugs, admired the baby book, and reflected on their respective blessings. Then Hayley blew her nose. "End of the moment, girls; I hear the guys comin' back in."

Tom and Graham, their arms around each other's shoulders, appeared in a window, weaving and waving. "Y'all come out here for a minute!" they bellowed, then bent over in a fit of hilarity.

Amanda was not amused. "Wonderful. Looks like my cowboy and my husband have become drinking buddies."

"Heavens to Betsy, Amanda! Is that the man Tom was worried about?" asked Millicent Brooks. "You should have punched *him* for thinking you'd ever waste your time on such a scrawny ol' picker." Everyone stared at the woman whose breeding and countenance had, for years, made her the poster child for grace and decorum. "What?" she bristled. "That's what they're *called*, aren't they? Pickers? Meg's not the only one who can learn new words."

Amanda hooted, and threw her arms around her mother-in-law. "Oh, God bless Flopsy!"

"It's too cold to come out there!" C. J. yelled, shaking her head no and shivering violently to try and get her message across to the other men who were now peering in the windows. "Y'all come *inside*!"

"Oh, come on, Mommy Whale," Hayley encouraged, getting up to hoist C. J. from her seat. "Just for a sec. Let's go see what's got the boys all riled up."

The other women smiled knowingly as they rose to crowd in front, forcing C. J. and Hayley to bring up the rear. En masse, they made their way out the door and onto the lawn where, suddenly, the sea of bodies parted to reveal Pete, standing in the driveway next to a fire-engine red mini-van. "Honey, it's not a convertible, but it has the biggest sunroof I could find."

"Mom, look!" called Tommy and Diana as they popped up like giraffes through the open sunroof. "Isn't this *cool*?"

Pete motioned to the inside. "It has more cupholders than we'll ever need, and a built-in vacuum cleaner!" He stepped forward to embrace his wife, who was weeping happily as she made her way through the crowd.

Amid the cheers and ripples of laughter, Tipsy rubbed his hands together. "Whew! It's too cold out here for an old man, folks." He grasped Millicent by the hand. "Besides, I feel the need to make a toast. Let's go back inside!"

As Pete and Keith filled glasses all around (save for Tom's and Graham's, which Amanda had confiscated), Tipsy stepped up on the raised hearth of the fireplace and began to sway. He winked at Millicent. "Come on up here with me, sugar," he said, and held out his hand.

He raised his punch glass. "A toast to the finest group of women I have ever been privileged to know. Despite the fact that the Hot Flash Tour went down in flames, I appreciate the fact y'all didn't *totally* ruin my reputation. Here's to new beginnings!"

"New beginnings!" the group repeated as they clinked and sipped.

"And, on that note," Tipsy continued, "I have an announcement to make. I've found a new business partner who's not only rich and smart, but charming and beautiful." He turned and put his arm around Millicent, then looked directly at Hayley. "Hayley Gayley, Miz Brooks here wants to bankroll the entire "Essence" CD, all ten tracks. I get the credit, you and Jack get national distribution, and Millie gets sixty percent of the profit!"

The room erupted in applause and cheers. "*Say* hallelujah!" Jack whooped, scooping Hayley up in a bone-crushing hug.

The members of Road Kill echoed compliantly. "*Hallelujah!*"

"Let's hear it for the *next* 'it' couple!" somebody yelled, and both Millicent and Tipsy went pink.

Then Millicent waved a hand. "I don't know if I would call us the '*it*' couple, but we're certainly willing to mix business and pleasure, aren't we, Tipsy?" she teased, and was left breathless when her silver-haired beau swept her backwards for a dramatic kiss.

From the sofa where he sat on the other side of the room, Tom shook his head in confusion. "I think I've had *way* too much to drink. Did I just hear my mother declare she and that man are an *item*?"

Graham clapped his former adversary on the back. "Welcome to the family, buddy!"

From another corner, Pinky waved his arms high over his head. "Well, if this is Announcement Central, I've got one, too! 'Pinky's Palace' opens December 1st! It's gonna be clean, family entertainment, despite the fact that Road Kill will be the house band!" When the hooting and booing ebbed, Pinky continued. "And there's justice in the world, 'cause Cal Taylor's opening for us during 'Elvis Impersonator Week,' so y'all come on down! There's always a free ticket at Will Call with your name on it."

"And be sure to stop by the gift shop," Meg added, interrupting the applause, "where you can find the full line of Lola Midnight romances!"

Suddenly Amanda appeared between Tom and Graham. "Y'all are spending waaaay too much time together," she grumbled. "It's making me nervous." She grabbed her husband by the arm and dragged him off the sofa to follow her toward the fireplace. "My turn!" she hollered, motioning Tipsy off the hearth, then climbing up to take his place, "My big announcement is, as of last night, I am an unemployed, but blissfully happy, mother and housewife. I hope y'all enjoyed the Pig Pickin', 'cause it was my first and last!" As the gang cheered and whistled, Amanda turned to her mother-in-law and curtsied. "Thank you for all your help, Millicent, but you are now officially off duty and free to run on with your new enterprise or run off with your new boyfriend!"

"Hey! That's my mother you're talking about!" Tom protested as the two women embraced to another round of cheers and applause. He turned and came face to face with Graham, who had once again drifted to his side. "My mother can't have a boyfriend; she's seventy-five years old!"

"Love knows no boundaries, old boy," Graham said with a commiserating sigh, "an' as long as there's sheep in the pasture, we wolves are gonna howl."

Tom blinked. "You're a very profound man, my friend."

"I am."

"Excuse me!" Alice surprised everyone by raising her glass and making her way to the hearth. "My turn!" she announced, stepping up and smiling at the assemblage. "I want to thank everyone for your hospitality this fall. It's been great to be back home. Before I head off on my big jungle adventure, I want to toast my mom and Pinky, who will *definitely* be the 'it' couple of Pigeon Forge. I'm so sorry I won't be able to make the grand opening." During the collective, "Awwwwww," that followed, Keith poked Alice in the ribs and a brief, whispered exchange ensued. "Oh, yes, and the distinguished Dr. Keith Parker will be joining me on this medical mission."

"What?!" As that word was heard over and over around the room and all heads turned to Keith, he shrugged.

"What can I say? I'm needed." His eyes found Hayley's, and the message they sent was conciliatory, a tad rueful and, perhaps, a smidgen defiant. "Everybody else is having a midlife crisis; I figure

I deserve one, too. But I've got a buddy coming into town to keep y'all—and my practice!— alive and well till I get back."

And then Jack was on the hearth, pulling Hayley up with him as he went. "Well, I'm sure glad everybody else's careers are takin' off, 'cause mine's fallin' apart! Pinky's stole my band, Tipsy's sold my bus . . . I figure I better marry my meal ticket before she changes her mind and goes back to bein' a solo act. Everybody keep Valentine's Day open—it's gonna be a heck of a weddin'!" He turned and kissed Hayley full on the mouth, unleashing a flood of catcalls.

"You know there's gonna be a *real* nice wedding chapel at Pinky's Palace," Pinky offered.

Jack nodded. "Thanks, Pinky; we'll think about it. I know you've always got my back." Then he looked down at the woman beside him, the woman he'd always loved and almost lost. "You've got my back, but Miss Hayley here's got my heart."

EPILOGUE

- Rhett Wilson was charged with kidnapping and sentenced to six years in prison, but was paroled after three years for good behavior. He helped the prison build a karaoke studio, which proved to be a significant deterrent to negative inmate behavior. Soon after being released, Rhett moved to Compton, California, put together a team of photo stalkers, and created a "celebrity sighting" website which, at last count, was getting a million hits a day.
- Deena Pomeroy was charged as an accessory to the crime and ordered to perform 250 hours of community service for the Country Music Hall of Fame. She auditioned for, and appeared on, *New Country Superstar*, but was dismissed because the judges said she was "just a pathetic Hayley Swift wannabe." Devastated, Deena divorced Rhett, moved to Branson, got a job at the Hollywood Wax Museum, and sings in the choir at Woodland Hills Family Church every Sunday.
- 'Heather Red Hat' is now president of Hayley Swift Fan Clubs,

International. Her failure to recruit Hayley as a Red Hat remains her greatest regret.

• Keith Parker and Alice Dorris saved untold numbers of lives in the deepest, darkest rain forests of the world, then decided to marry and move back to Skerry. Keith sold his medical practice to his buddy and he and Alice bought out the Dairy Dip and expanded the operation. Chili Cheese Fries are still on the menu, but are now available in "Gorilla-sized" servings. Tommy and Diana Brooks work there every summer.

• Millicent Brooks and Tipsy Mack married on Christmas Eve—the first wedding held at Pinky's Palace. Their record company, "Sixty-Nine & Holding," is hugely successful. They divide their time between Nashville and Skerry.

• Sue Campbell and Louise White take one day at a time. They are loved and visited by many friends. Nurse Jackie reports the best way to calm them down on a bad day is to log onto Rhett Wilson's celebrity sighting website.

• Road Kill has planted firm roots in Pigeon Forge. Bo is a proud member of the Kiwanis Club, Willard married Pinky's fourth cousin, once removed, and Graham can be found every Tuesday at the Laurel Falls Senior Citizens home, where he serenades the only women with whom he can *really* be trusted.

• Pinky's Palace made *Garden & Gun* magazine's list of "Most Unique Music Venues" and Pinky had to hire fifteen more relatives to handle the increase in visitors. Lola Midnight's steamy tales enjoy brisk sales at the gift shop, but have yet to make the bestseller list.

• Cal Taylor was fired on his opening night at Pinky's Palace for groping Pinky's mother backstage.

• Fred the bus driver and Bernie the chauffeur retired. They meet frequently to go fishing on Percy Priest Lake.

• Amanda and Tom Brooks celebrated their fifteenth wedding anniversary by learning to ballroom dance. They spent Amanda's fifty-fourth birthday at the World Championship of Ballroom Dancing competition in Boca Raton, where they won Second Place. Amanda's closet now boasts *several* twirly pink costumes.

• C. J. and Pete Fleming spend most of their days enjoying little Weldon Louis, whose big brother Skip plays Triple A baseball for the Greenville Drive. Weldon's doting big sister Wendy is married and eagerly awaiting her own chance at motherhood. The red minivan surpassed the hundred-thousand mile mark and is still going strong.

• Bubba Troutt parlayed his hands-on experience, business acumen, and time management skills into creating the largest pool maintenance company in the Southeast. He continues to serve as Manager of Everything for the Bisbees; Suzette, however, is no longer in the picture. At last word, she was investigating a promising career in the world of female wrestling.

• Hayley and Jack have appeared on the cover of every magazine published on six continents. As their fame increased, so did Jack's need for a bigger Happy Place, and renovations were swift. "Essence" went double-platinum, won CMA's Song of the Year, Album of the Year, Songwriter of the Year and, together, Hayley and Jack won Entertainer of the Year. Jack retired from performing after his first awards show, and now spends his time writing songs, producing them for Hayley, and scouting bands for Tipsy and Millicent when the call of the road becomes too strong. The Bisbees adopted a two-year-old orphan Keith and Alice rescued from a jungle village destroyed by fire; Jack is teaching him to play guitar.

About the Author

Jayne Jaudon Ferrer wrote her first story at the age of six, earned her first byline at nine, and has been writing ever since. A former advertising copywriter and freelance journalist, she is the author of seven books and the founder and host of www.YourDailyPoem.com, a website designed to share the pleasure and diversity of poetry with those who are skeptical. The happily married mother of three grown sons, Jayne lives in Greenville, South Carolina, where she enjoys gardening, hiking, and watching old movies.

Lightning Source UK Ltd.
Milton Keynes UK
UKHW010752120622
404255UK00002B/350